DICE WITH DOMINATION

I have enslaved all sorts of men, from refuse-disposal technicians to parliamentary candidates, and used every sort of bond, literal and figurative, to enslave them in my little games: my sweet-tasting feet, my smooth sturdy legs, cold chains, rough, chafing ropes, tight, pinching clamps, even the cruel bond of orgasm denial. But most commonly I have found myself standing over a trembling, naked professional man as he begs for the sweet contradiction of punishment and mercy.

DICE WITH DOMINATION

P.S. Brett

This book is a work of fiction.
In real life, make sure you practise safe, sane and consensual sex.

First published in 2006 by
Nexus
Thames Wharf Studios
Rainville Road
London W6 9HA

www.nexus-books.co.uk

A catalogue record for this book is available from the
British Library.

ISBN 0 352 34023 1
ISBN 9 780352 340238

The paper used in this book is a natural, recyclable product made
from wood grown in sustainable forests. The manufacturing process
conforms to the regulations of the country of origin.

Typeset by TW Typesetting, Plymouth, Devon

Printed and bound by
Clays Ltd, St Ives PLC

You'll notice that we have introduced a set of symbols onto our book jackets, so that you can tell at a glance what fetishes each of our brand new novels contains. Here's the key – enjoy!

cp (traditional)

cp (modern)

spanking

restraint/bondage

rope bondage/hojojutsu

latex/rubber/leather/enclosure

fem dom

willing captivity

medical

period setting

uniforms

sex rituals

One

'Well now, Kirsty,' I said in my stern, businesslike voice, 'it seems that we need to have a little conversation about dress code.'

Kirsty, clearly feeling uncomfortable, looked down towards her flat-soled shoes. Her dark hair hung in front of her, hiding her delicious features.

'Do look up, Kirsty,' I told her, disappointed that such a sumptuously endowed young lady could be cursed with such a shy streak.

'Yes, Ms McKnight,' she mumbled, looking up slightly and allowing me a clearer view of her dark-brown eyes.

'I don't appreciate having to call a girl into my office in only her third week,' I admonished her, hoping to put her in the mood to take criticism in a receptive spirit.

I turned to look through my office window, mostly for effect, I must admit – life has always been a performance for me, a series of poses and postures calculated either to intimidate or to titillate in some form or another.

I clasped my hands behind me, rested them upon my curvaceous, skirted buttocks and looked out across the twinkling Clyde at the buildings on the south bank as they shone in the evening sun, a mosaic of sand, rust and ivory. I allowed myself a satisfied smile in the corner of my cherry-lipped mouth. The view always reminded me of my first day's work as owner of The Paddle-Boat Casino; I had stood here at this window on that day too, and watched the people crossing the Jamaica Bridge or queuing for the River-bus. So many changes had been effected since then that it seemed like years ago. One of those changes, of course, had been the dress code for my sweet little croupiers.

I picked up a sheet of paper from my desk and glanced over the pink handwriting.

'Miss Jarvie, in her capacity as Head Croupier, has handed me a wee report that states she has had to warn you on three separate occasions regarding your attire.' I spoke in a way that demanded an answer.

'Yes, I'm sorry, Ms McKnight. I am trying to adjust to working here but I'm finding it a little difficult,' she said in her crisp, smart English accent.

I did not reply immediately, merely stepped towards her with my hands on my hips, ensuring that my black patent heels clacked clearly and loudly on the wooden floor. I pinched her black pencil skirt at the side with my thumb and forefinger and drew it slowly up, teasing myself deliciously as the hem crawled slowly over her knee and up her full thighs, exposing one curved hip and one opulent buttock. I held the skirt there, enjoying the spectacle of her cheek under its casing of nylon hose and cotton smalls.

I clicked my tongue, again for effect, and released the crumpled skirt from my grasp, reaching instead for the decorative collar of her white blouse, which was buttoned to the very top. I flicked it dismissively with my finger.

Kirsty wiggled prettily as she smoothed her skirt back down her legs and I had to bite my lip to stop

2

myself crying out with lust. I could have pounced on her and pushed my warm, thirsty tongue into the crease of flesh where her swaying arse met her jiggling thigh, but it disappeared once again beneath that non-regulation black skirt and I managed to keep my composure.

'I am sure you are aware that Casino dress code demands skirts above the knee, stockings rather than tights, a minimum two-inch heel and an unfastened top button on the blouse,' I said, returning to my desk. 'Need I remind you that we are trying to attract a certain brand of customer here and the dress code is a vital part of that strategy?'

'I know, Ms McKnight,' she said contritely.

I smiled warmly to put her at ease. I wanted to get to the bottom of the reasons for her misdemeanour and felt that the best way to begin was to get her to relax. I find that an admonishment followed quickly by a warm bosom, so to speak, is most effective in this respect. 'Now, Kirsty, is there a reason why you persist in frumping yourself up like this?'

She paused to gather herself for confession and her lovely breasts heaved with her preparatory breath. 'I'm sorry, Ms McKnight, but the other croupiers are so much more slim and shapely than I. I feel so plump and unattractive in comparison to them.'

How sweet to hear this luxuriously figured lassie profess such genuine modesty about herself! At that moment I vowed inwardly to have her parading her stuff about the establishment like a wee hussy before the month was out.

I interview all my croupiers personally. I find the time invested pays off in the end, for I have something of a knack for sensing when a girl has what it takes to become a Paddle-Boat croupier. It matters not how shy or introverted a girl is in that first audience – I can always tell if they have 'it', however deep 'it' may be buried. I think it must be in the eyes; a glint of the fantastically bizarre gives them away.

Kirsty was no different from any of the other girls I had picked out. In spite of the unflattering attire she had chosen to wear, and the deferential, unconfident eyes that seemed unable to meet my gaze for more than a second at a time, I saw the sexual beast within and knew that in the coming weeks I would enjoy coaxing it out.

I had anticipated that Kirsty would have problems with our dress code, not least because of her larger figure. Girls, for all their delights, will seize upon any weakness and the other croupiers would not make allowances for her shyness. It does not help that girls are bombarded with media images of waiflike females with willowy bodies, and it is not uncommon for the curvier lady to lose all confidence in the magic of her mouth-watering form.

I already had a plan in my delectably dirty little mind that was designed to help her begin her journey. I smiled again, a matronly, even motherly smile, with reassuring authority.

'I understand, Kirsty, really I do, and I will do my very best to help you to adjust.' I stood up again and sat on my desk, as close to her as I dared.

She seemed confused. 'Will I have to diet?' she asked, concern etched over her alabaster face.

'Jings, no!' I cried, stretching out a warm palm and resting it on her hip, feeling for the first time the warmth of her body, 'Diet? And lose those beautiful contours and this almost edible figure of yours? Over my dead body.'

She seemed very pleased to hear me praise her body in this manner and as she blushed I wondered if I might even be the first to do so.

4

'Kirsty, my sweet,' I continued, 'there are two things I intend to do with you today. I'm afraid that later we must agree on a punishment for your misdemeanours – after three separate breaches of the dress code, I must be seen to be keeping discipline among the staff – but firstly, and most importantly, I intend to demonstrate to you how gloriously sexy your fulsome figure truly is.'

I reached over to my telephone and rang the extension of the Head Croupier. She answered immediately and I wondered if the cheeky minx had been sitting at her desk waiting for my call from the moment Kirsty had entered my office. I would have to check the video cameras later.

'Hello, Gemma,' I said. 'Would you bring your good self and the lingerie hamper back up here, please?'

The redheaded Gemma was soon at my office door, a small basket in her hands, which she set down on my desk before removing its woven lid; the soft wickerwork creaked quietly.

Gemma was my most striking girl and it was with great pleasure that I had made her my Head Croupier, knowing that she would become a shining example to the others. She was breathtaking in a skirt cut with ruthless cunning to be short enough to allow a hint of her stocking tops as she moved. She knew the value of a high heel, opting for the highest pair of black sling-backs that the style would allow, and how well she used them to sculpt her luscious legs and throw her tight firm buttocks into a seductive dance as she walked. Her waist was so unnaturally cinched that it was hard to believe she was corsetless. Gemma would often let her long flame of hair dance and sway over her small round breasts while her light-brown eyes beckoned from beneath her fringe. No wonder, then, that she was my best poker girl. What man could steel his mind from the distraction of having her across the table, all puns intended? Why, none.

'Come on now, Kirsty, don't be shy, take your clothes off,' I snapped, hoping that curtness would jolt her into action before she knew what she was at. It seemed to work: she turned slightly to the side, out of her natural modesty, I'm sure, and began to unbutton her blouse. Gemma, so used to my naughty little games, had already anticipated what I was up to and was making herself busy picking out an ensemble for Kirsty. There was little else for me to do but return to my seat behind the desk and enjoy the show as Kirsty stripped down to her sweet white lacy bra and knickers, throwing her tights, blouse and skirt on to a chair.

I felt a thin film of my essence ease itself between the walls of my sex and I crossed my legs as tightly as I could. I have perfected the art of rhythmically squeezing my clitty between the tendons in my thighs in this position, and I felt this would be preferable to brazenly frigging myself in front of such a retiring neophyte.

Gemma had picked out rather a racy set of sheer silks to go with an ornate suspender belt and matching bra, all of them in a deep chocolate colour that I knew would suit Kirsty's pale skin and dark hair and eyes. I gave my thighs an extra hard squeeze at the thought of seeing her slip into the outfit and felt the first drop of dew collect on my petals.

'What are we waiting for, Kirsty? Slip yourself into the clothes Gemma has picked out for you.'

Kirsty looked down bashfully but did as I asked her nonetheless. I leant forwards and squeezed my thighs even harder. For me, watching a young lady climbing into saucy underwear is just as erotic as watching her peeling it off, and my mouth and pussy watered as I gazed intently. To my right I noticed the shameless Gemma brush her own breast with her hand and I glared at her to desist for the time being.

Kirsty was naked for only a second or two as she removed the fancy but unflattering white underwear. Her hips and breasts rippled seductively as she stepped out of the knickers and Gemma and I gasped simultaneously at the sight. She must surely have heard our involuntary expression of appreciation.

Kirsty slipped into the dark-brown panties and fastened the bra around her bust; the support pushed upwards and outwards, making her puppies sit up and beg to be played with. Her body was pristine, uniform white against the darkness of the fabric; she looked like gateau and whipped cream.

The show continued as she rolled those sheer, coffee-coloured stockings over her feet and up to her thighs. She had forgotten her suspender belt in her nervousness and they rolled back down her legs again as she reached to slip the belt up high around her waist. Gemma and I were treated once again to the view of her rolling those diaphanous silks back up her thighs to be fastened.

In my distraction I had forgotten about shoes. I sent Kirsty to my cupboard to fetch a pair of my own heels, telling her to pick the pair she thought would work best. As Kirsty made her way there I sensed that we had overcome her initial shyness and nodded to Gemma to signify that it was safe now to let herself go. A look of relief swept across the frustrated redhead's face and, after perching herself on the corner of my desk, she lifted her tight little skirt, pulled down her damp, skimpy knickers and began to rub her clitoris with the pad of her middle finger, throwing her head back as she felt the first ripple of pleasure.

Kirsty stepped into a pair of dark-tan ankle-strapped heels that I had forgotten I had and teetered back around the desk to where she had been standing, smiling coyly and flushing slightly. Gemma followed her path as a sunflower follows the sun, massaging her bud all the while. Kirsty gave us a twirl in her new ensemble.

I had discovered Gemma's little foible of wanking in the presence of an audience a couple of months ago. It was a peccadillo that I had had plenty of fun developing and exploiting – even discovering that a little verbal admonishment as she played helped to enhance the experience for her immensely.

Mock-playfully I remarked, 'Oh my, look at what the sight of a beautiful girl in her underwear has done to our little whore of a Head Croupier. She's completely lost control of herself and seems to be frigging her errant little clitoris without the slightest regard for her dignity – did you ever see such a disgraceful display?'

Gemma squeaked and gasped as I roundly insulted her, while Kirsty took in what was happening, half amused, half incredulous. When I felt Gemma had reached the first plateau of pleasure, I decided to rein her in a bit.

'That's enough now, Gemma. Stop. I think your loss of control has demonstrated to Kirsty exactly how bountiful her beauty is and given her the confidence to dress more freely in future. Am I right, Kirsty?'

'Yes, Ms McKnight,' admitted Kirsty, looking down to admire herself and, I noticed, giving a satisfied smile.

'Good. Now it is time to discuss discipline.' I stood up and walked around to the front of the desk. Gemma stood up also and adjusted her skirt and

8

underthings. She sighed deeply and looked up at me longingly. I ignored her – I had more important things to do than provide opportunities for her to masturbate.

'As you will be aware from your contract, Kirsty, the official penalty for non-adherence to the dress code is a fine equivalent to half a day's wages, but, now that you are a fully initiated Paddle-Boat croupier and you've seen the way we operate in here, I am able to offer you the choice of a more physical reproof.'

Gemma, knowing her part well, reached into the hamper again and pulled out my thick leather strap, handing it to me respectfully. I held it so that Kirsty could see it clearly and I could tell by the widening of her eyes and nostrils that she was both frightened and excited by the sight of the instrument. I slapped it softly against the palm of my hand.

'You may not be aware that, here in Scotland, undisciplined schoolchildren were not chastised with the cane, as in England, but with the belt,' I told her, slapping it against my hand once more for effect. 'The choice is, of course, yours. If you would prefer to take the fine then I will ask Gemma to make the necessary changes to payroll, but I recommend you seriously consider the benefits of a shorter, sharper lesson. Learning to appreciate your own beauty is a promising first step but sometimes the only way to agitate the mind or free the soul is a brusque beating.'

I could tell from looking into those deep-brown eyes that the soul they framed was in crisis, desperately wrestling for the courage to agree to the punishment that I longed to administer.

'How many will I have to take?' she asked.

'Why, no more than a half-dozen,' I reassured her.

'On my *bare* arse?'

'Of course.'

Kirsty bit her lip and drew a long, deep breath into her bosom before releasing it through her nostrils, eyelids fluttering. 'I shall take the belt, Ms McKnight,' she said.

I was hugely relieved at this response, and the frisson rippling through my quivering vagina was delightful. Gemma too was clearly pleased, but then any Scots lass is pleased at the news that she will shortly witness a straight-laced English girl receiving six stripes of the belt on her ample hind.

'I know it is no longer the fashion to cane a schoolchild's buttocks, but did your parents ever give you a beating?' I asked her.

'Once or twice, Ms McKnight, my mother or father would occasionally spank me.'

'That is hardly the same thing. Let us get to business. Please bend over the desk, Kirsty, and stretch your arms out wide.'

Kirsty did as she was bade and Gemma, relishing the moment, made her way around to the other side of the desk to lean heavily on Kirsty's hands and thereby hold her in place. I like the buttocks to quiver and squirm a little with each impact but prefer it if the subject can be restrained, or can restrain themselves, to stand fast for their punishment.

Kirsty was now bent over my desk and, thanks to the weight of Gemma's hands, spread-eagled upon it. Her feet were on tiptoes, just barely supporting her, and I couldn't have wished for a more pleasing sight than those generous, stockinged legs leading up to that gorgeous backside. I could not fight the urge to reach down and tweak my love-berry for just a second. My finger came back wet – I hadn't expected that and I licked it clean. Gemma swallowed hard on a smirk, not wanting to displease me by displaying any amusement at my randiness, but I spotted her enjoyment and vowed that she would very soon pay for it.

With that same hand I slowly unfastened the clasps of Kirsty's suspender, while I playfully slapped the belt against my thigh with the other. I knew that she would be able to hear the leather striking my leg.

'Lift your buttocks,' I told her, and as she obeyed I pulled down her knickers to leave them around her legs, just above the knees. Her white mounds of virgin strap-fodder gleamed up at me and I became almost giddy with the anticipation of slicing six ripe ones over that cleavage.

I wound up for the first blow, before snapping it down swiftly across her crack, which clenched and reddened. Kirsty gasped at the bracing sting of her first taste of real discipline. I let her recover before applying the second in the same place, mapping it precisely on to the red glow which now bloomed on the surface of her rump. She arched her back as her buttocks clenched once more in response.

I applied the third and fourth in quick succession, lengthways, one to each buttock. The change of angle caught her off guard, as I knew it would, forcing two pussy-moistening gasps from her. Again, I allowed her time to recover.

'There will be two more strokes across the buttocks, but I want your legs farther apart.' I made it sound as if there were some scientific thinking going on, whereas the truth was that I simply took a notion to see how her labia were reacting to the waves of impact and sensation that I was inflicting.

Kirsty was now grasping the edges of the desk so tightly that Gemma was barely needed to hold her in place. I sensed that she would not soon forget her first session with me.

11

The fifth stroke was applied as low on her buttocks as I dared go and the crack of the leather on her flesh was followed quickly by a gasping moan. I saw the very slightest glistening of moisture on her petals and silently rejoiced that the new addition to our fold was blessed with such a reactive wee flower.

I swept the belt across her once more, again as close to her mound as I could place it, and was pleased to hear another sexy little groan. The moistness on her delicious lips was now unmistakable. I could have covered both her full bottom and her shuddering pussy with a thousand kisses, but I had a busy day ahead of me and there simply wasn't time.

'Well done, Kirsty, you coped splendidly. Now put your clothes back on over the lingerie. You can wear it for the rest of your shift, but I expect to see you in regulation attire the next time you come in.'

'Yes, Ms McKnight.'

'You may take a minute or two to recover if you need it,' I reassured her.

'No, I really am fine, thank you, Ms McKnight – I think I could have taken half a dozen more,' she said proudly, giving me another coy look. But there was more to it this time: the suggestion of a now unfettered imagination taking its first step into the light?

'I knew the moment I saw you that you'd take to it. I'm so glad I was right,' I commented before turning to Gemma.

'If you'd like to take up the same position on the desk, Gemma,' I said matter-of-factly.

'Miss?' replied Gemma, somewhat taken aback.

'You are to receive a cut across the backside for your impudence.'

'What for, Miss?'

'I distinctly remember seeing you smirking at me for touching myself and I don't welcome your cheek, especially as you had just been fiddling with yourself like a docker's daughter.'

Reluctantly Gemma lifted her skirt and pulled down her panties, taking position on the desk with her arms out wide. The sight of another fine bottom prepared for a lacing increased my moistness to a trickle, which I could feel beginning to collect on my thighs. I was half-tempted not to bother with the punishment and ask her to put her tongue to me, but I fought the urge.

Gemma was far more experienced than Kirsty and I resolved to wale her sharply from above the shoulder, just to remind her to show a little more deference to the boss. The impact released quite a thwack, matched in volume by Gemma's cry as her buttocks clenched and her body bucked in response. It was delectable.

Gemma stood up and adjusted herself to remove the fluster from her appearance. I noticed that her nipples were hard, a reaction to a beating I had not seen before in her. Perhaps there is something to be said for the single, sharp stroke.

Kirsty was now dressed again in her skirt and blouse, although the unflattering underthings she had been wearing when she had entered the room remained on the chair.

'Now you can both return to work,' I told them, smiling and returning to my desk. 'Leave your tights, bra and panties here, Kirsty. You won't be needing them again.'

Two

I waited on the mezzanine, in the grandest of the four private dining rooms that were built into it, and opened the privacy shutters to look down on to the gaming floor below.

The casino's keen regular gamers and gamblers were all at their favourite perches as my girls busily, joyfully and sexily did what they do best, both on the floor and downstairs in my basement: helping hapless gentlemen to part with their money and offering them in return the thrill of the game, a frisson of danger and the rush of playing on the edge.

The Paddle-Boat was now beginning to resemble the vision I had for it on the day it had first come within the grasp of my long red nails. Certainly, the staffing problem was all but resolved; the long process of observation and sexual profiling had begun on my first day and any of the incumbent staff who were too frumpy, or prudish, or unadventurous, had been replaced – through natural wastage of course: I would never have dismissed anyone just because of their personality. Although I must admit that I was not beyond making life a little more uncomfortable for someone if I felt the Paddle-Boat might benefit from their sudden compulsion to find themselves alternative employment – it is amazing what the effect of finding your boss's spunky knickers in your locker, or opening your payslip to find a photograph of Michael, the usher, masturbating in the shower, can be on you when you're a starchy and priggish young virgin. None of them seemed to bear any grudge, though, and they always smiled politely as I escorted them out of the revolving door on their last day.

So my croupiers had been whittled down to a select eight. Eight miniature goddesses, all teasing the punters with their open blouses, carelessly leaning across the roulette table from time to time, or bending down to retrieve a deliberately fumbled chip, thereby exposing just the right amount of stocking top to any man lecherous enough to glance, which in my experience means any man at all.

Bringing in the right sort of clientele followed naturally from there. I sent Michael on missions to the saunas in town to spread gossip about our establishment across the massage tables – he practically begged me to send him once I'd suggested it, so I could not back down. Once rumours had spread their way around the right circles, I soon found myself looking over this very same balcony and smiling as lawyers, dentists, journalists, medical practitioners and architects began to wander on to the gaming floor. The professional man has a certain tendency towards the fetish, and especially towards the need for punishment. I have enslaved all sorts of men, from refuse-disposal technicians to parliamentary candidates, and used every sort of bond, literal and figurative, to enslave them in my little games: my sweet-tasting feet, my smooth sturdy legs, cold chains, rough, chafing ropes, tight, pinching clamps, even the cruel bond of orgasm denial. But most commonly I have found myself standing over a trembling, naked professional man as he begs for the sweet contradiction of punishment and mercy.

Perhaps the affluent professional is more able to pursue and develop his fantasies and desires, there being no financial limits to his exploration into the taboo. Or perhaps it is the natural need in us all for balance – the yang of the positive attributes of a professional man's everyday life, such as propriety, power and reward, must be balanced with the yin of misbehaviour, submission and punishment.

It is all speculation. Like the tigress who waits at the jungle trail for her prey, I cannot pretend to know where the creatures come from who pass my way; I merely know when to pounce.

I do not usually have time to sit down for lunch, but today I had something arranged with the prospective new chef, Peter.

Peter was a sweet young lad, if a little gangly and untidily coiffed, who had been the first to respond to my local newspaper advertisement for a new chef. I had intended to devote a titillating afternoon to interviewing (and teasing) a number of male applicants for the position but, as I've always been an admirer of keenness, especially in young men, I decided to reward him by closing the vacancy for the time being and giving the doe-eyed young fellow a week's trial.

'You seem very eager. The advertisement can only have hit the stands about twenty minutes ago,' I said to him, perching myself on my desk so that I could look down on him.

'I find I get more work that way,' he replied in a very suave manner that seemed at odds with his ungroomed image. I gave him a suggestive smile.

'I like eagerness in a young man,' I told him, and it was true: I find as a rule that the more enthusiastic a chap is about life, the more energetically he enters into his sexuality, and the more actively he tends to respond to the bite of my fingernails on his buttocks.

'I like women who like eagerness in a young man, so we seem a perfect match,' he countered, returning with interest the suggestive smile I had given him.

'Of course, eagerness is not enough to secure the position on its own,' I warned him, taking a more aloof tone to see if he would maintain his flirtatious demeanour or be discouraged.

'Oh, I have much more to offer than just eagerness. I am quite sure once you see the full package you'll want to take me up,' he said, smirking presumptuously, his eyes smouldering with all the possible meanings behind the statement.

'. . . Permanently,' he added.

I began to get the distinct impression that Peter was a little on the confident side, and decided to test that confidence with a proposal I hoped would appeal to him.

'You seem very sure of yourself,' I said, which seemed to make him smile even more coolly. That smirk was somehow both infuriating and exciting, and I vowed on the spot that one day I would wipe it off his face, even if I had to press my dripping sex over his nose and mouth to do it. 'Are you sure enough of yourself to accept a more demanding challenge?' I asked. 'Of course, if you'd prefer the relative safety of a week's trial, that's fine.'

'Sounds interesting. What did you have in mind?' he asked, I think half-believing that I was going to propose some sort of brash sexual challenge. I took great delight in disabusing him of that notion.

'For your first duty you would prepare a meal for me and serve it to me in one of the private mezzanine dining rooms. If I approve of your performance I'll

17

start you on a contract; if not, then you'll be back down to the agency in the morning – or whatever sordid activity you get up to between employments.'

I intended the final comment to bring him down a notch or two, but it just bounced off him like a squash ball off a wall.

'Would there be anything else at stake?' he asked suggestively, glancing up and down my gloriously sexy body as a hungry man glances up and down a menu. It was as if he was choosing a joint from a butcher's window, not addressing a sophisticated woman, future boss and, inevitably, Mistress.

If I had been in the mood for giving in to impulse I would have slapped him across the face with my open palm, but then I would also have had to give in to the other impulse vibrating through me at that instant, to ride his young cock like a randy cowgirl – and that really wasn't the behaviour of a modern businesswoman with an image to uphold.

'The challenge is just as I stated,' I insisted. 'Take it or leave it.'

He smiled again, his tongue planted firmly in his cheek this time – perhaps that helps him think – before replying. 'I accept.'

I did not need to be an expert at reading a face to know that more than a couple of impure thoughts were going through his head.

Perhaps I should explain a philosophy of mine that will help to illustrate exactly how unusual my attraction to young Peter was: as a dominant female I do not have sexual intercourse with Beta-male specimens.

On reflection, perhaps that is the wrong place to start. I should begin by saying that, for me, the male race falls into two categories, the Alpha male and the

Beta male. They are both naturally submissive to the authoritative woman who understands the power of her body and mind over the body and mind of the often superficial, stimulus-driven male.

My security staff are prime examples of Alpha males. I have picked them for their physical attributes, their lean muscular bodies and their masculine features. I rank them above Beta males, who tend to be young and scrawny or old and overweight; they are not true men in the physical sense of the word and, while they have their uses, I consider sexual intercourse a privilege that is above their station.

Should I choose to take a partner in the future, perhaps to raise a daughter, it shall be with an Alpha male. And when, from time to time, I feel I would like to take advantage of the pleasure that can be derived from sexual intercourse, it is always with an Alpha male.

So it was most unusual that Peter, apparently a Beta specimen, was having such a titillating effect on me.

I could hear Peter approaching along the corridor; the trundle and rattle of his trolley gave him away. I closed the shutters, quickly took my seat at the table and adopted the pose I wanted him to discover me in: cross-legged with my skirt-hem above my knee and my uppermost shin and instep glistening like a blade all the way down to the shoe dangling on my toe like the grapes that dangled above Tantalus.

It was my intention that when Peter walked through the door the vision greeting him would stop him in his tracks and momentarily make him forget himself. Life, as I say, is a performance.

He entered, wheeling the trolley carefully through the door. Peter was dressed casually that day, with a white, sauce-stained T-shirt and frayed jeans; his hair was mussed from working in the kitchen and he smelt of cooking and sweat. The only item of the chef's uniform he seemed willing to wear was the small white apron wrapped around his waist.

'Hello again, Ms McKnight.'

I observed with satisfaction as his eyes lit on my slowly swinging shoe and then ran upwards to take in my lower leg, continuing right up to the hem of my skirt.

'You have something for me, Chef?' I asked.

'Hmm? Oh, aye. I have your starter, if you're ready to eat?'

'I am, but would you pour me some wine first?' I picked up an empty glass by the stem and twiddled it in the air with my thumb and forefinger. Peter reached for the bottle of Cabernet Sauvignon at the table and poured me a glassful of that rich, velvety fluid. I locked my eyes on to his as I sipped and smiled. He smiled back, and returned to his trolley.

'First course is something fresh and simple: a fan of honeydew melon, served with stem ginger.' He slid a beautifully prepared dish on to the table before me. Peter had sliced the juicy lime-coloured flesh into a fan of thin sheaves, and spread them across the plate like a peacock's tail. The melon was jewelled with slender, translucent coins of stem ginger, and the whole was drizzled with a gossamer trail of syrup and crowned with an intricately carved cherry. I was highly impressed.

'You must be very good with your hands.'

He took the seat next to me and casually placed one of those hands speculatively upon my knee. I decided to allow it for the time being and, taking my fork, tried the starter.

'They do say the first bite is with the eye,' he said,

20

brazenly fixing his own blue eyes on my legs and cleavage.

I continued to eat as Peter enjoyed his 'first bite' of me from the adjacent seat, all the while his fingers lightly caressing the inside of my thigh, just above the knee. Again, I knew I really should not have let such a cheeky and cocksure young man take such liberties but he was making my flesh moisten and run with juice in the same way as the melon slice ran with juice as my fork cut into it.

His hand began to roll up my thigh and I felt that the time had come to put him back in his place. I washed my palate with a sip of wine.

'Serve me the main course,' I said. It was an order – I deliberately made it so, just to see how he would respond to female authority. After all, I need my male staff to know when to be obedient and when to be boisterous.

'Yes, of course, Ms McKnight,' he said and returned to his trolley.

He made no attempt to hide his tenting trousers but deliberately turned the bulge towards me as he attended to the main course. Even when Peter was displaying some capacity for obedience his cock seemed to urge him to defy me.

'I don't know if you've picked up anything of the way things work around The Paddle-Boat, but I can assure you that, if you respond well to my authority, it will score in your favour,' I said, reminding him I hoped that this exercise was tantamount to an appraisal or job interview and not some tryst behind a bike-shed in the schoolyard. I like to give the new blood some idea of the kind of establishment I want The Paddle-Boat to evolve into: it saves time and embarrassment later on. One of the most important things I could teach this rather headstrong, self-fancying Lothario was that I was very much in charge – of my staff and my lovers alike.

He swung slowly round again. He had a large covered dish balanced upon his palm, which he slid on to the table in front of me before removing the stainless-steel domed cover.

'Ms McKnight, I present the main course: baked oysters with spinach and fennel puree and crisp fried shallots.'

There was a definite deference to his demeanour, which I liked – it showed that he was picking up my cues. I needed a breather from his outrageously presumptuous flirting anyway, otherwise I might struggle to maintain my level of decorum; the thought of giving in and letting him do all the wicked things that were clearly going on in his mind was turning me on.

I ignored the glint of mischief that still lingered in his eye and surveyed my plate. A dozen oyster shells sat on a bed of rock salt and salad in a hexagonal pattern, each covered with a rich, verdant purée and topped with a coronet of browned, translucent shallots.

My mouth watered in time with my pussy and I tried to hide how impressed I was with his efforts.

'I'm not sure if I can manage a dozen of these, Peter. Won't you take a seat and have three or four for yourself?'

He bowed his head slightly and smiled. 'I would be happy to,' he said.

I took the first shell in my hand and, using the small fork provided, transferred its treasure to my waiting mouth. The purée and garnish were the perfect complement to the delicious mollusc, and I barely had to chew: I simply pushed my tongue against it, pressing it to the roof of my mouth, and the morsel melted away. Peter took an oyster of his own and mimicked my action.

'Delicious,' I said in congratulation. 'But a tad obvious, don't you think?'

'I don't know what you mean.' His large blue eyes portrayed innocence for the very first time since I had met him.

'I mean, what do *you* mean by serving me an aphrodisiac for lunch,' I prompted.

'Well, sometimes being obvious is the best way to get what you want,' he said with a smirk, once again placing his impudent hand on my thigh.

I ate another oyster while I considered whether to allow this. Its delicate taste took my mind away for a moment and made me forget to protest at this latest piece of insolence.

'I have never prepared oysters myself – how is it done?' I asked him, pretending not to have noticed the warmth of his hand inching up my inner thigh.

'You have to *shuck* them,' he said, as his fingers spidered their way upwards.

'*Shuck*?' I queried.

'*Shuck*,' he confirmed.

'How exactly does one *shuck*?' I asked him, as I felt a fingertip hook itself under the lacefront of my knickers. I quivered beneath it.

'Don't tell me a lady as beautiful and liberated as yourself has never *shucked* before.'

'Well, I haven't.'

'First, you have to scrub the shell of the oyster.' I felt the soft pads of his fingertips press against my cunt-lips. I fought to retain my composure and, to distract myself, devoured a third oyster, knowing, as I savoured the flavoursome titbit, that I would be waiting a while before I tasted my fourth.

'Do you have any tips for scrubbing the shell?' I

gasped, closing my eyes as the words softly leaked out of me and I surrendered to the melting sensations in my loins.

'I tend to use little circles with the brush, not pressing too hard. It is important to apply firm but even pressure and sweep smooth curves.' He was whispering now into my ear and my neck tingled on that side. I could feel his fingers brushing my pearl as they described those same circles on to my petals, easing them apart.

'Then what?' I asked.

'Then you must slip your oyster spatula between the shells, at the hinged end.'

I felt his middle- and fore-fingers slide between my moist lips. He softly moved them up and down, again teasing me with casual brushes of my clitoris.

'What happens then?' I breathed, placing my hand on the back of his neck.

'You must twist the shells apart.'

His two fingers parted my labia with a scissors-like motion. I gasped as I felt the air against the entrance to my sex.

'You can then gently force the flesh from the shell.'

A third finger pushed inside me, encouraging me to moisten and dilate still further before two more fingers joined in the slow thrusting into my soft, warm canal.

I pulled him to me and kissed him. His fingers dug softly for the treasure of my g-spot, which I felt him brush lightly. I pushed him away, my hand now on his shoulder, and looked at him intently.

'You seem to have picked up quite quickly that it is not just culinary skills I am looking for.'

'Yes, Ms McKnight.'

'Do you feel you are up to the additional demands of the position?'

'Yes, Ms McKnight.'

'They will be arduous on you physically at times.'

'Yes, Ms McKnight.'

'There will be no room for your pride, modesty or jealousy.'

'I understand.'

'And you will be required to answer to my whims and fancies, and to show willing when it comes to the expansion of your horizons.'

'I am willing, Ms McKnight.' He reciprocated my intense gaze.

I am aware that a man will say just about anything when he sees that sexual intercourse looms on the horizon – I have often mused on what I could make a man agree to with the promise of my delicious body and warm pussy – perhaps give over his livelihood to me, who knows? – but Peter's earnest gaze convinced me that his intentions were genuine. I had found myself an obedient, rutting stag and, even if he looked to me very much like a Beta specimen, I decided to bend the rules a little that afternoon. It was time to put him to his first assignment.

I kissed him again. Our lips and tongues lapped each other thirstily and I could feel myself glazing his fingertips with my sweet juices. I wanted to feel him inside me without delay. I reached for the bulge in his denims, lifting the flap of his apron to get at the zip underneath. He smelt like a cocktail of masculinity, of work and sweat from his morning's chores, and I inhaled him deeply.

I felt the prominent head of his circumcised penis poking out of his boxers and caressed it lightly with my fingers.

Peter stood up, wrestling frantically with his apron, which he unfastened and threw to the ground. I stood too, to tackle his belt and button, yanking trousers and underwear down in one jerk; his penis sprang forwards, wobbling in the air like a springboard.

I wasted no time and bent myself over the table, pulling my skirt up to present him with my glorious rump. Perhaps it was the thrill of my power to arouse men, perhaps it was the contradictory excitement of my slutty actions, but whatever the reason, the heat rushed to my face.

Peter wasted no time either, and manoeuvred himself behind me to plunge his erection to the hilt into my juicy quim. He fucked me like an animal, just as I had hoped he would, and I squeezed and squirmed on his rod to grasp every spasm of pleasure that I could.

My hand pushed between the table and my belly, instinctively reaching for my clitoris as I rocked back and forth. Peter announced his piston-like thrusts with alternate growls and groans.

Soon I was nearing my peak; the tingle of pleasure radiated to my belly, and my tongue and fingertips also quivered with twinges of sensation. My gasps must have excited him because I could feel his cock twitching on the edge of delivery. He hesitated, apparently anxious not to spend too quickly after I had put so much emphasis on his need to perform. His thrusting slowed slightly as he teetered on climax.

I was not in the mood for prolonged intercourse or holding back. My sex longed for a consignment of his creamy sauce.

'Go for it,' I told him, almost snarling.

He did, ramming me hard with a dozen vicious thrusts until he bathed my womb with his come. I savoured the afterglow as he slowly pushed in and out of me until his cock had softened, and withdrew; I heard a smack as my labia blew him a kiss of farewell.

'Not bad, Peter,' I gasped. Truth was, he had done very well; none of the Alphas in the security staff had humped me so vigorously on their first attempts and I felt I had something of a find here.

I adjusted my skirt with a wiggle of my hips and returned to my seat. I picked up my fork and ate another oyster, my appetite renewed.

'You can start on a full-time basis tomorrow morning,' I told him as I ate. 'In the meantime I suggest you get yourself straight and set about getting me my dessert.'

'Of course, Ms McKnight,' he replied. He pulled his jeans up, tucked his sticky cock back into his shorts, zipped, buttoned and buckled. He was still wrapping his apron around his waist when there was a knock at the door. I began eating another oyster.

Chloe McIntyre came into the room in her croupier's uniform of black skirt and white blouse, top button open. She was pouting with her full pink lips as usual, but turned them to a smile on seeing me.

'Good afternoon, Ms McKnight.'

'Good afternoon to you, Chloe,' I replied, smirking to myself as Peter tried to tie up his apron without arousing suspicion. I could have told him not to waste his time; Chloe had been working for me for a little while now and was well used to bursting in on me just after some risqué activity or other – not for her the discreet withdrawal. She grinned and flicked her straight blond hair.

'Mr Finlay has been playing me at the poker table for the last hour and a half,' she announced.

'That's good to hear,' I replied. Jeffrey Aitkin Finlay was an affluent QC, who seemed to enjoy throwing his money around in my casino – it was always good news to hear that he was paying us a visit.

27

'He has asked to play for an hour at the *private* wheel,' said Chloe.

I smiled an even wider smile and reached into my bra for the basement key. Chloe tottered over in her heels to take it from me.

'This will be your first time playing alone in the basement, Chloe. Are you ready?'

'Oh aye, absolutely,' she replied enthusiastically. 'I'll give him an hour he'll never forget.'

I was pleased. This was the climax of many hours' practice with Chloe and my own clients – or with members of the security staff who had agreed to help in my training programme – in the basement play-room. I took immense satisfaction in seeing her graduate so willingly to a solo performance.

'I shall read your journal entry with great interest,' I told her.

Chloe thanked me and skipped out of the door. I returned to the balcony, to open the shutters and look down on to the floor below. Mr Finlay was sitting patiently at one of the poker tables. It was only the early afternoon and he was still wearing his smart pinstriped suit. I wondered where he had heard about our ancillary services; was it from a fellow profes-sional gent? From a whispered rumour at some high-falutin social function? Or maybe my ploy had worked and he had overheard Michael in the waiting room of a West End massage parlour?

Chloe appeared on the gaming floor below, flicking her hair again seductively. Mr Finlay stood and she took his arm, glancing up at me with a smile as the two of them made their way to the rear of the gaming floor and through the veneered door that led to The Cellar.

Three

I had planned to read over Chloe's journal entry the next morning, before beginning my work for the day. Indeed, if truth be known, I had been anticipating it for the rest of that afternoon, all evening and much of the night. My last thought before sliding my newly bathed feet and freshly moisturised legs between my pearl-coloured sheets that night was to imagine to myself what kind of sordid antics the leering Mr Finlay had requested that afternoon and how the blossoming young Chloe might have coped with them.

It will be appreciated how frustrated I was when I glided into my office, slipped my slender pins under the desk, softly parked my sculpted buttocks on the chair and discovered not Chloe's report facing me, but also my open appointment book displaying the pencilled details of a 9.45 a.m. engagement. It had not been there before and I was surprised to see it pop up overnight like a morning erection. Fortunately the writing was familiar to me – that distinctive hand had written a couple of playroom journal entries in recent weeks. I picked up the phone.

'Hello?'

'Gemma, my sweet, was it yourself who booked this nine forty-five appointment?'

'Yes, Ms McKnight. Mrs F rang in just after Gordon and I had opened up; she was quite anxious to speak to you as soon as possible.'

'Well, that can't be helped, I suppose. Thank you, Gemma.'

I put the phone down and sighed. It was nine o'clock already. I searched my desk for Chloe's report and bit my red lip in frustration when I discovered it was not yet there. If it were not put into my hand soon I would have to resign myself to waiting until after I had spoken to this Mrs F. Mrs F? Who was this Mrs F? When I came to rack my brains I could not think of a Mrs F that I knew. I picked up the phone again.

'Hello?'

'Gemma darling. Who is this Mrs F? Should I have been expecting her?'

'It's Mrs Finlay, of course – the QC's wife.'

I gave one of the mysterious smiles that I like to practise in the mirror from time to time and wished someone had been watching me to admire it.

'Well, well, quite a coincidence. I wonder what she could want. Thank you, Gemma.' I put the phone down again, and leant back in my chair.

There was a timid, almost apologetic, knock on the door. I decided to ignore it, forcing my visitor to be more bold. Boldness is a trait that must be encouraged in a Paddle-Boat croupier.

A louder knock followed and this time I deigned to respond.

'Come in!' I called.

Chloe McIntyre slid into the office like a woodland sylph appearing from behind a tree. Her straight blond hair shone from a morning shampoo and her face was dipped towards the floor.

'Morning, Ms McKnight. I've brought you the

30

report from yesterday afternoon,' she said, looking up and smiling.

I smirked back.

'And how did you enjoy your first time in the playroom?'

A flush came over her momentarily as she recalled her experience.

'It was most exhilarating, Ms McKnight.'

'Well, you've delivered this just in time, Chloe. I shall read it straight away,' I told her, taking it from her hand.

As Chloe turned to leave, a thought must have entered her head. She turned towards me.

'Ms McKnight?'

'Hmm?'

'I wonder, if you are working in The Cellar in the near future, that is to say, well, if you need an assistant for any of the scenarios . . .'

'I will be sure to consider you, yes,' I interrupted.

Chloe beamed and skipped from the room in her high-heeled pumps. I watched her close the door behind her and turned to her report:

Croupier: Chloe McIntyre
Date: Tuesday 15th June
Client: Mr Finlay

I cannot describe the nervousness that took me over when Mr Finlay asked me if I had 'the keys to the playroom'. I knew a client would inevitably proposition me some day, and that there is a first time for everything, but still I was shaking like a leaf as I pressed the button under the table for my replacement. It seemed like an age before Abrille Martin appeared and I could leave the table with Mr Finlay. By then I was a little dewy with the anticipation, I must admit.

This is my first summary, Ms McKnight, so please forgive me if it rambles a bit; I hope you can still find the information you need.

Mr Finlay is about 55. He is quite slim and of average height with dark hair (dyed, I suspect) and large greying sideburns. His skin seems weathered – perhaps from enjoying too many cigars or Mediterranean holidays. I guess you can gather from all that that he is quite well to do, with neat suits and a posh Kelvinside accent. Or maybe it's Milngavie.

As I led Mr Finlay downstairs I could tell he was getting quite nervous, from his breathing and because his right cheek twitched a couple of times – I've noticed this also happens at the poker table when he has a good hand.

I suppose I should have mentioned this at the start but Mr Finlay first came into the casino four weeks ago. He only plays poker and, although he seems to know what he's doing, I think he has frittered away quite a lot of money.

I noticed that he tended to play when I was on shift and would stare at me during play, especially if I was leaning over to deal. I began to suspect, even early on, that he would be the first client to ask me down to the playroom.

I should apologise: when he finally asked me, I was so nervous that I failed to remember to ask him where he had heard about the playroom. I know this is important to you, Ms McKnight, so I shall ask him next time.

When we were safely out of sight, I collected his fee and asked him if he had a preference for any particular game, or if he would rather let The Wheel decide his fate. Mr Finlay knew exactly what he was looking for.

'I understand you have a school room,' he said, a little shyly.

'I see. And am I to be the Headmistress or the naughty pupil?'

Suddenly, his executive arrogance disappeared and his gaze fell to his shoes.

'Headmistress,' he said hoarsely.

'And I suppose you are to be a naughty school-boy?' I said pleasantly – trying my best to make him feel comfortable.

'– girl,' he said.

I begged his pardon.

'School*girl*.'

Well, I did not expect that and I nearly laughed out loud – but I remembered what you said in our training, how important it is to ensure the client feels accepted and welcome, so I swallowed my amusement.

'Is she to be punished, this naughty schoolgirl?' Mr Finlay took a huge breath before replying.

'Yes. She wants to be punished until she is crying like a wee baby girl.'

It obviously took a lot of courage for Mr Finlay to admit his fetish to me and even more courage to ask for it and I must admit I felt a bit of admiration for him. Not too much, though, as it was important to maintain my authority.

'Follow me,' I instructed, and strode into the basement, past your specially modified roulette wheel in the centre of the room, and towards the walled-off fantasy area at the back of the dungeon: The School Room.

Once there I went straight to the props cupboard at the rear of the mock classroom and pulled the schoolgirl's uniform from the rack and the thick-heeled black shoes from the box.

'Dress yourself. You *can* do that, I presume, girl?'

'Yes, Miss.'

As he readied himself I took the gown and mortar board from the cupboard and put them over my croupier's uniform, hiking up my skirt to expose my stocking tops and undoing two of my blouse buttons. Being a traditional Scottish lass I picked the belt rather than the cane and slapped it once in my hand. I was ready.

I must confess, Ms McKnight, the combination of taking on a position of power and adopting such a strikingly sexual image had me feeling like a royal flush.

I left Mr Finlay changing his clothes and paid a quick visit to another of the fantasy rooms, The Boudoir. I felt that our little schoolgirl would benefit from some girly hair and make-up so I fetched some over to The School Room.

I assisted the wee girlie with the rest of 'her' transformation and, after she had stepped into her short skirt and pulled up her hold-ups, smoothing them on to her legs, helpless to hide her enjoyment of the act, I stepped in with the make-up. I felt she should have pink girly lips, some freckles over her nose and rouged cheeks. I threw Mr Finlay's posh clothes into the cupboard and, when his underpants caught my eye, it gave me a rather delicious idea – so I deliberately left my pupil without any knickers. I think my pupil found the idea of going knickerless rather titillating – little realising I would be using it against her later.

Now that we were both ready I immediately clicked into character, just as you have suggested works best.

'Sit down, girl. Don't just stand there,' I snapped.

'Sorry, Miss,' she squeaked, tottering over to the desk and taking a seat.

'Now I understand you have been placed in detention today for failing to adhere to the St Valerie dress code.'

'Yes, Miss.'

'Now you know, Headmistress McKnight is very strict about our uniform, Wendy.' I picked the name Wendy straight off the top of my head – I was thinking of the character in *Peter Pan*, of course. 'Even the slightest divergence is to be punished severely. Take fifty lines: "I must adhere to the strict uniform code of our well-respected educational establishment: St Valerie's Preparatory School." Afterwards I will inspect your attire to ensure that you have mended your ways.' I placed a sheet of paper and a stubby pencil on the desk.

While she wrote I could not resist slapping the belt in my hands. Indeed, I decided to give Wendy a bit of a show while she wrote and I perched on the teacher's desk, crossing and uncrossing my sheer nylonned legs, allowing Wendy titillating peeks at my thighs and my black lacies. Her tight little skirt began to tent and after a few minutes I felt the time had come for some more humiliating and perhaps even tactile punishment.

I swiped the pencil and paper from Wendy's hand – not bothering to count how many lines she had done – and told her to stand. She did so, blushing even under her cosmetically rosy cheeks as her knickerless erection pushed at her skirt. I pretended not to notice it.

'Good. Now I'm going to inspect your uniform. Stand up straight, girl.'

Wendy stood to attention, rather like that cock under that skirt, and I circled her, sucking through my teeth and tutting a bit.

'That skirt is far too racy and short. Are you here to learn, girl, or to act like a whore?'

'Sorry, Miss.' There was real shame in Wendy's voice.

Honestly, Ms McKnight, I could not believe how well the session was going.

'I bet you are. Spending your lunch-hour behind the bike sheds, playing with all the naughty boys' willies. I've seen you – don't deny it. Secondly, those shoes are far too high.'

'Sorry, Miss.'

'Your blouse is undone. You're showing far too much cleavage, you dirty little girl.'

I made a show of slapping the belt as I walked around her. Now I was standing behind her and I could see Wendy shiver a little and quicken her breathing.

I reached forward and, lightly scraping the top of her thighs with my fingernails, lifted her skirt up at the back to expose her bare arse to the cellar air. A gasp burst from her lipsticked mouth.

'What's this? No undergarments? Are you completely without shame, you nasty little girl?'

I walked round in front of her again.

'Ms McKnight's rules are quite clear on this subject, girl. I have no choice but to administer a corporal punishment. Six strokes for the skirt, six for the shoes and six for the lack of underwear.'

I knew eighteen strokes of the belt would be hard to take but I wasn't sure if they would be enough to make Wendy cry, so I quickly thought of a way to extend the sentence. Glancing down at the tenting pencil skirt, I pretended to notice that erect penis for the first time.

'What's this?' I demanded. 'A girl with a dingle?'

'Yes, Miss, sorry, Miss.'

'I hope you know that girls with dingles are not permitted at St Valerie's? Of course, I will have to report this – it's more than my job is worth not to.'

'Yes, Miss.'

'Although . . .' I began, pausing long enough for Wendy to contemplate her forthcoming ordeal, '. . . I suppose if, in return for my secrecy, you agree to be my special little helper about campus, I can overlook reporting you. I shall still have to punish you for your insolent attempt to flout our entrance rules. A further six strokes should do it. Don't you agree?'

'Yes, Miss.' Wendy's voice was barely a squeak by now, and getting quite girly.

'I'm so glad. Now, Wendy, if you would bend over your desk we may begin. Remember to count nice and loud,' I ordered her as I gripped the belt in my hand.

She was a good little girl and did not procrastinate as a lesser girl might; she bent herself over the desk, stretching on to the tips of her toes. With my free hand I lifted her skirt to expose her bare cheeks. As I wound up for the initial stroke, I noticed that Wendy was lying down on top of her erection. I decided that I would rather keep an eye on the excited member – it was disappointing to think that I wouldn't have the chance to witness the effect that Wendy's punishment might have on her erection. I stepped nearer.

'Lift up your tummy, girl.'

Obediently she did so and I reached underneath her, my hands encircling her penis and pulling it towards me until it was pointing straight down towards the floor.

'Good. Now back down on the desk with you,' I said. Now I could clearly see Wendy's quivering arse-cheeks, her nylonned legs and terribly excited penis all at the same time and I was ready to commence.

I let the first stroke fall across both cheeks, using a relaxed arm. I regret to report that Wendy forgot who she was and let out a very manly grunt. On top of that, she neglected to count.

'Now Wendy, that was not at all ladylike, was it?' I said. 'You must remember to cry out like the snivelling little slut you are, not like some hairy docker – and don't forget to *count*.'

I let the second fall in exactly the same way, and this time Wendy gave a high-pitched gasp, then called out 'Two!' in a similar timbre.

Numbers three and four fell lengthways on separate buttocks, which began to redden and quiver nicely. At this point I changed gear, and put my arm into cross-strokes five and six. Wendy's buttocks clenched and unclenched each time. Indeed, I noted that she had to swallow to compose herself before calling out 'six'.

'That was for wearing such high heels, Wendy,' I reminded her.

'Yes, Mi-Eah!' she gasped. I recalled your advice not to let the recipient get used to the rhythm and so delivered the seventh before she had finished replying.

'Seven!' she cried after a moment

I continued in quick succession, with number eight falling across the cleavage and nine and ten falling lengthways on each mound. As she gasped out the numbers, I watched her carefully. There were no tears as yet and I began to wonder if I had it in me to fulfil Mr Finlay's request. I noticed also that her cock was still erect, which surprised me.

I resolved that a more severe treatment was called for.

I lifted the belt above my shoulder and administered strokes eleven and twelve, cracking them on to the cherry-red flesh with more gusto. This time Wendy squealed and bucked a little and I knew I had found the correct range at last. Ms McKnight, I must confess that by now the feeling of power was making my pussy weep a little.

'Those were for having such a short skirt on. This is an educational establishment, not Blythswood Square,' I told her.

'Yes, Mi-Eeaah!' I caught her again unawares.

The next four strokes were delivered with the same ferocity as I had put into the previous ones, repeating the pattern of two cross-strokes followed by two lengthways, and the skin on Wendy's furry peaches began to rise up and pit like a tangerine peel. By now it was taking her three or four gasps to collect herself for the count.

'. . . Six – teen,' she squeaked, eventually catching up with me.

I walked around her to gauge how things were progressing. There were certainly tears in her eyes and I could hear a lot of sniffing, but she could not yet be said to be properly sobbing or crying.

I was astonished to see that her cock was still hard, and pointing stiffly downwards. I did not think such a level of arousal would be possible under such duress and I could not help but reach out and pump it a few times with my hand – more out of admiration than anything else.

I put everything I dared into completing the third set of six, each stroke beginning well above my head. Wendy tottered in her heels and quivered from the blows and, as she made the count, her voice was shaky.

'*That* was for going knickerless,' I told her. 'Now, your final six strokes, which you earned for not declaring your dingle on the St Valerie's Entrance Application Form.'

'Please, Miss, go easy,' said Wendy desperately. Her voice was breaking up and I knew that she was close to tears.

The first real sobs began after the twentieth stroke. I was amazed – they really were just like the wailing of a schoolie. After the twenty-first, Wendy begged me to stop, but I ignored her pleas, knowing they were all part of Mr Finlay's fantasy, and delivered 22 and 23 in the same way.

'*Please*, Miss!'

I let her cry for a little while before completing the punishment. Tears were now streaming down Wendy's face and she sobbed right the way through the final stroke, which, primarily for my own benefit, I delivered with a flourish.

Amazingly, Wendy's cock was still hard. I had heard of this crying fetish before – I can't remember the proper name – but I had no idea of the level of arousal that was possible under such duress.

I reached forward and milked her cock. It only took a dozen or so pumps before it thumped out three wads of semen on to the side of the desk.

I returned to the teacher's desk to allow Wendy time to recover and we began her transformation back into Mr Finlay, who seemed very peaceful and satisfied afterwards. I do believe, Ms McKnight, that my first assignment was therefore a success and I hope that any fellow croupiers reading this will find it useful, should they be chosen for a session with Mr Finlay in the future. Although I still can't remember the name of that crying fetish!
Chloe.

'Dacrophilia,' I muttered as I finished reading Chloe's fabulous report. It had quite turned me on, and the only pity was that, having read it, I did not have time to rub myself before Mrs Finlay arrived.

She did so just before 9.45 a.m., as the first whirr of the roulette wheel could be heard in the gambling area. I watched from the mezzanine gallery as her short, skirted figure moved past the Chinese gentlemen who had started early at the blackjack table. Gemma met her halfway across the floor and escorted her towards my office.

As quickly as I could, but without looking flustered, I made my way there to greet her as she entered. My usual pose sufficed, I decided: perched on the corner of my desk, serving up a generous helping of my crossed legs, displaying them as the tools of my sexual power.

I know she saw them as she entered but she quickly chose to avert her eyes. Behind her, Gemma stared intently.

'Good morning, Mrs Finlay. It is a pleasure to meet you. Would you have a seat?' I gestured with an open palm for her to occupy the chair in front of my desk. She sat, and I settled into my chair opposite.

'Thank you, Gemma dear. Please wait outside,' I said to Gemma, who dutifully closed the office door behind her as she withdrew.

Mr Finlay had been spending a lot of time with us in recent weeks – we now know why – and I fancied this might turn out to be an interesting conversation.

'How can I help you, Mrs Finlay?' I asked.

Her reply was snappy but not exactly direct.

'I do not approve of this sort of establishment,' she said, 'and I don't feel altogether happy about having to attend here this morning. Not least because I have had to ask the deputy head to take assembly this morning.'

I smiled to myself. The knowledge that Mrs Finlay was head teacher at a local educational establishment suddenly demoted Mr Finlay's need to play out female authority scenarios to somewhat less of a mystery. I wondered which part of the establishment was the subject of Mrs Finlay's disapproval. Had Mr

Finlay been loose with his tongue and mentioned our subterranean playroom? Or perhaps she simply referred to our overt gambling activities. She continued to play out the rope that my silence had given her.

'But needs must – things have reached their limit, I'm afraid. I am the wife of Jeffrey A. Finlay, QC. He is an intelligent and successful man, as you might have gathered, but this evil place of yours has its poisonous fangs in him and it threatens to jeopardise everything that the two of us have worked for.'

'I assure you, Mrs Finlay, that is just about the last thing The Paddle-Boat would want to happen. We are simply a place of enjoyment and entertainment, nothing more, and we are certainly not in the business of ruination. How can I help to allay your fears?'

'You can't. I have been a fierce critic of gambling all my life and nothing you can say will change that, but you can resolve this problem by cancelling my husband's membership and barring him from the building from this point on.'

'Mrs Finlay, I cannot very well do that without Mr Finlay's own authority. I'm sorry.'

'If you refuse to co-operate I shall have no option but to resort to more drastic means!' she snapped, sitting forward in her chair.

I had no idea what she meant, but felt that I could perhaps change her thoughts on the matter with a few well-chosen words.

'Mrs Finlay, I appreciate you may be distressed, but I have a feeling that your husband's gambling losses will very soon decrease. You see, Mr Finlay was not really here to gamble – he was more interested in another of our services – and, now that we have been able to help him receive that service, I am sure that things will settle down and you will have no further need to worry.'

'I am not sure I follow you.'

I glanced down at Chloe's report on my desk, but decided not to go into any more detail at that moment.

'I wonder if you would agree to meet here again in a few weeks to review the situation. If there has been no improvement I will gladly discuss with Mr Finlay the cessation of his membership.'

She seemed to hesitate, and I was aware that my mysterious answer was not helping her, but eventually she agreed.

'Well, all right then. I try to be a fair woman,' she said.

I asked Gemma to show her out and as she left I breathed a sigh of relief. I seemed to have bought us a bit more time with Mrs Finlay. I hoped that, now Mr Finlay was one of our special clients, he would be confident enough to simply request a session and his need to gamble would be reduced, all of which should cause this little storm to blow over.

I had toyed with the idea of letting her read Chloe's report. The look on her face would have been priceless, I'm sure, but I could not risk revealing the existence of the playroom to the uninitiated, although of course there was the possibility that she would have found the revelation something of an epiphany, finally opening her up to her husband's true desires and showing how she might fulfil them herself. Were it not for the risk, I would have handed her the report in an instant, for sexual freedom is surely the greatest gift any woman can give to a couple.

Four

'Muscles aren't really my thing,' said Maureen as she relaxed in the common room. 'I prefer a man to be smart, well turned-out, intelligent.' Mo was a local lass and I had given her employment as a croupier nearly three months previously. Our break-times seemed to have coincided that morning and I was treating her to a coffee.

Sometimes the pressures of work demand that I take my break in my office, where I can work as I drink my tea, but as often as possible I like to sit with the girls in the common room. This gives me the chance to get to know them a little better, so that I can better coach them to use their skills to their advantage; it's all part of the learning process for us all. It's also an advantage for me to learn about their foibles and weaknesses, so that I can judge how to use them to *my* advantage – and that of The Paddle-Boat as a whole, naturally.

'Thank you, Ms McKnight,' said Maureen as I handed her a cup of black coffee. I sat near by with my preferred cup of steaming, refreshing tea.

'So,' I said with a grin, 'what you're saying is that, if Michael made a move on you, you'd knock him back in the hope of someone more scrawny?'

Maureen's pink lips stretched into a smile. She

knew I had caught her out; Michael was my most deliciously hunky bouncer.

'No, perhaps not,' she answered, flicking her chestnut hair bashfully, 'but I wouldn't give up a slim, smart office boy that I already had in exchange for some beefcake!

I smiled and stood up, gesturing to the balcony. Unlike the other rooms on the mezzanine, such as the customer dining areas, the screens for the staff common room are rarely opened – I prefer my staff members not to be exposed to the public's vulgar gaze during their breaks. After all, the girls have an image to maintain and the last thing I want is for diners to peer across the gaming hall and see the gorgeously aloof Maureen or the stoically sexual Abrille kicking her shoes into a corner and puffing on a quick fag with her leg over one arm of a tea-stained sofa.

Maureen put her slender frame to work, helping me to fold back the screens, and we stepped out to the balcony rail to look down upon the gaming floor.

'Now, let's find out exactly what sort of man does it for you,' I suggested.

Mo smiled and shrugged, which I took to mean that she had no objection to the idea.

'See anything you like?' I asked.

Maureen pursed her lips in concentration as she scanned the floor below, cogitating and evaluating the appearance of our customers as, oblivious to us, they focused their attention on the roulette wheels, the cards and, if they were that way inclined, the croupiers.

I spied one gent playing poker at Abrille's table who seemed to fit Maureen's description. He was clean-shaven, wearing an unfeasibly well-pressed charcoal-grey suit, a silk tie and gleaming black shoes. I drew Maureen's attention to him. She replied with a non-committal sniff.

'Hmmm. No, I think perhaps not. I would go for someone a bit younger.'

Agreed, the man I had targeted was greying and halfway to a double-chin, but her preference for youth was one she had not previously mentioned. I continued the search until my eye lit on a stockier fellow, explaining the rules of roulette to his female companion, who seemed a little nervous of playing the game. He was younger, certainly not over thirty, with short-cropped, spiky blond hair, and he met the smartness prerequisite – his cufflinks sparkled against the darkness of his navy-blue shirt and tie. I pointed and Mo eagerly followed the line of my finger.

'Too, er, portly,' she said politely, of course meaning fat. 'I like someone a little more lithe' – of course meaning slim.

Maureen was turning out to be a fussy young lady, and I wondered if any of the folk present would appeal to her. Just then she gasped and I turned to witness her purring with approval at a slim, dark-haired fellow who had stepped into the hall below, dressed in an expensive-looking suit and smart shoes. There was poise about him as he unbuttoned his jacket, exposing an eye-catching purple shirt and lilac silk tie. He surveyed each croupier at work and stepped on to the gaming floor, wandering casually between the tables.

'Ohh, yes, please, take me now,' gasped Maureen.

'I've never seen him before. Do you know him?' I asked curiously.

A smile spread over Maureen's elfin face. 'Yes, I do. It's Stephen Koenig. He owns the Kasbah night-club – a few of my friends and I used to go down there just to gawp at him all night.'

'He's rich then?'

'– as cream custard,' she confirmed.

I smiled another of my satisfied smiles. Lately The Paddle-Boat's allure to the affluent was surprising even me, and I wondered if Mr Koenig had strolled into the casino in the hope of a bigger thrill than could be afforded by simply letting a grand or two ride on black.

'That's him there.' I said to Michael, pointing to the black-and-white screen in the security room. Michael's hamlike hand pressed on the zoom button to afford us a close-up view of Mr Koenig at the blackjack table. He was unaware of our interest in him. I let a casual hand rest on Michael's solid shoulder; I do so enjoy feeling his muscles, and I like to steal these little gropes whenever I can get away with it.

'Mmmm, he does look good in glasses,' commented Maureen behind me.

'Do you remember him from your travels at all, Michael?' I asked, ignoring Maureen's lustful observation.

'He does seem familiar,' answered Michael, who seemed a tad uncertain.

I was hoping Michael would remember our new visitor from one of his rumour-spreading missions around the city. I wanted some clue that my hunch about Stephen Koenig might be correct – that a careless word in a sauna or massage parlour had piqued his interest, and his sexual curiosity had led him into the casino to case the joint.

I could have been wrong about him, of course. I would hate to lure Mr Koenig down to our basement wonderland to discover that he was just a genuine gambler looking for a drink and a flutter. Mind you, the last time I read the signs wrongly – placing someone under my heel who was not quite expecting it – they wound up discovering that they liked it. That is another story, however.

'He's still checking out the girls,' observed Maureen. 'I should get back to my table and see if I can catch his eye.'

I let her leave. The poor girl's damp knickers were practically squelching as she walked, and I was not going to cheat her of her opportunity to get a little closer to her sex idol.

'Aye,' said Michael.

'Aye what?' I said, squeezing his shoulder.

'I mind him now, I was in a waiting room with him and another man in a sauna on Park Circus. I must have got him curious.'

I needed no more encouragement. I thanked Michael with a nibble at his earlobe and made my way on to the floor to speak to our intriguing patron.

'Can I not tempt you into playing a game or two?' I said, with a look that fairly sizzled with suggestion. Really, if his cock didn't tingle at the sight of my pursed, smiling lips he must have been made of stone. 'I've seen you wandering the floor, but you don't seem to want to join in.'

'I've never played before. Perhaps I shall join a table in a little while, once I've plucked up the courage.' He spoke politely and with confident assurance, in spite of his timid words. And he was handsome. I could understand Maureen's interest – his calmness implied protectiveness, his glasses intelligence, the expensive clothes security. Even his afternoon stubble lent him masculinity without detracting from his elegance. And in one so young, how rare.

All the same, my attraction to him was different from that of a younger woman like Maureen. For my

48

part I was overcome with the desire to mess him up, fluster him, deconstruct his suave demeanour, subjugate him.

'What does a man of your means have to fear from losing a few pounds on the spin of a wheel?' I goaded him.

'How would you know if I am a man of means? I *could* be a pauper.'

'Only if the patrons of your nightclub purchase their drinks with beans,' I whispered in his ear.

He smiled. 'You seem to know a lot about me.'

'You seem to have a lot of admirers,' I retorted.

He thought about my reply for a second and seemed to catch the gist. He glanced around at a couple of croupiers, Abrille and then Maureen, who had returned to work her table after her break.

'Anyone you'd care to introduce me to?'

'Now that would be making it too easy. I'm Valerie McKnight. Ms,' I said, offering my hand to be kissed in a manner that was too, too old-fashioned for words but so, so enjoyable. He took my cue and leant to press his lips to the backs of my fingers. As he did so I lowered my hand slightly, forcing him to bend and make his first deferential gesture to me.

'What brings an apparent gambling neophyte to The Paddle-Boat?' I asked him as he extended himself again to his full height, his eyes gazing at me like a flower growing towards the sun. Those irises betrayed that somewhere deep within himself he had enjoyed bending his knee to me.

'I heard so many good rumours about the place.'

'About the place, or about the croupiers?' I asked cuttingly.

'Both,' he replied, smiling and unabashed.

I cursed myself for squandering the advantage I had gained with the hand-kiss, letting the conversation return to one of equals. Perhaps I could discomfort him with a little paranoia.

'My security guard manager swears he's seen you somewhere before.'

'Perhaps he saw me at my club. I'm often at the bar.'

'He never goes out. It can't be that. No, he's the sort of chap who prefers to unwind with a bath, a sauna, maybe even a massage. Do you ever attend such places?'

'Perhaps –'

'Do you like to play?' I asked suddenly, as he struggled with his reply.

'I've never really gambled before.'

This was very amusing. I knew that he knew the true meaning of my question but he still dared not dream that he had found what he was looking for. He was, I think, still wary of offending me by responding directly to my apparently suggestive tone.

'Oh, I think I'm going to have to punish you for that little fib – I am quite sure you've gambled in a casino before. The income from a popular social establishment can pay for an awful lot of holidays in the South of France,' I observed, certain that the Riviera's own gambling houses had tempted him in on many occasions. 'But the question is: do you like to *play*?'

I think Maureen may have heard my voice, because she looked across at us as she dealt a hand at her table, clearly jealous of my closeness to Stephen Koenig, but I was sure the nosey little girl would be unable to make out anything meaningful from where she was. There was no reply from Stephen and I continued.

'I can't help wondering why a young gent would come to The Paddle-Boat and so transparently feign ignorance of gambling. Perhaps you are hoping I will offer you some other kind of game?'

He remained silent, and again I took this as licence to go further.

'We do have another game-room, a very private game-room, but I should warn you that the house always wins, the pain will not only be felt in your pocket, and the games we play there are not for the proud.'

Stephen was now breathing slowly and deeply through flared nostrils. I flushed slightly at the feeling of control this gave me – bringing a man to heel by arousing him beyond his will to control himself is surely woman's greatest power. I leant and whispered in his ear.

'Are you willing to submit yourself to the whim of The Wheel?' I knew he had only a vague idea what I meant, but I trusted that his curiosity, and his tingling cock, would control his decision.

'Yes,' he replied hoarsely, as if choked with emotion. I stepped back and glared at him like an officious librarian to show that his response was inadequate.

He breathed a voiceless whisper: 'Yes – Mistress.'

'Follow me,' I told him, and proceeded to leave the gaming hall, strutting like a catwalk model, swinging my arse rhythmically as the helpless supplicant was drawn into my wake.

Maureen watched as we left together and I whispered to her as we passed, 'Leave your table in thirty minutes and come to the basement. Dress appropriately for whatever playroom you find us in.' I would not wish her to miss this opportunity to have the object of her lustful desires at her feet.

'Do you submit to the whim of The Wheel?'

I paced behind Stephen as he knelt, now naked, in front of The Wheel.

'I do, Mistress.'

I had taken my substantial fee from him moments before and folded it over my finger to slip it into my bra. It is my philosophy never to undercharge my clients. Men want to submit to dominant women in all ways possible: physically, emotionally, sexually and also financially. Indeed, the burst of adrenalin that pumps around his body as he relinquishes his fee – just that bit more than he knows he can probably afford – forms part of a chemical cocktail that addicts him and enslaves him to return again and again.

'Stand, but keep your head bowed,' I commanded.

He did so. He could now see The Wheel and its eight specially made segments, inscribed with the names of the eight basement playrooms. I am sure he was trying his best to read each of them without raising his head, curious to have some clue to his fate. The bowing of the head, necessary when a slave is allowed to stand, serves an obvious purpose in displaying submissiveness, but has the useful by-product of keeping many of the goings-on in the room a mystery, as he cannot clearly see what his Mistress is preparing for him. The imagination then runs free.

The Wheel whirred as I spun it with a flick of my slender hand, its colours merging and dancing in the periphery of my slave's vision. I picked up the black roulette ball and placed it in its culvert, setting it on its orbital path around the wheel.

Stephen watched with his head bowed and his eyes straining upwards. He was nervous and, judging by his semi-erect penis, which twitched slightly with each of his heartbeats, excited. No doubt he was experiencing that exquisite mixture of dread and exhilaration that feeds a submissive's addiction.

The ball began to dance randomly as it fell from orbit, and my eyes danced too as they followed it to its final nestling place in one of the segments. The wheel clicked to a halt. I smiled as I read the result – the ball had come to rest in the section marked 'Stables'.

'Well, you are a lucky slave, Stephen, my dear. You are to be trained as a pony-boy. Get down on all fours.'

'Yes, Mistress,' he said as he dropped to the floor.

I stood over him, so that my high-heeled shoes and the exposed parts of my feet filled his field of view. 'Make your way to the stable,' I instructed, pointing to the appropriate area.

The Stable is situated between The School Room, where Chloe had dealt with Mr Finlay so admirably, and The Office, where my clients like to be emasculated by a ruthless, and sexy, employer.

I have had a small stable installed to the left of the area – it's about the size of a toilet cubicle – where my pony-boys (and girls) can be confined while I prepare myself for a scenario. I keep the stable stocked with straw bedding to increase the realism and therefore the dehumanising effect.

Stephen's slender but coltish body was the perfect image for a pony-boy, and I found myself getting quite excited as I opened the barred wooden door to allow him to crawl inside. I bolted it behind him and slipped a dish of water under it for him to drink.

'You are going to need it,' I told him.

Out of sight, I changed into attire more suited to breaking in a new pony: tight beige jodhpurs that drew the eye to the contours of my hips and thighs, and matt-black riding boots that lent me the calves of an Olympic athlete. I opted for the cream-white roll-neck rather than a blouse on top – without my bra, so that a hint of my areola could be seen through the thin weave as it stretched over my bust. I wore an open jacket on top and the classic black, velvet-covered riding helmet on my head – I wouldn't want to cause myself a mischief were I to come off my steed, now, would I? The playrooms have at least one mirror on the wall, so that a client can see his or her transformation or humiliation, and the riding-school mirror confirmed my theory that I was looking mesmerising.

The saddlery is kept on hooks and racks mounted on the back wall. Even on all fours Stephen would have been able to see the straps, bridles, stirrups, tails, crops and the specially made saddle on the far wall, all waiting to be used upon him. It must have been a thrilling sight.

I picked a riding crop from the array and unbolted the stable door to allow Stephen to emerge. He had finished his bowl of water while I had been changing. I tapped his buttock with the leather loop at the end of the crop, just lightly, to give him the impetus to walk out of the stable compartment into the play-room.

There is some debate amongst the pony-play sorority as to whether the pony should be upright or on all fours. Each has its merits and disadvantages. For example, the pony cannot be easily or realisti-cally ridden in the upright position, but is better able to pull a chariot or buggy at a reasonable speed. Further, if a Mistress chooses to humiliate her ponies with a dressage event, more realistic gaits and more graceful manoeuvres can be achieved by an upright pony than one playing quadruped. But something of the feeling of animality is lost when a pony is not on all fours, I feel.

I tend to go for a compromise between the two, keeping my pony-boy on the floor for the majority of the time but allowing him to stand upright if the performance or task is more suited.

'First of all, I think we need to get you feeling like a pony,' I said, reaching once more to the wall. I have three pony-tail butt-plugs, each with a differently coloured plume of horse hair cascading from the base. I felt Stephen would best suit a black tail.

'We cannot have a pony without a tail,' I decreed as I lubricated the stubby little phallus. I then allowed the strands of coarse hair to brush over his face and along his back, finally letting them tickle his anus for a second or two.

'Feel free to whinny or bray if it helps,' I said, as I slowly eased the tapered plug into his twitching hole. He let out a very human-sounding grunt as it slipped into place, for which I gave him a sharp tap with the crop.

'Now that was not a very equine sound at all. Do try again.'

Stephen collected himself and produced a neigh-cum-bray that was much more to my liking, although he still clearly needed some practice.

'Good boy. The next task is to assign you your stable name. I think from here on you will answer to the name of, let's see, Florin. Whinny and paw the ground if you understand.'

Florin understood. I could tell he was getting used to the idea of our little game. I tapped his hind quarter and stroked his scrotum with the crop as a reward.

'Good Florin. Now let's get you ready for your first ride.'

I took the special saddle down from the wall, along with the bridle and the soft brush, and laid them on the floor so that Florin could clearly see what awaited him.

'Now, if we're going for a ride, you need to be presentable, so I'm going to brush your coat. Many ponies find this quite pleasurable, so be sure to neigh or whinny to show me how you enjoy it.'

The brush I like very much – I pretend to brush the coat of my mount, just lightly and with a much softer brush than would be used on a real pony. The bristles play over the skin and have a very activating effect on the senses, especially around the buttocks and inside the thigh. Florin whinnied a couple of times during the process and it was most gratifying that by the end his penis was no longer dangling freely, but trying its best to cling to his belly.

I had purchased a number of bridles and saddles in fetish shops on various trips to London. A couple of the bridles were decorative, with brass rivets and plumes and even bells attached, but the one I had picked for Florin was of functional dark leather and cold steel, with blackened blinkers. They are, of course, made for a human head and are much smaller than the equine equivalent; they have a band over the nose and a bit for the mouth, and fasten behind the head.

'Open,' I commanded as I slid the bit into place between his lips and fastened the buckle.

I have two saddles, again designed for the human back, smaller than a real saddle, with softer leather and the stirrups high and forward so that the rider's feet do not drag on the ground. By far my favourite saddle is the one with the dildo attached, spearing upwards from the seat. I asked about the possibility of adding a dildo to the saddle in the shop and the mature female shopkeeper was surprisingly accommodating, asking me to return the next day. I was delighted with the finished effect and now I can ride my pony-boys with this lovely black rod inside me, grinding my pussy as my steed's gait causes his shoulder blades and hips to rock it from side to side.

I buckled the saddle securely around his shoulders and under his belly, pushing his erect penis out of the way for the moment.

'Good boy,' I purred, patting him on the flank lovingly. 'Now we're going for a little trek around the basement and I'm going to teach you a few manoeuvres.'

I stood astride him and pulled down my joddies, not far – just enough to allow the air to get to my moistening pussy – and lowered myself on to the cock-shaped rubber prong. Once it was inside me and I was able to squirm on it without it slipping out, I lifted my booted feet into the stirrups, transferring my entire weight on to Florin's back.

'Good boy,' I said, stroking his shoulder. 'Now let's begin with some basic pony commands, shall we?' I knew that Florin probably knew the basic commands already, for walking forward, turning left and right and so forth – who doesn't? But I proceeded to explain the rudiments of locomotion to him regardless, insisting that a neigh of acknowledgement follow each explanation.

'Good. Let's put this all into action,' I said as I dug my heels into his side.

Florin started forwards towards the far end of the cellar and I ground my pussy on to the dildo as, with each of his steps, it rocked and rolled inside of me. I began to sway to the rhythm of his ponderous gait and slapped his flank and buttock with the crop to encourage him. It was certainly one of the more enjoyable 25-yard journeys I have experienced. I pulled on the reins to bring Florin to a halt at The Dungeon Room opposite.

Maureen had arrived and, when we stopped, I spied her watching us from the stairs, no doubt admiring Stephen's firm arse. When she saw that I had noticed her, she skipped quietly down and made her way to The Riding School. I am sure with his blinkers on Florin was unaware of her presence. I decided to give him a little more instruction at this end of the room, to allow Maureen enough time to change into boots and jodhpurs.

'Well, you seem to have the basics mastered. Did you enjoy that?' I asked.

Florin neighed and nodded his head – it really was just like a pony and I delighted to see him immersing himself in the role.

'Good, now let's try a few other moves. When I tap your left shoulder, I want you to bend down to the floor and when I tap you in the same way again I want you to return to your normal position.'

I tapped Florin twice to make him go down as instructed and twice again to return him to his previous stance.

'Good boy. Now, when I tap your right shoulder I want you to rear up, kick your forelegs in front of you and neigh for me.' Florin gave a quiet whinny to show that he understood.

I tapped him on the right shoulder and he reared up beautifully, kicking his forelegs out in front of him, for all the world like Champion the Wonder Horse, and once again there was true passion in the braying noise he made.

As the animal in Florin came to the fore, I was becoming very aroused and I began playing his shoulders like a pair of bongos, tapping to make him bow forward and then rear up, repeating the exercise some two dozen times. Obviously the rearing up of the pony-boy works the dildo into my vagina and, if

I concentrate, I can make it ply my g-spot as my mount leans forward.

I was soaking wet now and I repeated the percussion performance on his shoulders, working that stiff rod into all the right areas of my pussy. I reached for my clit and worked a finger into it. I must have looked like some sex-mad rodeo cowgirl trying desperately to remain on her wild stallion long enough to orgasm. I clean forgot that Maureen must surely have been watching and I came loudly, grinding myself down on the dildo with saturated satisfaction.

Breathing heavily, I started my pony up again and steered him left to head back to the stable. The slower movements of his back, oscillating the dildo inside me, were the perfect come-down for my orgasmic after-glow.

Back at the ranch, so to speak, I dismounted and looked around for Maureen. She was nowhere to be seen, which perplexed me. I felt sure she would want to take Florin for a ride herself and put him through his paces.

Just when I was about to conclude that she had changed her mind about Stephen, I heard the sound of bells jangling behind me, and out stepped an all but naked Maureen, in the upright pony position, with her hands up in front of her and her right foot pawing the ground. She gave a handsome, mare-like whinny and I felt a shiver of lust run through me. I can only imagine the effect she had on Florin.

She wore nothing but a decorative bridle, with bells and a purple plume atop the head and a long chestnut tail, which I suppose matched her own hair best. Her hair made a lovely mane, tied behind in a French plait. She wore also a pair of high-heeled ankle boots, which pleased me as pony-girls should always have on heels of some description. Her ample bush matched her chestnut hair and, although she was a slender lass, her hips curved most pleasingly.

I cannot recall how long I stood there, astonished at her choice of costume. I expected her to take the role of a riding instructor, and the sight of her naked flesh, quivering in excitement, was an unexpected enchantment. Despite the surprising nature of Maureen's entrance, I knew exactly why she had chosen that outfit and I wasted no time in putting her fantasy into motion.

'Ah, Florin, good, your stable-mate has arrived,' I said as I opened the stable door once more, leading him in by the reins and tapping him on his rear with the riding crop. Florin crawled inside and I tied the reins to a hook in the wall to restrain him; what he was about to see through the slats in the wooden door would turn him into a lust-crazed stallion and I did not wish to leave the wild beast unfettered.

I bolted the door behind him. If he strained his neck to the left he should still be able to see the action just beyond his blinkers. All the while, I was trying to think of a stable-name for the horny little mare.

I walked up to her, giving the crop a sharp tap against my boot as I strode. Tenderly I stroked her side, her breast, her stomach and her buttock, and leant to blow softly in her ear. 'Your stable-name is Bess,' I told her. It was the name of Dick Turpin's horse and it was the first suitable name that came to mind.

'This is Bess,' I said, loudly enough for Florin to hear. 'One of my horniest little mares.' I struck her sharply on her tight bottom, at which she whinnied gratefully. I spied Florin straining to see out of the corner of his eye.

'On all fours, please, Bess,' I commanded, repeating the stroke. She dropped gracefully to the floor and took up the stance of the quadruped pony-girl, neighing and shaking her head. I was most impressed at how far she immersed herself in the character.

Bess was facing the stable door, but I wanted Florin to get a more tantalising view from his compartment, so I ordered her about face, leading her to the left by the reins that she had obligingly attached to her bridle and applying the crop to her left buttock, driving her hind quarter to the right. Soon she was facing outwards, the curves of her rear now drawing Florin's gaze like a beacon.

I reached down and massaged Bess's moist entrance in miniature circles until my middle finger was slick with her juice. She gasped in pleasure and I slapped her, reminding her softly that human noises were forbidden to pony-girls.

I put my sticky finger in my mouth and, playing somewhat to my captive audience, thirstily sucked at it. 'Mmmm. Florin, we're in luck. It seems our little pony-girl is in season,' I announced. 'We had best prepare her for mating while we have the opportunity.'

I instructed Bess to remain still and walked across the cellar to The Dungeon opposite. This action had two purposes: firstly, The Dungeon Room is equipped with many, many restrainment devices, including the leg dividers I wished to use on sweet Bess to prepare her for mating; secondly, I wanted to leave my slave animals together alone. This is one of the more delectable humiliation devices, and can be extremely arousing for its victims. In my absence, Bess and Florin would be aware of each other's presence but unable to acknowledge it or communicate in any way. Bess would be able to feel Florin's lusty gaze upon her reddened arse, her plugged anus, her syrupy labia behind the strands of her tail; both would be intensely aware that, although they had never spoken, never met or been introduced, they would shortly be rutting like animals, uninhibited and absolved of responsibility, for what choice did they have? They were mere beasts following the wishes of their Mistress.

I returned with the dividers: two wooden batons, each with two cuffs attached to their ends. I forced Bess's feet and hands (or hooves) apart to the width of the beams and applied the cuffs to each wrist and ankle. Bess now had a metre of wood between her fore and hind legs and was unable to close them. I tied her reins tightly to a hook and, knowing that the redder her arse, the more fuckable she would look, I laced her with the crop five or six times. A whinny of torment followed.

I unbolted the stable door and untied the now mindless Florin. His frantic pony-cock was practically steaming with pre-come.

'There's my good little stud,' I cooed, stroking it with my fingertips. I waved the crop before his blinkered face. 'Remember, no human noises,' I whispered.

I led Florin and his swaying cock behind Bess, pulling him roughly up to climb on to her back. I lifted Bess's tail as Florin adjusted his hips, trying desperately to enter his mate. He needed my guiding hand to slide inside her.

Bess shook to the core and she neighed loudly, and, as though she had fired the starter pistol for a race, Florin responded by humping her vigorously, trawling the depths of her pussy with swift, buttock-driven thrusts up into her. I watched in awe, as though witnessing a force of nature, which I suppose I was.

The noises were the most arousing music: Bess's desperate brays of pleasure, calling Florin to action, and his high-pitched, gasping whinnies, indicative of an impending orgasm.

They needed no further encouragement from my crop. Florin gripped Bess's shoulders and clenched his buttocks as he spent ferociously inside her. I was most gratified by the display, and had I had any sugar lumps available I would have offered them to both as a reward.

I removed Florin by his reins, placing him back in his stall while I released Bess from her bonds.

'Was that what you were looking for?' I asked her quietly. She did not look up, but the pleasure on her face was obvious.

'Yes, Ms McKnight,' she gasped in gratitude.

I spanked her with the crop.

'No human noises,' I snapped.

Five

That evening, I stayed late: Stephen Koenig's antics had kept me away from some very boring, but nonetheless vital, paperwork. I let the security staff leave at three a.m., telling Michael and Gordon to lock me in for the night. I often make this little request, when work is getting on top of me. They usually make all sorts of fuss about my safety, bless them, thinking of the risk of fire and such mishaps. It's very touching, but ultimately just a bit too anal. I tend to give them one of those 'looks' that men love so much: cold, stern, unmoved, with one sharp eyebrow arching upwards. The tingling it gives them in their cocks seems to persuade them to relent.

I don't work all night, of course; I'll take a nap on the long leather sofa in my office or a wander around the mezzanine to stretch my legs. I'm not allowed down to the ground floor as Michael tells me it will set off the alarms and bring the constabulary trotting up to the door. You might think such an event would appeal to me but they're not allowed to hump on duty, so what's the point?

Another thing I do to clear the mind between bouts of paperwork is gaze out of the window across the rolling river, fixing my eyes on the reflected specks of orange and white lights as they dance on the restless surface. Or perhaps I'll go to the front of the building to observe, and maybe enjoy a private giggle at, straggling revellers or furtive alleyway shaggers.

The Paddle-Boat shares its neighbourhood with the Clydeside cycleway, the Port Elizabeth Bridge, the grand, ornate red sandstone telephone exchange and the California Fitness Club, a sparklingly modern building with a vast glass frontage and metallic external support structure. The club can be most entertaining during the day or the busy evening, as much of the apparatus is in full view through the huge, slanting window panes. Often, if I fancy a wet-on in the afternoon, I nip to the window to watch an athletic girl bouncing and joggling on a running machine, the sweat collecting between her breasts and thighs, or ogle at a glistening hunk as he works his pectorals on a bench. At four a.m., though, there is nary a soul in the building and the herd of exercise bikes is shrouded in the strange blue darkness of the city night. This night, however, was different.

My eye was suddenly drawn by the sputtering of strip lighting coming on above the weights area on the first floor of the health club, and I saw a long-haired young man walk into the area in a white towelling gown, as if he had just come from a steam bath or sauna. He seemed handsome even from this distance. His dominant jaw-line and the clean, square lines of his face were clear to me and, with the rebellious dark mane of hair that ran to his shoulders, gave him the look of a Pictish warrior.

I watched intently. He swaggered over to a piece of Multi-Gym apparatus and casually untied his robe, hanging it on the adjacent machine. He was naked. I exhaled through pursed lips as I admired his solid buttocks, and my hand drifted slowly, almost involuntarily, to my crotch.

The young Adonis took position on the machine and began his private little naked workout. I eagerly watched the sinews and muscles bulge as he performed a set of chest presses, half amused, half aroused by the surprising display, and began to speculate who this gentleman might be and what he was up to.

I concluded he must be someone of authority at the club – who else would have such access after closing time? A member of management, perhaps? In any case, it was someone who clearly enjoyed the freedom of pushing and testing his body in its natural form, naked and unfettered.

During his next performance I stared longingly at his cock, nestling in its cradle of dark-brown curls, as his torso pumped the bar up and down. This was royal entertainment, and I began to rub myself through my skirt and knickers.

His first set of exercises complete, our exhibitionist neighbour stood and began to shoulder-press a heavily laden bar above his head. He was now facing the window, giving each lift the full juice and letting it all hang out. I was very moist indeed and yanked my panties down to my thighs. My middle finger snaked under the hem of my skirt and to my love button. Borrowing some pussy juice from my moistening love-lips, I wet my clitty and really began to enjoy the show as this male specimen worked his body, seemingly for my sole enjoyment.

During the last set of these exercises, I received something of a shock that made my belly flutter even more: unmistakably, and excitingly, he noticed me watching him. I had forgotten a Peeping Tom's first commandment: 'watch in darkness'. The body-builder's eyes (I call him a body-builder but, to be frank, it seemed to me that he was wasting his time as his body was already built) must have caught the sight of me in the window, framed as I was by a rectangle of yellowish light.

If that was not confounding enough, then his reaction to my presence was: he carried on regardless! Should I not have expected some display of embarrassed apology? Was he not exposing himself unlawfully to an innocent female citizen and in doing so violating her rights? Apparently he felt he had nothing to be ashamed of, and he continued with another exercise, this time placing the bar behind his neck and turning his back on me to perform deep, powerful squats with his not inconsequential leg muscles.

I quickly forgot my indignation and my thoughts returned to my weeping petals. The view afforded me now was of a granite-hewn derrière clenching and unclenching with extreme physical effort, and I found myself fantasising that each powerful contraction was propelling his cock into my juicy hole. I was left with the choice of storming off in disgust at his brazen behaviour and calling the police, or making the most of the show and wanking myself silly. I chose the latter.

I was nearing my peak when the squats finished and the showman laid the bar down on the gym floor. I was excited by the prospect of what physical demonstration might follow and received another of those electrifying visceral flutters as he turned once more to face the window and revealed his trembling cock rising through the horizontal and growing thicker by the moment. It was clear that the presence of an audience was turning our exhibitionist on somewhat.

By the time he had taken a seated position back on the Multi-Gym apparatus, his cock was fully erect and almost taunting me – defying me to act as most females would and call the police, professing shock and offence.

To be fair, it was a glistening and fitting monument to the raw sexual attractiveness of its owner. Even at this distance I could make out a vein or two, the contour of his urethra and the curving 'w' shape where his glans and shaft met. The sight pleased me greatly. I really wanted him to wank it.

I put my stiletto heel on the window sill and set my thumb and fingers to work on my clitoris and vagina. I prayed he would respond by performing every man's favourite bicep workout and I was not disappointed. Without deigning to acknowledge me in the slightest, and as though acting out a nocturnal ceremony of long standing that was by now second nature, he pulled on his shiny thick penis with slow rhythmic handfuls.

I found myself praying that he was a quick finisher – I had quite a head-start on him and, as the loud squelching of my pussy confirmed, I was almost ready to spend. But, ever greedy for more pleasure, I wanted the thrill of seeing him spout first.

I held off as long as I could, biting my lip and moaning to myself as drops of my love-juice speckled the floor, but I soon felt my tunnel spasm uncontrollably and I had no choice but to give in to the moment, throwing my head back and giving a throaty wail of pleasure. As the waves of bliss receded, I saw my horny athlete spray a fountain of white foam into the air, his teeth gritted as though he were pumping iron again, not cock. Watching it was the perfect way to savour my orgasm.

I straightened myself out, affecting once again the appearance of the lady I most assuredly am not. I watched my 'lover' as he stood up, placed his robe around his ample shoulders and left the gym room, extinguishing the light behind him, again without so much as a wave or acknowledgement. I had never felt so used in all my days, and I'm not one to forget such insolence easily.

Burly Gordon woke me at about nine a.m. I was asleep on the couch in my office, and the first thing I felt was his hand tenderly rocking my shoulder. A steaming cup of tea had appeared on my desk and Gordon had made a discreet exit before I had time to gather myself and thank him. I must have nodded off shortly after my nocturnal adventure at the window; there is only one slumber deeper than the sleep of the just, and that's the sleep of the just after.

I shook the grogginess from my head and made sure my fine crown of dark hair had the required body and bounce by plying it a few times with my fingers. I was a long way from my best, but at least I was presentable. I returned to my desk, my tea fuelling my recovery, and picked up the last item of paperwork I had been working on before falling asleep.

It was the training plan. With both blonde Chloe and brunette Maureen now started off in the basement, and Gemma, the Head Croupier, already fully proficient, I needed to allocate some time to make a careful choice of whom, from the remaining female staff, to 'promote' to a move downstairs.

I remembered sucking thoughtfully on my pen in the middle of the previous night as I considered the subject. That must have been when I dropped off. I had whittled the choice down to two of the other five girls, Abrille and Amber. Shy Kirsty Hankin was obviously nowhere near ready, and I did not feel that either Nhyla Sarker or Lily Wang was quite fully comfortable with her existing responsibilities, so I had decided to give them a little more time gaining experience at the tables, distracting players with glimpses of cleavage and flashes of stocking tops.

Abrille or Amber? It was a difficult choice and I could understand why I had slept on it. But a decision had to be made one way or another and I came to the rather romantic conclusion that chance should decide.

I took myself down to the gaming floor. I was looking a little less refined than usual after my night on the couch, but I rationalised that very few people would have time to look at me closely enough to read the story of the night before on my features, if I was quick. Gemma was setting up the nearest roulette table and I strode over to her. She was looking divine: her red wavy hair was down and the deepest russet shade of her lipstick seemed somehow to make her look even more voluptuous. Is it possible, I wondered, for a perfectly chosen and applied lipstick to make you look curvier? Perhaps it is. Perhaps it was her unbuttoned blouse and short black skirt that was achieving the effect.

'Bad night?' she said with a grin, deliberately trying to provoke me. I ignored her; she was only doing it to give me cause to spank her that bit harder next time.

'No punters yet?' I asked.

'It's a bit early.'

'Spin the wheel for me, would you, just for fun.'

She shrugged and did so, sending the little ball off in its counter-orbit as the wheel whirred.

I watched the ball course around the blurring colours of the spinning wheel. Black, I determined, would mean Abrille. Red would mean Amber. The rules of the game determined, I waited. The ball dropped on to the wheel, dancing its random waltz before nestling under a number.

'Seventeen. Black,' announced Gemma.

So French beauty Abrille Martin it was.

'Thank you, Gemma,' I said. 'Send Abrille up to my office when her shift starts, would you?'

On my way back up the carpeted stairs towards my office, I overheard voices coming the other way that caused me pause. The newly appointed chef, Peter, was chatting to someone on the way down.

So soon after Gemma's little jibe, I did not relish a potential image-shattering encounter with Peter; my plans for that young man were quite clear in my mind and, while he was most definitely a good shag, I wanted our relationship to end up with him submiss-ive at my feet, preferably begging for permission to relieve himself from the agony of an as yet to be determined prohibition. A vital prerequisite for achieving that goal was the preservation of my image as a goddess of eroticism – an image I could hardly uphold at the back of nine a.m. and some eighteen hours since I last touched up my war-paint. I hid in the small recess under the first flight of stairs.

I could hear Peter's voice over the creak of the stair and could tell from the tone that he was in the process of charming, or attempting to charm, someone. I should not have been surprised. I listened more intently. It was a jolly conversation between Peter's friendly Scottish accent and a sultry French female purr. It was Abrille, the very girl I wanted to speak to! As they came nearer I began to make out sentences.

'. . . Aye, everybody seems very nice here. I'm enjoying it,' said Peter.

'Ah yes, the social life is one of the great things about here. It can be very "interesting", let me assure you,' agreed Abrille.

71

'Yes, I know . . .' Peter replied knowingly, and from the faraway echo in his voice he was clearly casting his mind back to a certain lunchtime romp. 'I must say, I never worked in a place where the ladies were so strikingly sexy, yourself especially, Abrille.'

Now I could hear their footfalls on the stairs directly above my head.

'Oh, thank you, that is very kind. You know, we must all arrange a night out on the town together. must we not? It would be fun,' suggested Abrille in her usual friendly manner.

'Yes, it would – provided I get a good warning. I need to get a few early nights in to prepare. I've been having some terrible headaches in the mornings lately.'

'Oh, you poor thing. They are not self-inflicted? Not hangovers I hope?'

'No comment,' said Peter with a laugh. They had reached the bottom of the stairs.

'My shift is starting. I shall speak to you later, I'm sure,' said Abrille, making her excuses and heading for the game floor. Peter sped off down the corridor in the other direction and I emerged from my hideaway and made my way upstairs. I estimated I had enough time to pick an outfit from the cupboard in my plush office and get myself looking divine again before Gemma sent Abrille back up to my office.

'Hello, Abrille. Sit down.'

I was posing again on my desk, my beautiful legs encased in a new pair of light-tan stockings, my tight navy-blue skirt constricting them at the thighs and giving me that 'mermaid' look. My simple black heels tapered to a stiletto and gave my ankles that perfect contour. It was a conventional look that I had gone for, matching the skirt with a smart royal-blue silk blouse. Red lipstick and light-blue eye-shadow completed the transformation.

I allowed Abrille a few seconds to admire me before I spoke. I like to be an inspiration to all of my girls and I'm sure these moments spur them on to improvement. I can only imagine, as she gazed up at me from her seat, how much she must have yearned to carry the same air herself one day.

She did indeed look lovely, with her cascading black curls and shining brown skin. She was clearly very much at home in the croupier's uniform, wearing the blouse open at the neck and the skirt as high as is feasible. I could have died from gushing pussy syndrome when I saw her cross her legs: toes pointed, graceful hands, eyes focused on infinity, her poise exuded the sexual power that it is my mission to instil in my girls. Any man alone with her at that moment would have been dancing to the tune that his loins were playing, falling to his knees on the floor to kiss the tip of her black pumps and pleading for further pleasures, such as the taste of a toe or the feel of her instep on his tongue. Yes, I knew at that moment that The Paddle-Boat had made the right choice for graduation.

'Abrille, I won't beat about the bush. I think you are ready to participate in a basement session.'

A smile spread across Abrille's chocolate face, like the rays of dawn spreading over a dewy meadow. I sensed she had been anticipating such a development.

'Oh, Ms McKnight, I'm so pleased. I have been waiting for you to offer me the opportunity.'

'Yes, it did not go without notice how assiduously you have been adhering to my instructions on game-floor deportment, and now I judge the time has come. The first session will be a mock exercise with myself and a male member of staff. I will let you know the details when they are arranged.'

I was about to dismiss Miss Martin back to her table when I was struck by a wicked idea.

'Abrille – how do you feel about helping me do a session right now?'

Abrille gave a Gallic shrug. 'Why not?'

'Oh, I am so glad! I have a plan to lure young Peter into a session. It should be rather fun. Go down to the kitchen and persuade him that you're something of an expert at holistic medicine and offer to help him out with those morning headaches he was complaining about.'

Abrille stood up. 'Yes, Ms McKnight,' she said.

'Tell him to meet you in The White Room in the cellar in twenty minutes, and do your best to make him think he's got a chance of fucking your fragrant French fanny. Be flirty,' I told her, unbuttoning the third button on her blouse and revealing her lacy bra and the shimmering capuccino-coloured flesh between her breasts.

Abrille was about to leave when a frown crept over her features. 'Ms McKnight, how did you know about the headaches conversation?'

'Never you mind,' I said, slapping her firmly on the buttocks. 'Now go, and report straight back here.'

Six

The White Room, as they call it in our business, is an area equipped and decorated for the purpose of acting out medical fantasies. The Paddle-Boat's White Room is situated in our Cellar Fantasia, between The Dungeon Room and The Office.

I had spent the past few months equipping the room to give it the cold, clinical atmosphere of a surgery. There was a treatment table, with an inclinable section that allowed me to choose whether our lucky humiliated patients would sit up or lie back, and a pair of stirrups to hold the feet and legs in place during an examination or treatment.

I bought everything over the internet, except the sink with shower-head and the white porcelain child-sized toilet and bidet. Those were installed by Alba Kitchens & Bathrooms. Their representative was very discreet and didn't ask any awkward questions about this or any of the other rooms. At the small cost of one pair of used knickers and two silk stockings, I was able to persuade him to sign a secrecy contract. The internet is lavishly stocked with sources of clean, safe medical supplies to add authenticity to any White Room: swabs, catheters, bandages, enemas, straitjackets, blood pressure monitors, straps, anaesthesia masks, first aid boxes, speculums, kidney dishes, medical wall-charts, gloves, pipettes, funnels, syringes – you name it. I keep most of the equipment on the walls, like in The Stable Room, as this adds to the atmosphere and gives the first-time entrant a full view of the possible fates that await him or her. One of the prerequisites of a successful session is that the subject's imagination is allowed to race right from the start. For that reason, and to give the expectant patient a flutter of adrenalin, perhaps even fear, I hang a few items high up on the wall for display only: scalpels, a bone-saw, a huge hypodermic syringe.

The uniforms are kept in a tall white cupboard. I have a white coat for when I want to play doctor, and a white dress uniform for when I want to play nurse; it's a one-piece, cut high at the hem and low at the neck, made of rubber and emblazoned with a large red cross, should anyone be in doubt as to its wearer's medical qualifications. I had bought it from a wonderful lingerie shop in Royal Exchange Square called Pyjama Party. The owner, Lynda Stenhouse, is a lovely woman, so helpful and understanding – it really is pleasant to go in there from time to time and chat with her. She had always advised that the nurse uniform be worn with flesh-coloured stockings, but I wondered if that advice would hold for a mocha-tinged skin tone such as Abrille's. I decided it would and handed Abrille the dress, the hat, the white high heels and the stockings.

'Put these on,' I said.

She took them eagerly and I watched and salivated as her semi-naked flesh squirmed into the second skin of the rubber dress and the stockings were tenderly rolled up her legs. There is something very attractive about a smooth dark skin encased in white nylon or a silk that carries a Caucasian flesh hue. I think it is because the natural skin tone bosses the overall effect, whereas the tones of we whiter girls are crowded out by the tone of the stocking. Whatever the reasons, Abrille's thighs and calves were a glorious sight, creamy as *chocolat chaud*. If you could have bottled her it would have put Pfizer out of business: Instant Erection.

'Are you not getting changed too?' she asked as she slipped on the white pumps.

'Of course,' I said, biting my lip to fight the lust she was firing in me.

I reached into the cupboard and took the doctor's coat from its hanger, putting it on over my skirt and blouse. There was a pair of dummy spectacles in the breast pocket, which I slipped on to my nose. I tied my dark hair back to a pony tail to complete the image.

'There. I will be Doctor McKnight, you can be Nurse Martin,' I announced.

'What is the plan?'

'I shall hide in The Dungeon Room next door with the light off, so when he arrives you will appear to be alone in The White Room. Get him strapped on to the table – it shouldn't be too difficult to get him prone if you give him the impression that you intend to ride his cock – and then announce that the doctor will be in shortly. I'll take it from there. My only advice is: follow my lead, watch and learn. How do you feel?'

'Excited!'

I kissed her full on the lips. I don't know what possessed me to do so, but I do know that I let my bottom lip linger on hers for the tiniest moment too long. Turning on my heel and swishing my coat, I left her.

I found a shadowy corner in the unlit Dungeon Room, which would afford me the luxury of being able to hear the proceedings next door. I made myself comfortable. Soon Peter appeared, poking his curly mop around the door to peer down the stairs. Seeing the lights in The White Room, he entered, closed the door behind him and made his way down the stairs, his footsteps echoing around the chamber.

Abrille stalked out on her white heels to meet him and posed provocatively in the entrance to The White Room, one foot pointing forwards, the other out to the side, a hand on her hip. Peter stopped in his tracks as his jaw fell and his eyes widened; he even put a steadying hand on The Wheel to keep his balance. I could not blame him for feeling giddy.

'I was wondering if a little treatment from Nurse Martin might cure your headaches?' she said.

'I'm really not sure, but it's worth a try,' replied Peter, almost absently – he was still shell-shocked from the vision of Abrille.

'Come and lie on the treatment table and we shall see if massaging your poor head with my cleavage has any effect.'

Mesmerised, Peter complied, placing himself on the table and craning his neck forward so as not to waste one second of the opportunity to gaze at the amazing Abrille.

Abrille climbed astride him, her knickerless pussy resting on his stomach, and pressed her succulent cleavage on to his nose and face. I heard him inhale deeply and moan with pleasure and I watched as Abrille's furry beaver and firm brown globes poked from under the bright white uniform. Then she sat back and pulled Peter's sweatshirt over his head, revealing his slim, fit-looking torso. He was still entranced and gazed at her in disbelief. He was now most assuredly under her spell and Abrille seized the opportunity like a true professional, strapping his wrists to the sides of the table just as I had asked. He

78

was too dizzy with lust to object. Cruelly, she ground her crotch on to the bulge in his trousers as one last parting tease, and dismounted.

'The doctor will be with you in a minute,' she advised and left him, treating him to a wonderfully tantalising display of her wiggling arse.

'What? Abrille!?' I heard him call as she joined me in the darkness of The Dungeon Room.

I hugged her in appreciation of her performance, casually allowing my hand to linger on her breast as I released her.

'*Magnifique*,' I said. 'We'll give him a few seconds to contemplate his situation.' I wanted Peter to take in his surroundings, the *mise-en-scène*, the equipment, and for his imagination to start running before I made my entrance.

'Abrille? Where are you?' Peter called.

'Introduce me,' I whispered to Abrille after a second or two.

Abrille strode back into the surgery. I admired her swaying buttocks as I followed a yard or two behind.

'This is Doctor McKnight, who will be conducting the examination today,' she proclaimed.

Peter took a look at me in my white coat and dark-rimmed glasses and gave a rueful smile, letting his head fall back on to the padded table and causing it to puff out air at the sides.

'I might have known,' he said, which I thought rather too outspoken for one in his position.

'Nurse Martin, I would be grateful if the patient would only speak when asked to. We have a lot of procedures to get through and can't waste time,' I said, deliberately directing the comment away from the patient, although it was obviously meant for his ears. I picked up a clipboard from the side work-surface and pretended to read it.

'I see,' I said as I considered the imaginary notes. 'Frequent headaches. I think we shall begin with an examination to determine the cause of the neuralgia and then prescribe a suitable treatment. Would you remove the patient's lower garments please, Nurse Martin, while I prepare?'

'Yes, Doctor,' Abrille answered, stepping up to remove his shoes and socks. As she did so I bent down to discreetly whisper her first lesson in running medical sessions. 'Tease him with glimpses of your body, but do not make eye contact,' I said, lightly brushing her earlobe with my soft lips.

Abrille nodded quietly, placing the patient's shoes under the treatment table and proceeding to undo his belt, button and fly. I busied myself collecting some apparatus for the examination as Abrille pulled his trousers off and then unpeeled his underpants releasing his almost fully erect circumcised penis, which sprang upwards, then lolled slightly to the right. By now the patient would have guessed that he was unlikely to be fucking the incredibly fuckable Abrille any time today and I was gratified to see that in spite of this disappointment he was still excited by the situation.

My hands squirmed into a pair of disposable gloves, and I pulled the cuff down with a snap, 'The patient appears to be ready. I wonder if the excited state of his penis might indicate that it has some significance in the complaint. Nurse, would you take a swab sample from the patient's urethra?' I handed Abrille a large cotton bud or swab. 'Down to about a centimetre's depth should be enough.'

Abrille carefully inserted one cotton-covered end into the slit at the top of the patient's penis, slowly twisting it until the white head of the swab had disappeared inside. The patient's hands flexed in their straps and I heard him gasp at the sensation. I am sure Abrille was now growing to appreciate the three most important ingredients of medical play. First there is humiliation, or dehumanisation, making the customer or participant feel like a specimen, not a person. Secondly, pleasure, which can be delivered through both visual and physical media. The visual stimulus is provided by the nurse or doctor, the physical by invasive treatments or examinations in the erogenous nerve centres of the body, such as the genitals, nipples or anus. Thirdly, pain, which should be applied carefully to the same nerve centres. The third ingredient is most effective when delivered simultaneously with pleasure, as our patient was now experiencing.

I held out a kidney dish for Nurse Martin to put the swab in. She eased it out of the patient's penis expertly and dropped it into the shiny metal dish.

'Good. There should be plenty there for the girls in the lab to analyse,' I said, placing the dish on the side, to be sent to some imaginary laboratory.

'Thank you, Nurse. Would you measure the penis for me while I take notes?' I handed Sister Abrille a tape measure and she gingerly took the patient's penis and reported various measurements of length, circumference and testicle size (although I'm not quite sure how she obtained an accurate reading of *that* particular dimension using only a measuring tape). The humiliation of the patient was clear to see on his flushing face.

'Are there any distinguishing marks on the penis or scrotum, Sister? Darkened areas or lighter patches on the skin?' I asked, hoping that Abrille would take the hint and reply in the affirmative.

Abrille began a fingertip scrutiny of the patient's scrotum and penis.

'Yes, Doctor, there is a darkened patch on the anterior of the shaft,' she replied, pointing to the smallest of blemishes that I had trouble seeing even when I peered at it over my glasses.

'Yes, there is,' I agreed with enthusiasm. 'Penis shows evidence of frequent handling,' I said out loud as I wrote the details on my clipboard.

'Sister, would you prepare the patient for anal examination by placing his feet in the stirrups?'

As Abrille carried out the task I picked up some lube and a speculum and positioned myself so that I was more or less standing between the patient's suspended feet. In full view of the patient I lubricated my gloved finger and then slowly but firmly twisted it into his anus past his sphincter, pulling it in and out steadily to open him up. The gasps of simultaneous pleasure and discomfort were music to my dominant ears.

Having loosened the anus, I took up the chrome speculum and clicked it to the closed position, applying generous lubrication to its surfaces. I took to my knee so that my eye was the right level and, with Abrille's sweet breath at my ear, as she watched intently over my shoulder, I began to insert the scope.

The patient's gasps grew deeper as I eased the implement into his arse, forcing it, like my finger seconds earlier, past the constricting muscle. I let it rest in the position for a moment to allow him to get used to its presence, and then began to apply even pressure to the thumb lever to open the scope and stretch the orifice for viewing.

The patient groaned and gasped. Now, perhaps, pain, pleasure and humiliation were in perfect proportion. I continued to ease my thumb downwards until both nurse and doctor could see clearly inside his most intimate areas. Abrille placed a hand on my shoulder.

'If you look inside at the rectum wall, Sister, you can see some reddening in certain areas,' I said, concocting a feature or symptom for us to discuss.

Could our compliant patient possibly have felt more excitement and humiliation than he was experiencing now? He was restrained, and two beautiful, sexy women, apparently unconcerned by his evident lust for them, were examining his rectum and discussing it in his presence with complete disregard for his dignity.

'Oh, yes, Doctor,' said Abrille, playing along. 'Is that normal?'

'Only in cases of frequent digital insertion,' I replied. 'I think we shall apply a balm to soothe the area, while we have access to it. Would you hold the speculum for me, Sister?'

I went over to the sink, where I filled a large needle-less syringe with warm water. Kneeling behind my assistant, I aimed the syringe into the opened anus and squirted the warm liquid into his sensitive canal.

As someone who has had a similar experience herself (during her experimental youth), I know that there are few sensations more overpowering than this. Assuredly, the patient's groans were now ones of pleasure.

'Good, that's done. If you would ease the speculum out for me, Abrille.'

Abrille tenderly removed the speculum and placed it in the sink. I watched the patient's gaping anus slowly closing like an iris in the sunlight. How cute. His cock was now fully erect and pulsating slightly. I wondered if, were it not for the strapping on his wrists, he would now be stroking it.

I felt the time had come to provide a diagnosis and prescribe a treatment. As before, we discussed the matter as though he was not there.

'Well, Sister, this patient has clearly been wanking excessively, and probably likes to finger-fuck his anus while he does so. We can only conjecture what other sordid practices he gets up to in private – I'm afraid an examination can only reveal so much.'

'I suspected he might be a frequent masturbator when I first saw him,' commented Abrille in an almost musical French accent. She was playing along wonderfully and I squeezed her hand in encouragement. She responded by stepping closer to me.

'Yes, me too, but the examination was nonetheless necessary in order to be certain.'

'What treatment would you recommend, Doctor?' asked Abrille, really getting into her role. I felt her breath on my face and goose pimples ran down my neck.

'The only treatment available which might reduce the incidence of masturbation is a complete system flush – to release pressure in the anus and testicles. We shall begin with an enema,' I told her, with so much authority that even I believed it might have some basis in medical fact.

There are many varied ways of delivering colonic irrigation to a patient, but my preferred tool is the gravity enema, which administers a steady, titillating trickle into the patient's bowel, unlike many of the other methods, which involve a pumping action and cause the chosen liquid to enter in bursts. My patients assure me that the combination of an alluring female towering over their supine, oft-times restrained, body and the sensation of gradual pressure building inside such a vulnerable area is extraordinarily wank-inducing. And this is in spite of, or perhaps because of, the ultimate admission of sexual supplication that giving in to the auto-erotic act represents.

I wanted to see if the patient, so confident and

assured in everyday life, would succumb to the urge and debase himself before us.

'Remove the patient's right strap, please, Sister,' I said, 'and while you do that I shall prepare the enema.'

The enema apparatus is a four-sided, opaque container made from thick plastic sheeting, which holds a maximum of three pints of fluid. A four-foot tube runs from the bottom of the container, ending in a simple tap and tapered nozzle, which is inserted into the anus. The rim of the container section has two loops which allow it to be held at a suitable height, or hooked on to a stand if the arm is tiring. When the tap is opened, gravity gets to work and the fluid enters the anus, filling the patient with sensation.

By the time the apparatus was filled and ready for use, Abrille had removed the strap as requested and the patient's right hand was free. I took the opportunity to drop him a hint.

'Sister, if the patient's testicles are still full after the enema, we shall perform prostate massage to empty them, although I am sure the patient is aware that this will make him ejaculate without orgasm. Follow me, Nurse, and I will demonstrate the enema.'

We positioned ourselves between the suspended feet of the patient and I bade Abrille insert the nozzle while I held the container, now filled with warm water, up to the height of my curving breasts.

The patient took in a small gasp of air as the nozzle entered his rear and under my whispered instruction Abrille delicately twisted it until it was securely inserted.

'Open the tap,' I said.

The patient's eyes narrowed as he felt the first trickles of the balmy fluid invade him. Soon he was groaning, a low, croaky groan with lips slightly apart, and as his head lolled I noticed his hand instinctively move to his cock.

I glanced at Abrille and gave her an encouraging smile to show that things were going well. I hoped my smugness did not show too much, but I was rather pleased at having achieved so soon my goal of reducing this particular patient to a masturbating submissive. I am sure, once the patient's fingers had encircled his cock and begun their pumping motion, Abrille could work out for herself how well it was going, so perhaps she did not need my smile of encouragement.

I watched the level of water slowly falling as the patient received his humiliating dosage and performed his shameful ritual. Abrille posed brazenly for our frenzied little masturbator, with the hem of her skin-tight uniform raised to the top of her thighs and one foot forwards, presenting her gleaming shank to his greedy eyes. I wished I could run my tongue along that thigh myself, but unfortunately I was in the middle of a delicate medical procedure that required at least a share of my attention.

'We must leave some notes on this one's chart regarding his inappropriate behaviour during treatment,' I told my nurse. 'I'd hate it if less liberal or tolerant medics were confronted by such a pitiful display without warning.'

Still holding the equipment aloft I stepped behind Abrille and rather naughtily reached under her dress with my middle finger and caressed her sex with a side-to-side motion. She did not complain and barely seemed distracted by my action.

'It will at least save us the time of applying a prostate massage,' observed Abrille, remaining in character.

'Yes, I suppose that's true, Nurse.'

By now there was just an inch or two of fluid left in the container and the myriad sensations were bringing the patient close to orgasm.

'Fetch the sample cup, please, Nurse. We might as well send everything we can to the girls in the lab today.'

Abrille picked up the small plastic cup and placed it under the patient's penis, ready to collect a sample of his jism. The patient responded to her closeness by increasing his rhythm and we did not have to wait too much longer for a tooth-gnashing climax as he deposited five or six threads of semen into the receptacle. Abrille's look was one of distinct satisfaction, and she pumped the last few drops from his penis into the cup with her own hand.

While the patient recovered, I disengaged the enema and Abrille unstrapped the patient's other arm. He lay practically still in a state of post-orgasmic nirvana.

'Please come back in two weeks' time if there is no improvement to your condition,' I advised. Then Abrille and I left him to compose and clean himself, giving him a parting instruction to tidy the surgery before returning to work.

'Yes, Doctor McKnight,' he breathed.

We both felt the burning of his longing gaze on our swaying arses as we disappeared upstairs.

The unmitigated success of Abrille's first session painted a grin on my face that I was scarcely able to hide. Any of the staff passing by and seeing me during the rest of that day must have wondered what I had been up to, to be beaming so widely. I doubt they would have guessed exactly, but probably presumed it had to do with humping a bouncer in the store-room, or something like that.

By the time the late shift had started, I had reached the conclusion that, given Abrille's immediate proficiency at the task presented to her, I might as well go ahead and give Amber her chance too. Abrille was clearly going to need much less attention than I had anticipated, so there was plenty of time for me to take on another apprentice. I glanced at my watch; Amber's shift would be starting soon, so I went in search of the beautiful lassie.

Amber, a petite Scots girl with short, bobbed, blond hair and a firm, well-proportioned body, is a bright, friendly sort, if a little loud at times. Like many of the females in this city, she has an obsession with keeping her body in a constant state of bronze. Nonetheless, I took her on as a Paddle-Boat girl because of her forwardness and outspoken nature; I hoped that the ability to speak and act so honestly would assist her in communicating feelings and desires with future clients.

She was not one for tardiness and I knew she would be somewhere in the building preparing for her shift. I started looking in the bar.

'Have you seen Amber?' I asked as I peered inside the bar area.

Maureen was perched demurely on a barstool, leaning her chin on her hand and playing with a drink. Barman Jack muttered something amusing into her ear that made her smile and flick her auburn hair. Maureen had gone bare-legged that day and the contrast between the black skirt and black shoes and her cream-white pins was striking. I pitied poor Jack, who would have been unable to feast his eyes from his vantage point behind the bar. Perhaps that was why he was leaning so far forward.

'Have either of you seen Amber?' I asked.

They both shrugged and I left them to their drinks, thinking to try the common room on the mezzanine.

It tended to be empty after a shift change as my staff either head home or for the bar at the end of their tour of duty.

As I approached the door I was surprised to hear playful giggling coming from within. Curious, I slipped off my heels and went silk-footed so as not to be heard. Luckily, the door was ajar and I was able to widen the gap ever so slightly without being heard, and peer inside.

The blond-haired Chloe McIntyre and the fit, handsome Gordon were sharing one of the armchairs. Chloe was in Gordon's lap, her legs over one of the arms and one hand behind his neck. There was a lot of soft laughter and low talking. Still curious, I watched on.

Chloe was rattling some dice in her free hand, and they seemed to be sharing a very private joke. Clearly, I was not the only member of the establishment to have noticed the tendency for this room to offer privacy just after the evening shift-change. Chloe rolled the dice on the coffee table and then Gordon picked them up and did the same. The second result caused a great rush of playful slapping and laughter, though Chloe seemed more pleased about it than Gordon. Then, to my amazement, Gordon took to his knees and began burrowing his head under her skirt, like a ferret up a rabbit-hole. Chloe was clearly enjoying herself – her legs were now splayed over the arms of the easy-chair – but for some reason seemed obsessed with keeping an eye on her watch. I had no time to see how things might develop as I needed to find Amber and I made a discreet exit.

I felt rather threatened by what I had seen in the common room. Perhaps it was just jealousy, or even a misplaced feminine emotion, but to see two members of my staff involving themselves in sexual pleasure without my knowledge, participation or even permission seemed to shatter my self-image as Queen of this nest of iniquity. Red-faced and distracted, I stormed away, heading for the Accounts department.

Amber and Gemma were there, sorting out the chips that had been collected from the roulette table. Having tracked Amber down at last, I snapped at her, 'Amber, can I see you please?'

The poor cherub was quite taken aback by my tone and I suddenly realised that I had no reason to be so abrupt. My mood was nothing to do with her. I felt doubly stupid when I realised I was still carrying my shoes.

'I'm sorry, Amber, I did not mean to sound angry,' I said apologetically. 'Actually, I think you might find our conversation quite pleasing.'

Amber came out into the corridor, still looking a little worried.

'Sorry about that. Amber, how do you think your time at The Paddle-Boat has gone since you joined us?'

'Aye, not bad.' She smiled. 'It was awful strange being asked to flaunt myself at my job at first, but now I like it.'

'That's awful good to hear. Would you say it has changed you at all? Changed your attitudes?'

'No half, by the way,' she said with a laugh. 'I've found I love the attention, the feel of a man's eyes upon me, the power it gives me. It has changed me, so it has.'

I was flushed with pride to hear this and forgot my previous worries. Amber certainly seemed eager enough, and I suppose that was something I never doubted about her.

'How would you feel about coming in with me to do a session, downstairs in the basement?' I asked her. 'You could watch, or take part, whatever you're most at home with.'

Amber seemed to pause and I feared she might be showing some trepidation, but the glint that then appeared in her eye suggested she was merely imagining some of the possibilities.

'Aye. Aye, why not?'

'I'm so glad. I shall send for you when an opportunity arrives.'

Seven

The opportunity arose a couple of days later when I received a visit from Austin Barrowman, a dentist from Wishaw, the client who had been my very first personal customer. Austin had first come to see me for a session many moons ago, well before The Cellar was equipped as now, but I still had access to most of the implements and toys any submissive could hope to have used on him. After one session Austin seemed to latch on to me, the poor helpless, hormone-driven mutt.

Austin is 42, I think, quite attractive for his age, usually smartly dressed and coiffed, but strangely, whatever the time of day, always with a shadow on his jaw-line that suggests he last shaved twelve hours ago.

In those days The Paddle-Boat was an ordinary casino, albeit with an extraordinary manageress, and I had to advertise in the local press for custom. I kept the tribute amount high to avoid oversubscription and ensure the right class of clientèle, and I ran my sessions in the evenings from a rented flat until The Cellar was properly equipped.

By now Austin's familiarity meant that he was rarely a walk-in customer; his preference was to ring me in my office to arrange an appointment, usually for the next day. Since I have been able to provide a service on the premises, a routine has emerged where I trot down to The Cellar to spin The Wheel in his absence and then ring him back later in the day to advise him what Fortune had determined his fate should be. The calls are always brief.

'Austin. It's Mistress Valerie.'

'Good evening, Mistress.'

'The Wheel has determined that you will spend tomorrow's session in The Dungeon Room.'

'Yes, Mistress.'

It was then Austin's task to consider the fantasy he would like me to provide for him in the ordained setting. I did not tell him that Amber Johnson would be observing, and perhaps participating, on this particular occasion; I was sure we could work her into the fantasy.

The time approached for Austin's appointment and I summoned Gemma up from downstairs to help me into my costume; the attire I wear in The Dungeon Room is tight, with many fastenings, and a tradition has grown out of my need for assistance in putting it all on: Gemma lends her helping hands.

The curvaceous redhead arrived in my office in moments, eager to please me, not least because serving me gives her a flutter of pleasure in her belly, a flutter she cannot replicate elsewhere.

When she entered, I was standing in the centre of the room striking a regal pose. I allowed her a second or two to admire me.

'I shall be working in The Dungeon Room in about an hour. Dress me,' I said.

No words passed Gemma's glistening red lips. Immediately she skipped over to fetch the full-length mirror from the corner and place it before me.

'What shall the Mistress be wearing today?'

'Fetch me the red bodice top, the black leather skirt, my long black gloves, the red suspender belt and matching stockings and some red shoes.'

'Yes, Mistress.'

'No, wait. Make it the black knee-high boots.'

'Yes, Mistress.'

Gemma entered the office wardrobe to collect the items specified. She made several trips back and forth, bringing out the lingerie hamper and laying some items carefully on my sofa. Her hips were swaying and her red hair swishing beautifully and I was tempted to send her back for something else just to watch her movements, but logic prevailed: there would be plenty of other opportunities to gaze at her figure.

Gemma knelt to remove my high-heeled pumps, running her alabaster fingers down my nylon-covered calves as she did so. I flexed my toes in their stockings as they became free of the tight shoes, and in response she took them in her hands, massaging the soles firmly with her thumbs.

'You may inhale,' I told her.

Gemma did so, pressing her nose to my toes and breathing deeply so that I could feel the cool of the rushing air passing between them.

'Continue,' I said.

'Mistress,' she responded, bowing her head.

Sensuously, she pushed her hands up my thighs to reach under my short pencil skirt and unfasten the clasps of my suspender belt. Delicately she unrolled my stocking, kissing the tips of my toes as they became exposed. She repeated the ritual with the same intensity for the other leg, and then knelt before me, looking up with the pleading innocence of a puppy on a doorstep.

Now that I had her full attention, I thought I might

start a discussion about something that had recently been playing on my mind.

'The plans for The Paddle-Boat seem to be going very well, don't you think, Gemma?'

'Yes, Mistress.'

'I am especially pleased with the way the croupiers appear to be relaxing into the roles I have come to demand of them; many of them seem more comfortable about themselves.'

'Yes, indeed, Mistress – the atmosphere has changed noticeably on the games floor, and in the bars and staff areas.'

I had feared that Gemma might make such an observation.

'Oh. How do you mean?'

'Pardon me for saying so, Mistress, but I believe your liberal personality is rubbing off on some of our colleagues.'

Her comment gave me pause, and I considered what I had seen in recent days around The Paddle-Boat: Abrille and Peter being flirty on the stairs, barman Jack whispering into Maureen's ear over a drink and, of course, the antics of Gordon and Chloe in the common room.

'Continue with your task,' I told her as I ruminated on the situation.

Gemma unzipped my skirt, before carefully guiding it to the floor around my ankles, where I made her wait for some three or four seconds on her knees, frozen in time, before I deigned to step out of it, allowing her to continue. Standing, she dutifully unbuttoned my blouse, lifting it carefully from my back, leaving me in just my black bra, suspender belt and invisible knickers.

'What about this dice game I have seen being played?' I said at last, fishing for gossip.

Gemma's face turned immediately to a radiant smile. 'Oh, have you been told about it? Isn't it fun, Mistress?'

I snapped my fingers loudly to show that no Queen expected such a jolly demeanour in her lady-in-waiting. She bowed her head immediately and reached around to unbutton my suspender belt and place it on the couch. Then she approached me again, still with her head bowed, and began to unclasp my bra. It fell away into her hands, freeing my fresh, ripe breasts. Instinctively, Gemma knelt in homage to my naked beauty.

'Lower your head still further,' I commanded.

She did so wordlessly, lowering her eyes towards my feet.

'Now tell me about this dice game.'

'Yes, Mistress. Michael and Maureen got together last week, Mistress: sexually, Mistress.'

I was unaware of this development and a tad shocked that the lascivious Maureen, having denied to me that muscular Michael was her type, should feel the need to be rogered by him, apparently within hours of receiving similar treatment from horny pony-boy Stephen Koenig.

'The wee slut.'

'Shortly after their little fling, Mistress, Maureen told the other croupiers of a sex game she and Michael had come up with – involving dice.'

'How does the game work?'

'Two dice are used, Mistress. Maureen would roll them, then Michael, and the highest scorer would receive oral pleasure from the other for the number of minutes shown on their dice.' Gemma kept her head bowed as she reported to me, but she must have been tempted to extend her neck and look upon my naked splendour. I revelled in teasing her like this.

'I think I follow you.' I was impressed at the creativity shown by my staff in coming up with the game, but disappointed with the vanilla flavour of the forfeit activity. Surely the score on the dice should determine the number of strokes across the buttocks received by the loser, or the number of ice cubes melted on the genitals or in the anus.

Ambiguity reigned inside me again: on the one hand I was pleased to hear that my staff were growing in sexual maturity, following my example, but on the other my ego was bruised – I was affronted that my drones and workers were making honey without my royal assent.

'And how many have tried this game?' I asked.

'Chloe and myself both sought out Michael to try the game with one of the original players, Mistress. Then Chloe tried it with Gordon, and I tried it with Jack Moyes.'

Gemma was now blushing slightly and perhaps sensed my displeasure at what she had revealed. Regretfully, I had no time for further interrogation, as I needed to be dressed. I decided not to pursue the matter.

Reaching down, I lifted her chin with one slender finger and kissed her full, pouting red lips as she came to her feet.

'Dress me.'

She began with my red bodice. It is not appropriate for a slave-girl to place a garment over her Mistress's head, which might seem the logical way to perform the task, so she knelt for me to step into it and drew it up my legs, over the arc of my hips, up to my breasts. The cups of the garment snugly enveloped my breasts like a lover's hands. Walking around me, Gemma tightened the laces at the rear, forcing my mounds together, where they kissed in a torturously teasing cleavage.

She fetched the delicately made but boldly coloured red suspender belt from the couch and knelt down to encircle my waist with it. With her arms around my waist and her cheek pressed to my subtly convex abdomen, she fastened it behind my back. I felt her excited breath on my hip.

She must have feasted her eyes on the pink lips of my sex, half hidden in my dark bush, as she straightened the four clasp-straps so that they dangled freely down my thighs, fore and aft.

Gemma will be Gemma, and I knew she must be bursting to play with herself; she always wanted to, but especially now that her Goddess was towering above her, next to naked. It cannot have got any easier for her as she collected the seamed red stockings and once more knelt at my feet. She rolled one of them in her hand.

I lifted a pedicured foot on to the top of her thigh, allowing her to place the diaphanous extra skin over my toes. She smoothed it up my leg with her soft hands, lightly massaging and caressing my flesh as she went. I felt her graceful fingers attaching the clasps to the silken scarlet band at the top of the stocking.

I changed feet, again pressing my sole to her shank as she prepared the stocking. My sex softened with moisture as Gemma repeated the exercise. I and my pussy enjoyed the erotic sensation that goes with having one's legs adorned in silk or nylon.

Gemma fixed the clasps to the second stocking and, bravely for a slave, ran her palms and fingertips up and down my calves and thighs in a light massage. I was in sensual heaven, and Gemma inched nearer, allowing the inside of her leg to brush against my calf. If she could, she would have humped my leg like a horny dog.

'Stand,' I commanded her. She stood, head bowed.

Once more I lifted her chin with my finger and kissed her mouth, this time parting her ruby lips. Our tongues writhed like naked lovers and I cupped the back of her neck with my hand, increasing the passion and forcing her head back into a passive posture. Her mouth was warm and comforting and I found contentment exploring it. Finally, I placed my free arm around her waist and leant my torso forwards, requiring her to bend backwards and relax the weight of her body on to my arm. I kissed her still, adopting the pose of the suave, irresistible hero from some black-and-white movie, with her as the helpless heroine, swept off her feet. Then, when I sensed her appetite for more had peaked, I released her.

'Continue your duties,' I said.

Gemma obeyed, fetching my leather skirt from the arm of the couch, then knelt to place it on the floor before me. Again I made her wait there, unmoving, until I was ready to step into the short black garment and allow her to fasten it around my waist. The smell of the leather filled my nostrils.

It really is short: if the straps of my suspenders are extended to full length, which they nearly always are, then the skirt will fail to cover the clasps and stocking tops. The sides of the skirt have openings, held together by criss-cross lacings, which allow a flash of the side of my buttock to be seen. The contrast of black leather and my soft, white flesh draws the eye irresistibly.

Gemma prepared my black knee-high boots, which are quite tight and must be unlaced before one can put them on; they are then laced back up over the leg. This takes time and care, and while Gemma busied herself I took the chance to liaise with my Head Croupier.

'It does not worry you that these naughty little trysts amongst the staff may distract everyone from what we are trying to do here?' I asked.

'Mistress? No, Mistress,' replied Gemma, looking up from her task. 'Surely it will only serve to extend their sexual imaginations and help them to create better sessions.'

I was unconvinced, but decided to wait and see how things developed rather than rule the place with an iron heel.

'So be it, slave-girl. We shall play it as you suggest for the time being, but, if things escalate and I find that eyes are being taken off balls, I shall have to step in.'

'Yes, Mistress.'

My boots were now fitted and I took two or three experimental steps on the stiletto heels to ensure that they were comfortable.

'Good,' I said, satisfied. 'Now before I put on the gloves, strip so that your buttocks and genitals are exposed, bring me the belt from my desk and bend over the arm of the sofa.'

'Mistress?' responded Gemma, a little confused. 'Have I not pleased Mistress today?'

'Today, yes, but I recall a cheeky comment or two in recent days, for which you will be receiving "pelters" – six, to be precise. Count loudly.'

Gemma was well trained and, in spite of her confusion, had handed me the belt and taken position almost on auto-pilot, while I had been explaining the situation. My mouth and pussy watered as my eyes were presented with her full round moon.

I thwacked it forehand and then backhand in quick succession.

'One. Two,' she said loudly as she gathered herself from the sudden shock.

She was more braced for the third, again a forehand stroke, and so I increased the venom for the fourth, on the backhand.

'Three . . . four,' she called.

A red stripe announced itself where the belt had fallen, and her globes clenched involuntarily from the sting.

The final two strokes were on the forehand and spaced by three seconds, as I wanted the full pang of the fifth to be experienced before the sixth was applied.

'Five . . . six,' proclaimed Gemma. 'Thank you, Mistress.'

'You may dress, and then away and give Amber these instructions for the session.'

I handed Gemma a slip of paper and as she covered herself up again I pulled on the final items of my outfit: the long black shiny gloves.

Austin Barrowman was escorted to my office by Gemma. I could hardly walk out into the public areas to meet him, the way I was dressed now, unless I wanted to attract a gaggle of Mrs Finlays, waving placards outside and trying to close us down.

As he entered, so suave-looking in his smart trousers and open-necked shirt, he was greeted with my dominant image draped over the sofa, my arms stretched out and my feet resting on a footstool.

'Good morning, Mistress.'

'Good morning, Austin,' I replied. 'Please sit.'

I moved my booted heels from the footstool, allowing him to squat down on to it.

'What is your poison today, slave?' I asked, smiling.

'Inescapable bondage and physical punishment, Mistress,' he replied shyly. It was a fantasy that fit

The Wheel's chosen room perfectly. I always admired Austin's commitment, versatility and imagination – as well as his money.

'Your tribute.'

Austin reached into his pocket and proffered a handful of bank notes, which I took.

I spat in his face.

'Loser,' I said.

Austin is one of those men I referred to earlier, who receive a thrill from the act of paying a female for their fantasies. Austin had asked me to remind him in some way of the significance of his weakness every time I took money from him.

I counted the money and secreted it in my bodice.

'Excellent. Let us go,' I said, leading the way.

Few words were needed after many months of regular sessions with my most long-standing client.

Amber was already in The Dungeon Room, where I had instructed her to go to dress and light the candles. My directions were that the black heels, skirt and stockings of her croupier's uniform were fine as they were, but she was to replace the white blouse and bra with a black bodice. I added that she could add an accessory of her own choice to the ensemble and, on coming down the stairs, with Austin obediently following, I was pleased and amused to see she had chosen a feline eye-mask. With her blond hair contrasting with the black outfit, and the tanned flesh exposed around her midriff, she looked very sexy indeed.

'This is Mistress Amber, who will be assisting me in your punishment. Greet her,' I said to him.

Austin bowed his head.

'Greetings, Mistress.'

Amber flushed with pride at her first experience of being called 'Mistress'.

'Greetings, slave,' she replied.

'Undress,' I commanded.

Immediately Austin made his way to a corner and began to disrobe, folding his clothes neatly like a good slave.

To decorate The Dungeon Room I had had the plaster stripped away to reveal the bare brickwork. Each brick was then painted black and the pointing purple. The floor is a chequered pattern of purple and red tiling. There are many candle sconces of blackened metal around the walls, as candlelight is more conducive to the ambience than the strip lighting available upstairs. I have consulted with Michael about having torches put in but he starts quoting all sorts of boring and unsexy fire regulations at me, so I've let it drop.

Other fixtures include a whipping bench, a wall-mounted St Andrew's crucifix, a small metal cage and a restraining bench called a 'spitfire'. I have two hooks in the ceiling, which often come in useful, and, of course, the toys of the trade hanging on the far wall.

While the slave stripped I collected some items from their wall-mountings and handed them to my assistant to hold, keeping a flogger in my own hand.

'This slave wants to feel completely at our mercy, and to receive severe physical punishment from which there is no escape,' I whispered to Amber to give her an idea of what to expect.

By now the slave was prepared and kneeling naked with his head bowed.

I sat on one of the three chairs and gestured to Amber to take another and place the items I had given her on the third chair. I cracked the flogger on my boots.

'Crawl to us, slave, and taste Amber's delicious shoes.'

The slave did exactly as he was told, crawling to where Amber sat cross-legged and applying the tip of his tongue to the toe of her shoe, then more boldly licking the sole and sucking the heel.

Amber had never before seen anyone prostrate themselves in this fashion and perhaps had not imagined the submission would be so utterly unquestioning. She looked at me with a little surprise as the dust and grime were licked from her shoes.

After this quick introduction I was ready to restrain the slave for his ordeal.

'Cease,' I said.

The slave resumed his kneeling position.

'The Mistresses look stunning today,' he said.

I could not believe my ears. Had this slave actually spoken without permission? Perhaps the presence of another Mistress was blurring the etiquette for the slave, and making him forget himself.

'Do not speak unless you are asked or instructed to speak, slave,' I warned him, and swung the leather strands of the flogger across his back sharply. 'You are supposedly an experienced slave – conduct yourself like one.'

'Yes, Mistress.'

That, I thought, would remove any ambiguity. I took a moment to consider the session. The slave had asked for inescapable bondage and I wanted therefore to put him in a humiliating and uncomfortable pose, in which any movement would cause his bonds to tighten and remind him of his complete vulnerability.

I began by shackling his ankles together with two chained leather cuffs; the maximum separation that the metal chain between them would allow was perhaps less than six inches, so his feet were in effect glued to one another.

'Raise your chin.' I ordered.

Amber guessed my next move and handed me the leather collar. I buckled it around the slave's neck, tightly enough to be uncomfortable but well short of restricting his anxious breathing.

'Place your head on the floor and grasp your ankles,' I told my slave.

'Yes, Mistress.' Now his backside was perfectly exposed for punishment.

I noticed a curiosity-filled Amber peering at his scrotum and penis as they dangled between his legs.

'Pass me the red rope,' I said. 'Believe me, this slave is going to want to wriggle free once I get to work on him, so it may take quite a bit of rope to ensure he is held fast.'

I began on his right wrist and forearm: with his palms outwards, I bound the wrist to the ankle using a firm knot and then his forearm to his foreleg with many coils of the cord around both, finishing with a knot to secure the elbow joint to just below the knee.

'Another, please,' I said to Amber, who passed me a second length. I repeated the exercise, binding the left forearm to the left foreleg in the same way.

'Now pass me the yellow cord.'

My ropes are colour-coded for length. The yellow cord, a little shorter, was fed through the loop in the slave's collar. I knotted it in place, and then around the chain separating the ankle cuffs, so it was short enough that if the slave attempted to lift his head he would feel pressure on his neck from the collar and the rough, taut rope would press into his genitals.

The slave now seemed fearful. The undeniable adrenalin rush of his vulnerability was coursing through him. I walked around him, examining my work.

'The slave has submitted himself to whatever whimsy we see fit to inflict upon him. Good. We can begin the pain.'

I decided to begin on the genitals, which were dangling so invitingly between his legs that it was impossible to start anywhere else.

I pressed the top of my foot to his cock and scrotum. The cool shiny surface of my boot may have been pleasant at first but grunts of discomfort soon began when I commenced a repeated light kicking motion, gradually increasing in power. The pangs would eventually start to radiate from his cock and balls, perhaps into his abdomen and buttocks, and I let him experience this for almost a minute.

To mark the end of the ordeal, I slapped the boot of my standing leg with the flogger, making a loud crack. I was pleased to see that his penis was erect, although it has always amazed me that such treatment can be interpreted as pleasure, even by an organ as needy as the penis.

As Amber watched, I began with the flogger, swinging the leather strands in a wheel-like motion through the air, so that they struck his testicles as they arced past. I was unrelenting, and the dozens of blows fell like rainfall. The slave became agitated, crying out, wriggling, writhing, trying in vain to lift his head, to find some more comfortable position, but there was none, no relief and no escape.

The beauty of this form of flagellation is that the pain becomes more and more acute as the barrage continues and the scrotum's sensitivity increases.

'Listen to his pathetic whimpering, will you, Mistress Amber,' I commented as I increased the frequency of the flagellation. I knew the sensations must be white-hot by now and the feeling of helplessness in our slave, brought on by his position and our lack of pity for his predicament, must have been more paralysing than the bonds that held him. He continued his sobbing and whimpering until I finally ceased.

'I think the time has come for Mistress Amber to try her hand,' I said. 'Mistress Amber, would you apply some strokes to this scrawny little backside? Twelve should do it.'

Amber took the flogger, tentatively at first, and stood behind the slave, where she could see clearly for the first time his bright-red scrotum.

Grinning, she copied the way I had swung the flogger and cracked a beauty on to the slave's upturned backside. His breath escaped him, seeping out through clenched teeth.

'Good. That's one,' I called.

Amber was encouraged by her first attempt and laced him again with a similar result, causing his lower back and buttocks to redden. How our slave must have felt to know that he was our plaything and that our only game was his discomfort.

'Two,' I called.

Amber was gaining in confidence and turned herself sideways-on, so as to lay the vicious strands across the buttocks. By now she had mastered my technique of allowing the strands to circle in the air and she delivered a salvo of strikes in quicker succession.

'Three, four, five, six.'

After the sixth I laid a steadying hand on Amber's arm to halt the beating.

'I wonder if I could ask your opinion on something, Mistress Amber.'

'Aye, of course,' replied Amber loudly; she had cottoned on that many of the conversations between Mistresses during a session are meant primarily for the ears of the slave.

107

'I wonder if we should stop the beating there and do something about this unsightly erection, or continue to the full schedule of twelve lashes?'

'Aye, it's unsightly all right,' Amber agreed.

'If we do stop, however, I think the slave would have to owe you the full twelve lashes for next time.'

'Oh, definitely.'

I reached down between the slave's legs and roughly grasped his undercarriage, pulling his penis downwards between his legs so that it poked outwards like a puppy's tail.

'First let us see if the erection can be discouraged with a few bites of the flogger,' I suggested, pushing downwards at the base so that the penis remained in the dog-tail position but my hands were out of the way.

Amber struck carefully down upon it, wielding the flogger as though it were a conker and string. I let her apply the same blow twice more, a second or two apart. The unnaturally positioned penis wobbled like a diving board on each occasion. The slave's high-pitched wailing was not unexpected; the pain must have been searing his loins for a good few seconds.

'That appears to have been unsuccessful. It seems we will have to resolve this another way,' I said as I began to pump the now supremely sensitive member with my hand.

I gestured to Amber to take over and after a short while we were taking turns to milk the slave's errant tail. His moans and grunts retained their high-pitched timbre as we steadily, almost metronomically, pulled on it.

By now the helpless slave, who, in his restrained position, was totally reliant on us for both his pleasure and his pain, must have felt himself nearing orgasm. I decided the time had come to apply the final cruelty.

'No, it does not seem to want to go away,' I said. 'I give up.'

'Me too, Mistress Valerie.'

'Blow the candles out and we can discuss the slave upstairs over a cup of tea. Perhaps by then the erection will have gone and we can set him free.'

Amber walked around The Dungeon Room, extinguishing the candles one by one as I stood over the slave. As darkness closed in around us, I spat firmly on the slave's back.

'Loser,' I said.

I took Amber's hand and we walked across the room, past The Wheel, which still held the little black ball in its Dungeon Room segment, and up the stairs.

Eight

Gemma tapped lightly on my half-opened door. I knew it was her; I could see her waving red hair through the crack. I beckoned her in.

'Come in, Gemma. What can I do for you?'

It was the following day, early in the afternoon and I was going over some 'paperwork' at my desk – a lingerie catalogue, if truth be known. How lucky that I can shop for seductive underwear and look at pictures of beautiful young women in the name of my job.

'Good afternoon, Ms McKnight. I came to let you know that I have a client waiting for me.'

The news intrigued me. I stood up.

'Who is it?'

'His name is Campbell.'

'Is he rich?'

'He says he's a businessman; that's all I've got out of him so far.'

'Let me see him.'

Gemma and I walked around to one of the function rooms on the gallery level, where the gaming floor can be watched from above. Leaning on the rail, Gemma pointed to her table. I followed the direction of her outstretched arm to a table where Amber was covering in Gemma's absence, keeping the poker hands coming for the gamblers still present.

A short dark fellow sat impatiently playing a hand; he glanced anxiously over his shoulder towards the door where Gemma had disappeared moments earlier. He clearly could not wait for her return.

He wore no suit, just an open-necked black shirt and dark-brown trousers. His hair was short and receding at the front, but otherwise he showed all the marks of good living and healthy lifestyle.

'Did he say where he heard about the service?'

'Not yet, Ms McKnight. I'll be sure and put it in my report. I'd best go down.'

'Yes, good luck, and have fun.'

As Head Croupier Gemma has her own key to The Cellar and I did not need to fetch mine for her, so I stayed there looking at the gamblers and watched as she crossed the floor to escort Campbell downstairs. He seemed very eager indeed, throwing in a hand he had already paid ante for, rather than play it to its conclusion.

After they had disappeared below I continued to 'people-watch', a pastime I enjoy hugely, especially when I have trained a fair proportion of those people in the arts of tease and seduction; I like to observe the girls and see the tricks and deportments I have imparted to them being put into action.

I smiled to myself as the once shy Kirsty leant across the roulette table with her brilliantly white cleavage on full show, deliberately trying to catch the eye of one oriental gentleman. Amber was sitting on the raised stool behind her table – the poker table she had just taken over from Gemma – crossing and uncrossing her legs and causing her skirt to rise a little higher each time, distracting her punters more and more as each hand was played. I saw one gent catch a glimpse of this behaviour and alter his course from the punto banco table to take a seat with her.

He was a large fellow, broad across his shoulders and chest, and young, with a mane of dark hair down to his shoulders. As I examined him and his square-set jaw I began to wonder if this was the first time I had laid eyes upon him. He was a handsome young Alpha specimen indeed. Could he possibly be my naked athlete from a few nights ago?

I was not close enough to see his features clearly on that memorable night, so simply staring at him from this distance was not going to solve the mystery – I would have to go down, chat him up, amaze him with my beauty and raw sexual magnetism, of course, and get the answer from the horse's mouth.

'Always nice to see a new customer.' I said, smiling at our visitor with my red-lipped mouth.

The broad, rugged fellow looked up from his cards. From the way his pupils dilated on seeing me, it seemed that my appearance inspired his lust, but if he recognised me he was able to hide it.

'Please keep your cards over the table, sir,' said Amber from the dealer's chair. In his distraction, the gentleman had forgotten this important rule, but he corrected his error immediately, returning his elbows to the table.

'What makes you think that I'm a new customer?' he asked.

'Because I would certainly have remembered if you had been here before,' I told him, casually laying my hand on the curved bar on the back of his stool.

'I'm Valerie McKnight – the proprietor.' I added, demurely offering my free hand.

He took it. His handshake was firm but friendly, and I wondered if his embrace would mimic those qualities. I withdrew my hand, allowing it to stroke the back of his own.

'I'm Marty, by the way. Do you give this sort of VIP greeting to every new customer?' he asked.

Marty smiled a lot, I noted, revealing a hint of teeth and two dimples. He was not at all the assured, vain, smooth operator I had imagined and I liked the edge of vulnerability that his winning but somewhat nervous smile gave him.

'Only the handsome, hunky ones.' I said.

He seemed unable to suppress another self-conscious smile.

'Well, then, I'm very flattered.'

Amber finished playing the hand, and my new friend turned to watch proceedings, throwing in his hand when Amber's two Jacks had apparently out-stripped him.

'I don't seem to be very lucky today.'

'It's early in the day. You've barely started. Things will pick up,' I consoled him. 'Tell me, how did you get such a wonderful figure?'

I was keen to get the conversation on to the subject of him. After all, this was supposed to be a fact-finding mission first and a flirt-offensive second.

'Oh, that,' he said, regarding his arms as though he had never seen them before. 'I help to run the gym across the street – it's only natural I'd put on a bit of bulk, spending all day there.'

'And all night?'

'Sorry?'

'Nothing.'

By now it was becoming clearer to me that this was indeed the exhibitionist body-builder with a penchant for pumping iron and cock at the same time. I knew he would not be certain, but he would be forming at least some suspicion that I was the mysterious female figure who had watched his antics from the window that night.

113

'Are you the manager?' I asked quickly. I wanted to keep him talking, lest his mind ruminate too much on the possible consequences of recognition, and scare him away: for all he knew, I might be some frightful prude trying to entrap him into a confession and have him carted away by the local force for indecency.

'Not really, but I own a share of it.'

I now had his complete attention – he had not bothered to lay a chip down for the next hand, being content to concentrate on me. Not even the sight of Amber's tanned flesh above her stocking tops could distract him.

'I was thinking of joining your gym myself. I'm always telling my croupiers that a woman should do her best to maintain her figure. Don't you agree?'

'I think you're doing a pretty good job of that already – although you'd be very welcome.'

'I'm not much of an expert, I'm afraid. All I know about weight-training and fitness is what I see across the street from our window on the second floor,' I said, flashing my eyes to show that the true significance of the comment was behind the words. Marty drew back his head – not far, just an inch: enough to tell me that any doubt or ambiguity had been dispelled. We proceeded with the conversation, both now knowing we had 'met' before but neither acknowledging it explicitly. Marty coughed slightly to compose himself.

'It's no problem. If you're a novice we do a half-hour induction course to show you how to use the equipment.'

'I like the sound of that, provided it's you that does my induction.'

Marty looked me up and down.

'I'd love to.'

114

I placed a hand on his leg, just above the knee.

'Is the induction course done naked as well?' I asked impishly, squeezing his leg to show I remembered his show from before.

Marty looked me straight in the eye, but took an age to respond. He was like a rabbit frozen in the headlights of my directness.

'Depends on how busy our floor is,' he answered finally.

'Is it likely we will find a private corner when I come over?' I asked, running my fingers up his leg like a naughty little spider. I was simpering now, to accentuate my availability, and to turn him on even more.

'We're open twenty-four-seven. Just after midnight is one of our quietest times – how does that sound?' I suspected Marty's genitals were now talking for him; I noticed his breathing was becoming deeper and his lips were fuller, more pouting, but I was flattered by his keenness and accepted.

'Then I'll meet you at midnight,' I whispered.

I keep a bright-pink sports bag in my office cupboard, containing a supply of sportswear. As I said to Marty at the poker table, I am a firm believer that a woman should do what she can to maintain her body. It is, after all, her duty – not to please men, but in the interests of womankind, for it is our mesmerising desirability that drives to the heart of men's flaws and allows us to control them as we do.

Personally, I can't stand pretentious membership-only fitness clubs; I tend to frequent the municipal facilities and leisure centres, which have an altogether more down-to-earth ambience: the air smells of fresh sweat, for one thing, not cologne. Still, I was willing to make exceptions for the right reasons and Marty seemed a solid enough reason to me.

He was waiting outside as I strode through The Paddle-Boat's revolving doors. He was dressed in a pair of tight black cycling shorts, trainers and a hugging white T-shirt. I heard the 23:59 trundling out of Central Station and disappearing over the river and was impressed with his punctuality. I had changed already into my training shoes, loose white sport socks, high-waisted black dancing briefs and a bright pink lycra crop-top with a Y-shaped back. I wonder if even a tenth of my flesh was covered, and had it not been a balmy summer evening I daresay I would have perished from exposure in the few seconds it took to cross the street.

The eyes of the security guard at California Fitness barely flickered as Marty and I strode by, I presumed the 'ID Cards Must Be Shown' sign at the desk did not apply to Marty and the other owners, whoever they might be.

I followed Marty to the lift, choosing not to comment on the apparent contradiction between maintaining one's fitness and using the lift to go up two floors. Instead, I grabbed him and treated him to a warm, wet kiss, before pulling away in time to compose myself before the doors opened.

We entered the gym on the second level and, as promised, it was almost deserted. In fact our only company was a slim, athletic-looking auburn-haired woman on an exercise bike. She was very sweaty from working out in the summer night, which I liked. Unlike most women, who tie their hair back while training, she had hers down and her workout was giving it quite a mussed-up appearance, as if she had just been rogered vigorously by three body-builders, or so I imagined.

Marty went over to an adjustable chin-up bar, and moved it down to a setting just below hip level.

'We always begin with stretches, Valerie.'

'Ms McKnight,' I insisted.

It must have puzzled him that I would deny him the use of my first name when I had just had my tongue in his mouth, but I did not care what he thought, as long as he obeyed.

'Ms McKnight,' he said, and shrugged.

'What should I start with?'

'Legs first. Put one foot on the bar in front of you and lean forwards, with your back as straight as possible, and touch your toe.'

I performed the exercise with my left leg and watched in the mirror as Marty gazed at my arse: specifically, the movement of my left buttock as it stretched to allow the motion.

'You are very supple.'

'It can be useful,' I replied, changing legs.

'Good,' he said hoarsely. 'Now try standing with your legs about a metre apart and reach down to the floor with both hands – keeping your legs as straight as possible.'

I performed the exercise right in front of him, reaching down to the floor to look up at him through my firm legs. The contours of my hamstrings must have been a glory for him to behold, although I suspected his attention might be drawn towards my arse cheeks, now forming that beautiful love-heart shape unique to the lithe woman.

I imagine Marty was also getting his first glimpse of a nice little surprise I had prepared for him before leaving the casino: my dark-pink labia were pulled outwards and peeping out on either side of the black gusset of my briefs.

'Oh, man . . .'

'What's next?' I said, looking up at him from between my legs and swaying my buttocks and thighs from side to side.

He stared at me, hypnotised, before returning to lucidity. 'I think we'd better try you with some free weights now,' he said expressionlessly, like a man in a trance.

He reached for a rather light-looking bar with two small, round, plastic weights at either end. I glanced across the room at the auburn-haired woman. She seemed totally uninterested in us. This pleased me, because it meant we had some licence to fool around a bit.

I lay down on the bench on my back and Marty stepped over me, still holding the bar, and stood astride me. I heaved my bust with a lustful gasp as he leered down at me.

'Hold your arms up,' he instructed.

In response, I rubbed my hands over my breasts to make my nipples stand out under the bright-pink crop-top.

'Hold your arms up,' he repeated. 'This is an exercise to develop your chest.'

I continued to run my palms and fingers over my nipples.

'So is this.'

'C'mon, hold your arms up.'

I gave in and reached up so that my hunk could lay the silver-grey bar in my hands.

'Breathe in as you lower the bar, and out as you make the effort to raise it.'

I did two repetitions as Marty lowered himself on to my mound, a distinct bulge appearing in his tight shorts.

I continued to work my pectorals, grinding my crotch up against his buttocks in time with each effort.

'That was good,' he said after ten lifts. It was not clear if he was referring to my exercise technique or my crotchwork.

'Let's try a back exercise,' he suggested, getting up and resting the barbell on two hooks. I stood up as Marty reached for two small dumb-bells and crouched to place them on the floor in front of me. As he rose, he did not neglect to run the back of his fingers up the inside of my thigh, as I would have expected any accomplished seducer to do, and a wave of pleasure rippled through my loins.

'Good. Now bend forwards with your legs straight and pick up the dumb-bells. Keep your back straight and try to look straight ahead.'

I followed his instructions and immediately felt my hamstrings stretch slightly from the added weight of the dumb-bells. Marty walked around me, gazing lustily at the contours of my arse and hips. He had positioned me so that a Multi-Gym apparatus was between us and the other woman, who pumped away on her exercise bike. The apparatus conveniently obscured my hind quarters from her view.

'Now lift the weights up to your chest, working the muscles in your back, slowly at first.'

I performed one repetition of the exercise as I felt Marty edge closer and push his thick quadriceps against the gusset of my briefs.

'Don't stop,' he said quietly.

Slowly I repeated the exercise several times, becoming aware of Marty's hand creeping down to rub the soft flesh of my sex through the black elastane of my skimpy sports garment. I began to seep cream on to the gusset and it must have soaked through to his fingers. By the tenth exercise I was gasping with pleasure. The auburn-haired woman would naturally assume that my moans were induced by the workout, or so I hoped.

'Take a few seconds' rest and then another set of ten,' said Marty, rubbing slowly but firmly. I wished he would get the nerve to expose my pussy and do some proper work with his insolent fingers.

Once I had recommenced my exercises, he peeled away my gusset and, moving it to the side, pushed the tip of his middle finger downwards, over the opening of my vagina, and around, until it met the reddening bulb of my clitoris.

I used the effort of my exercises as cover for my groans of pleasure, but I was becoming so turned on that I secretly craved the excitement of being seen.

'OK, let's try something else,' he said at last.

I put the weights down and stood upright, not bothering to fix my briefs. As I turned I saw Marty licking his fingers and, seized with lust, I kissed him again, pushing my tongue against his for three exciting seconds. I tasted again the kiss I had tasted in the lift, only this time with a twist of pussy juice to bring out the flavour. I don't know if the woman on the bike saw us kiss, only that Marty glanced furtively in her direction as I pulled away.

'Now, I think we should have a go at some squats,' Marty suggested, as he lifted the barbell from the bench hooks. 'Hold it like this and lift it on to your shoulders like this.'

I watched him, my pussy bare to his gaze, as he squatted down on his haunches with the bar across his shoulders. He then drove his body to its full height again, pushing the weight upwards with ease. I rubbed my clitoris in appreciation of the show.

The weight was not heavy – Marty had been kind to me for my first training session – and it was no struggle for me to take the bar from him and rest it behind my neck. I had not readjusted my gusset and he was about to get the show of his life; this excited me, and I felt a thrill in my torso akin to first-night nerves as I prepared to squat.

The sweaty auburn-haired woman had moved to a treadmill and over Marty's broad shoulder I could see her bobbing up and down. I thrilled at the thought of her seeing me show my pussy to this masculine specimen as I performed the exercise. Sometimes there can be no greater excitement than behaving like your free sexual self in the sight of a third party.

I looked him squarely in the eye and, locking him in a stare charged with electricity, squatted down, opening my legs as wide as I could without sacrificing my balance, and allowed my folds to display themselves to his greedy eyes. Marty licked his lips as I returned to the upright position.

I went down again, holding the position to let him feast his eyes and stare right into me. I felt he was gazing into my very soul. I have something of a one-track soul and I guess, by offering him this vista, I was giving him pretty much the best view of my soul that any mortal was likely to get.

Marty's mouth fell open in awe at the show he was getting and I began to feel an animalistic urge welling inside me as I went down again. My vagina yearned for cock. I snarled this time, with all the primal energy inside me, like a tigress on heat.

Marty's cock was now fully erect, pushing desperately at the fabric of his shorts, and when I saw it twitch involuntarily I was not for waiting any longer. I put the barbell down on the floor.

'Is there an exercise I can do where you could fuck me at the same time?' I snapped.

Marty manoeuvred me behind the Multi-Gym apparatus once more, to obscure us from view, and turned me around so I was facing away from him.

'Legs apart,' he said, and I complied.

'Touch the floor in front of you as though stretching your hamstrings.'

121

I began the exercise he had suggested, slowly lowering myself to touch my toes. The woman on the treadmill would now be able to see my shoulders and head bobbing up and down around the side of the machine and I tried my best to look as casual as possible – yes, I was just innocently doing a warm-down after a light workout, that's all, and if any onlooker had the impression that the hunky long-haired brute behind me was about to fuck me, that was just an example of an imagination running away with itself.

I casually continued my stretches as my briefs were pulled over my buttocks down to my knees. Then the soft caress of Marty's fingers gently parted my petals.

I heard the sound of his cycling shorts being pulled down and then, at last, I felt the head of his penis, that same penis I had watched being wanked from across the street a few nights before, press against me. My juice lubricated him and at his second thrust he slipped inside me. I stifled a gasp as he pulled away again. On his third thrust he pressed even further into me, moaning softly, trying his best to avoid attracting the attention of our athletic female friend.

On the fourth stroke he slid all the way up me, and the real fucking could begin: long, savouring, firm strokes in to the hilt and almost out again. I groaned, and did my best to sound like someone testing her body rather than a woman enjoying a nice hard shaft. I am sure my form became ragged as Marty's deliberate, insistent thrusts became more and more pleasurable for me, but I did the hamstring exercises as best I could. After all, it was my activity that was giving us the cover for the real workout.

Perhaps it was no accident that, as my succulent pussy enjoyed more and more of Marty's cock, my stretching exercises became less and less convincing for, once again, I began to hope, secretly and inwardly, that the woman would spy us surrendering to our urges.

In the East, they say that an energy centre, a chakra, is located just above the navel, only an inch or two away from the very spot that Marty's cock-head was pressing against at the zenith of each thrust. I like to call it my Fetish Chakra, and it throbs with excitement whenever a kinky or deviant thought enters my head. It pulsed now as I imagined the woman standing over us, watching me shamelessly welcoming Marty's cock into me time after time.

I had to fight myself not to look in her direction – if I did she might become suspicious; it might attract her attention and spoil our party. I continued to savour Marty's efforts and he began to break his silence, grunting quietly as his cock explored the tender caress of my soft pussy.

I could not help myself, and throwing caution to the wind I turned to look in the direction of the treadmill, hoping that even an unreturned glance would satisfy my yearning to be seen by her. I got more than I bargained for.

She was standing not five metres away, watching us and, judging by the way her wrist had disappeared into her sweat-trimmed shorts, enjoying herself. She looked half at, half through, me and, as I realised that the kink I was craving was now fulfilled, my Fetish Chakra began to hum and send spasms through my abdomen and loins. The ruse of my stretching exercises was now rather redundant and I stopped, concentrating instead on staring back at her, return-ing her gaze with interest. I did not look away, even when my mouth opened and a scream of pleasure escaped me. My anus twitched, spasms went though my vagina and I experienced a solid and juddering orgasm, as if nirvana had taken the form of a juggernaut and driven right through me. Never once, through the whole sensation, did I look away from our onanistic spectator.

My crescendo had its effect on Marty, exciting him beyond control, and he exchanged his deliberate technique for a wilder bucking motion, ramming me with shorter, quicker strokes. The voyeuse enjoyed this immensely and frigged herself more keenly as she watched him.

I liked it too and placed my hands on the floor to offer him more support for his efforts and more resistance. His angle changed slightly, and he pushed his cock upwards with a sudden spearing motion – usually a sign that a man is about to spend.

'Yes!' I called. 'Let me feel it!'

He redoubled his efforts, almost lifting me off the floor as I both heard and felt him come.

I closed my eyes, concentrating on the strokes of his sensitive cock as he came down from his high. I opened them again as I heard the sound of a door closing. Our audience had left the auditorium, apparently satisfied with the show.

'Who was that?' I asked Marty over my shoulder as he withdrew.

'Suzanne,' he replied. 'She's been a member here for a long time. We started training late at around the same time; she likes the rawness of a masculine man and we kind of reached an understanding after I caught her sniffing a pair of my discarded shorts: I let her watch me working out and I give her my clothes to wash afterwards. It turns her on.'

He sat down on the bench. I wondered if he was indeed as shy as I had first assumed on meeting him. I sat across his lap.

'Have you ever fucked in front of her before?' I asked.

'Oh, only a couple of times,' he replied modestly.

I raised an eyebrow.

Nine

It does not do to arrive late for work, even if you are the boss and even if you've been up late having glorious sex in a public place, so I took a briefcase in on the following morning. The joy of the briefcase wheeze is that it allows you to stride in at around 10.30 a.m. and look as if you had other business to attend to before you got to work. Some might consider that as the lady of the manor I should not be concerned about what others think I have been doing with my morning, but I know the importance of setting an example to my charges.

The place is quiet at that time and only redheaded Gemma and the once shy Kirsty were running tables. I gave them a bright, friendly wave as I passed and made my way up to my office.

I had completely forgotten about Gemma's session with Campbell Pinkerton until that moment. It was only the sight of her report on my desk that reminded me, and the thought of starting the day with a fix of first-hand erotica really helped to pick me up. I prepared a coffee and sat down to read.

Croupier: Gemma Jarvie
Date: Monday 21st June
Client: Campbell Pinkerton

Miss McKnight, after leaving you on the gaming floor I took Mr Pinkerton directly downstairs. He seemed very compliant, following me like a dutiful little hound without needing so much as a word from me. As we descended the stairs in the dusklike gloom, I turned to ask him how he heard about our service.

'I heard someone talking about it in a sauna waiting room,' he answered.

'When was this?'

'A couple of months ago. It's taken me this long to pluck up the courage to come down.'

'It will take more courage than that to submit to the whim of The Wheel,' I told him.

'Yes, I know.'

I glared at him.

'Yes, I know, Mistress,' he said, correcting himself, and I noticed that shudder of fear and pleasure that ripples through every slave on their transition to submission.

'You paid females to provide relief for your "problem" at this sauna?' I asked, glancing at his crotch as I spoke, to indicate my meaning.

'Yes, Mistress,' he confirmed.

I did not reply, but continued down the stairs. The high-heeled courts that are part of my uniform echoed around The Cellar's space and I imagine in the gloom it all felt rather spooky for Campbell.

I turned on the lights and strode towards The Wheel. I did not have to check to see if the slave was behind me, as I knew he would naturally follow in my wake.

'Kneel,' I said. I spun the roulette wheel casually at this point for effect.

He was already kneeling when I turned around.

'Do you submit to the whim of The Wheel?' I asked.

I forgave him the single surreptitious glance upwards to look upon The Wheel that he had heard talk of those weeks ago.

'I do, Mistress.'

I picked up the ball and sent it running around the already spinning wheel. It rattled and finally came to rest.

'The Throne Room,' I declared. I was rather pleased at The Wheel's choice, Ms McKnight. 'Follow me on your hands and knees,' I commanded, and led the way.

I made our new slave remove his clothes at the entrance to The Throne Room, fold them and leave them in a pile by one of the support pillars. Then I bade him face outwards, away from the play area, towards the centre of the room, while I chose my attire.

I had an image in my mind, Ms McKnight, of how I wanted to be worshipped: as a gloriously adorned Queen in jewelled and feathered regalia and striking, extravagant make-up. The make-up is where I started. I commanded the slave to put his head to the floor so that the transformation process could not be viewed at any stage.

Note for future Mistresses of this slave: he is very patient and barely moved a muscle as he waited on my pleasure.

I walked across to The Boudoir and spent five minutes or so applying a lavish gold and bronze eye-shadow and an autumn-red lipstick. I returned to The Throne Room and from the clothes that were there I chose a golden head-dress with a mounted peacock feather on top and a teardrop of sparkling gold that dangled in the centre of my forehead, a merlot-coloured bikini-style outfit, with gold links tying each separate triangle of fabric, a sleeveless gown of a similar hue and finally the glistening heeled sandals with the criss-cross strapping all the way to below the knee. My beautiful white legs, my rounded cleavage, as well as glimpses of other tender areas, were all on view. Ms McKnight, your taste in, and feel for, clothing is beyond the ken of most; I truly felt like a goddess as I floated to the Throne and sat upon the red cushion, allowing my upper limbs to drift to rest on the arms of the royal chair. I put one of my feet on the foot-block.

'Slave,' I called.

'Yes, Mistress.'

'You may now address me as Majesty,' I told him. I really must have been feeing full of myself to come up with that one, but I deserved it – I am here to be worshipped by the paying slaves, after all.

'Yes, Majesty.'

'You may now turn to face me, on your knees. You will be allowed a brief period to admire your Queen and fully appreciate her beauty and consider your relative position in nature. Do it now.'

The slave turned and knelt at the entrance to The Throne Room, lifting his eyes to view me. I could see the sweet yearning sorrow in him as he longed for the unattainable.

'Crawl to me,' I said when his penis had shown its first signs of independence. 'Eyes to the floor,' I commanded as he arrived. He could no longer look upon me, although I made sure a blurry image of my outstretched foot still remained in the periphery of his vision: I remember you telling me, all those months ago when you trained me, that this was important.

'It is fortunate for you, slave, that I appreciate the worship of a servile tongue and mouth, or you would never enjoy the privilege of physical contact with your Queen.'

'Yes, Majesty.'

'Your first duty as my subject is to keep my feet and shoes clean of the dust and perspiration they can pick up during my courtly duties. Use the tip of your tongue: be delicate and do not leave behind any of your slavering.'

'Yes, Majesty.'

'As you serve, I wish to hear how breathtaking I am – but I warn you, if you simply repeat a boring phrase like "Oh, Majesty, you're so beautiful" over and over I will take a dim view of it. Be imaginative.'

'Yes, Majesty.'

I like to give slaves something challenging to keep their minds on the move while they serve me, Ms McKnight.

The slave began by cleaning my shoes; he ran his tongue around the edge of the shoe and then, like a child with a lollipop, he licked the little dust that had collected on the soles since I had donned them, swallowing without hesitation.

It has always fascinated me that dust or grit can seem so delicious to a man purely because it has found its way on to the sole of the shoe of an attractive woman. After all, he would not lick the same grime from the floor before I had trodden on it and picked it up.

'It is a privilege, Majesty, to be granted the duty of licking your shoes clean,' he said, before diverting his attention to the gold-coloured finish of the straps.

The slave made a very thorough job of cleaning, nay polishing, the shoe. The tip of his tongue buffed the leather in a side-to-side motion, working over the foot area and criss-crossing my shins and calves along the straps. He was very imaginative, saying things like: 'My tongue exists purely to perform these tasks for your most gracious Majesty,' and 'Majesty is too kind, permitting me such liberties as to taste her shoe leather.' I think he may have done something like this before.

Soon he was nearly finished and I imagine his mouth was watering at the thought of receiving the dessert to this main course: contact with my beautiful flesh.

'You may begin by sampling the morsels under each to-nail,' I instructed him.

Campbell extended the tip of his tongue and allowed it to sort of patrol back and forth under the overhanging part of my painted big to-nail. His eyelids drooped as he tasted the confiture of my body's secretions, his tongue digging as deeply as it would go. I allowed him to feast in this way on all ten of my toes – the sensation of the warm, wet tongue on the tips of my toes was not an unpleasant one and I made sure I enjoyed the experience to the full.

'Good. Now clean the sides and tops of my feet.'

'Yes, Majesty.' He delicately cradled my shoe with his nervous hands, ran his tongue along the smooth skin on the top of my foot and gradually worked his way around to my sensitive instep.

I am particularly proud of the flawless sheen on this part of my feet, Ms McKnight – I am sure you can imagine how the flecks of pheromone-rich sweat sparkled like the tiny, twinkling silver deposits on a quartz crystal. I was not surprised to hear my subject moaning with pleasure as he savoured my unique flavour on his tongue.

The cocktail of sweat and pheromones between my toes had been maturing all morning inside the pressure-cooker of my regulation black court shoes.

I tried my best to maintain my aloof, regal posture, but the sensations on my feet were making it very difficult, especially as my pussy and clit were beginning to tingle.

I was pleased to note that the chemistry between foot and tongue was once again working its strange magic; my subject already looked mesmerised by the tastes and odours, and I wondered what level of trance he might enter during what was to come.

'You are being too quiet. Tell me how much you are enjoying the taste.'

'Majesty, my tongue tingles with pleasure – your feet are like nectar from a flower,' he said. Rather original, I thought.

'Yes, I suppose they are,' I responded. 'You may now desist.'

My worshipping subject put his head back to the floor and I could hear him rolling his tongue around in his mouth, so desperate was he to taste more.

'You may now sample between the royal toes with the tip of your tongue, and this time do not forget to tell your Queen how much you are enjoying the experience.'

'Yes, Majesty.'

Campbell then lifted his head from the floor and reached out with his tongue to slide it between the first two toes of my left foot. His cock rose towards full stiffness and I noted how a twitch coincided with the contact between his tongue and my sweet oils.

'Mmm,' he moaned, 'Majesty's beautiful feet are more intoxicating and captivating than any wine.'

Very poetic, I'm sure!

He moved on to the next toe, sliding his soft, hungry tongue between it and its neighbour.

He exhaled deeply, a sign, I think, of a dizzying contentment, and I felt the warm breath over my foot. My clit tingled again and I'm afraid in my weakness I could not help but rub it with my middle finger.

'Mmmm. The merest taste of Majesty brings electricity to my tongue and my mouth waters with desire. My neck tingles with thirst for you, Majesty.'

Campbell is quite lyrical when given a free rein, don't you think, Ms McKnight?

Once he had sucked and licked all the juices he was going to get from my toes I bade him stop and, looking upwards and away from his kneeling body, told him to make his final tribute to my toes. 'Do not look up from your sacred task,' I insisted.

I peered down at him as he pumped away on his cock, aiming it at my alabaster feet and my dark-red to-nails. I could not resist joining him, Ms McKnight: as discreetly as I could, I allowed my hand to creep down to the Royal Clitty and softly rub it in tiny circles. What with my subject pumping on his hard, bulging, veined cock and the anticipation of receiving his tribute, I was getting quite excited and struggled to keep my cold, regal composure.

Soon Campbell began to grit his teeth and sprinkles of his come flecked my feet as a prelude to the warm and sensuous feeling of his main load shooting on to, and seeping between, my toes. I gasped quite loudly as the experience set me off on a little orgasm, but I suspect my supplicating masturbator would have been too wrapped up in his own sensations to notice this little diversion from character that I had allowed myself.

I made him lick it up from my feet – this seemed like the right thing to do. I'm sure he would not have licked it up under any other circumstances, but the fact that it had been in contact with the Royal Feet probably made it seem like ambrosia to him. He certainly seemed to lap it up quite eagerly.

Gemma

* * *

133

Gemma's report was most enjoyable and I daresay, had I been as much of a slut as she is, I would have 'softly rubbed my Royal Clitty in tiny circles' too. I seem to spend my whole working day taking mental notes to do this, do that, hump this cock, lick that pussy, keep an eye on him, follow her, and so on, and I found myself doing the same thing again – Gemma's spelling was a little off-beam in her report and I felt a spanking might be in order, especially as she had clearly thrown in the little howlers on purpose – or are we to believe that she genuinely misspelt a word as simple as 'toenail'? As usual my Head Croupier was unable to stop herself 'fishing for discipline' with a minor, but deliberate, misdemeanour.

The morning was wearing on and it was only a matter of time before some pressing business began pulling on my sleeve, looking for attention. There was a knock at the door. Out of habit I looked down to check that I was fully dressed and decent before calling for my visitor to enter.

It was Gemma, so smart and sexy in her uniform. 'Mrs Finlay is here to see you again,' she declared.

My head jerked backwards in surprise. 'Really? How unexpected. Did she give any hint what it might be about?'

'No, Ms McKnight, she did not.'

I shrugged. 'Send her up.'

A few minutes later the short figure of Mrs Finlay was led into my room. I had taken my usual pose on the corner of my desk, just to rub in yet again how attractive I and my legs are, in case she had forgotten.

'Come in, Mrs Finlay. Please take a seat,' I said in the traditional fashion.

She did so, sitting rather timidly with her handbag on her knees – not at all the arrogant posturing she had employed on her first visit.

'What can I do for you this morning? I did not expect to hear from you again for another couple of weeks, if at all,' I said.

Mrs Finlay took a steadying breath before speaking.

'I have come to discuss the matter of my husband's reasons for attending your establishment, and to discuss also what you think I should do about it.'

'I'm not sure I follow you,' I said, employing again the tactics from our first conversation: feigning ignorance to draw her thoughts out of her.

'Ms McKnight, my husband has advised me, after much discussion and many unpleasant evenings at the dinner table, that the auxiliary service you have been providing for him is prostitution.'

Mrs Finlay's face was plum-red, partly through embarrassment, partly, I sensed, through outrage.

'I appreciate that what we may do here is not to everyone's taste, but I can assure you it is not prostitution, Mrs Finlay.'

'What do you call it then?'

'Mrs Finlay, think of all the businesses involved in delivering our dreams: property agents and banks to bring us that dream home, travel agents and tour operators for that dream holiday, private schools so our children can get the qualifications for that dream career. I am only providing the same thing: dreams and fantasies to men and women who need them. It just so happens that those dreams happen to contain a sexual element. Does that make me a prostitute? I think not.'

'It sounds like prostitution to me,' Mrs Finlay snapped.

'What has your husband told you about what he asked us to do for him here?'

'Jeffrey has not gone into the specifics of the activities he paid you for.' Mrs Finlay readjusted her

135

bottom on the chair and looked towards the window, unwilling to look me in the eye.

'Perhaps it would have been helpful if he had.'

'In what way?'

'Do you love your husband?'

'For Heaven's sake, is this relevant? Of course I do.'

'Very much indeed it is relevant. You love him, of course, and I presume you felt the same way when you were married, and wanted only to make him happy.'

'Must we –'

'What if I told you we knew a way, through our dealings with Mr Finlay, whereby you could make your husband, and quite probably yourself, happier than he, or you, have ever been?'

'What do you mean?' Mrs Finlay was still terse, but I sensed her interest had been piqued.

'Well, it won't be easy for you to see or hear – but if you truly believe that we marry to do whatever we can to bring each other happiness, then I hope you will let me show you a path that may take you and Jeffrey to that destination. Come with me.'

Mrs Finlay still seemed reluctant as I led her down to The Cellar. I suppose we cannot blame her for that; it had taken a lot of courage to even return to The Paddle-Boat, against the self-indoctrination of a lifetime of prudery, but in spite of her natural disinclination I knew that deep down she really wanted me to challenge her limits in this way and reveal to her this new world. Why else would she have come to me, asking for help?

Mrs Finlay was careful of her footing on the stairs, even after I had turned on the lights, and she concentrated on stepping carefully until her modest one-and-a-half-inch heels were safely on the basement

136

floor. On firmer, flatter ground, she scanned the array of rooms around her, and a look of astonishment came over her face – she had not quite grasped until now the scale and breadth of our services.

'What is all this?' she asked.

'These are the fantasy rooms: The White Room, The Office, The Stable, The Boudoir, The Throne Room, The School Room, The Nursery and The Dungeon. Having so many allows me to cater for just about any fantasy that my customers wish to name, and, if they're not sure, then The Wheel can help.'

'The Wheel?'

I showed Mrs Finlay The Wheel and watched as she tilted her head to read each section around the circumference; she would have recognised the names of the rooms I had just listed for her.

'Some of my customers enjoy the thrill of placing their fates under the whim of The Wheel. Jeffrey, however, had a very clear idea of his fantasy before he arrived.'

Curiosity had now overpowered indignation in the fight for Mrs Finlay's psyche. 'Which room did he choose?'

'I think you already know.'

'The School Room?' she hazarded.

'Of course. You see, Mrs Finlay, you may feel that your husband has cheated on you or been unfaithful to you by coming to see me, but the truth is that his perversion grows directly out of his love for you – he fantasises about being dominated by a headmistress and I am sure, were it not for the fear of rejection and losing you, he would have come to you for it, not to me.'

Mrs Finlay's hand went to her mouth as she considered what she had learnt. Her eyes were moist as I softly grasped her arm and led her to The School Room. She did not resist. I turned on the lights.

'Mrs Finlay, this is a lot to take in, I know, but I hope when you leave you will think about it, discuss it with Mr Finlay, and perhaps come back here and allow us to teach you how the two of you may bring each other's fantasies to life.'

Elizabeth Finlay said nothing. She simply stared into the mock classroom, at the desk, the blackboard and the belts and canes. I dared not shock her further with the specifics of Mr Finlay's foibles; she had seen quite enough for this visit.

'Can I offer you a cup of tea, Mrs Finlay?' I asked.

She nodded, and took her hand from her mouth, where it had been for some time. She nodded again.

'Please. And I wonder if I could trouble you . . . for a measure of your best malt?'

It was well into lunchtime when I escorted Mrs Finlay to the door to send her on her way. My parting comment to her made it clear that they were both welcome back at any time and if need be I would arrange for Chloe to see them both in The Cellar. She walked to her car, still dazed but, I felt and hoped, a new person.

As I strutted and wiggled back across the gaming floor towards my office, my sweet, oft-nibbled ears recognised a manly voice amidst a melody of female laughter, and I stopped to observe. It was Marty, the hunk from the gymnasium, my most recent shag. Strange that he had not made himself known, either on his arrival or as I had first crossed the floor escorting Mrs Finlay from the building. Even now he seemed oblivious to my presence, and I am not used to heads that don't turn in my direction. He was playing roulette, dressed in a suit, without a tie, and with his usually wild hair tucked into a pony-tail.

Blonde Amber with her perpetual tan was running the table, but the presence of two more of my girls intrigued me: dusky Abrille and shy English rose Kirsty. As far as I was aware, both were off-duty, so I had no problem with them being away from their own tables. Call it jealousy if you will, but I was most uncomfortable with the way all three of them were flirting with him, flicking their hair and giggling like schoolgirls – not to mention the way he was casually laying his hands on them as he spoke. My croupiers are free to socialise with anyone they like, and their sex-lives are of course their own, but I feel a certain responsibility for them and would hate it if some satyromaniac saw my establishment as a kind of pussy-farm where he could work his way through the livestock.

With a purposeful, and audible, stride I approached and laid a graceful hand on Marty's shoulder.

'I say, Marty, you do look smart,' I said in his ear.

Apparently unsurprised by my sudden appearance, Marty slowly turned to face me. There was a friendly grin on his face, which I returned with interest, and a look passed between us that recalled at least a modicum of the passion we had experienced together at our last meeting.

'Valerie. Nice to see you.'

'Nice to see you too. Enjoying the game I trust?' I smiled back.

'Aye, and the company,' he replied, flashing a look at Kirsty that betrayed his intentions for her.

I wanted to lay down a marker for Marty to let him know I was watching him. I decided that keeping things humorous would serve best.

'Well, I'd hate for my girls to get mixed up with the likes of you,' I said, winking at them. 'So let's hope your fun ends there.'

They giggled and Marty joined in with a smile.

'And so it shall,' he said.

Ten

On reflection I decided that Marty's fraternisation with a few of the girls was little more than a distraction – I still planned to get under his skin, whether he was involved with my croupiers or not, and I doubted that even their young bodies could provide enough of a decoy to keep him away from my unrivalled allure and expertise when I made my move. I saw Marty a couple of times in the casino over the next few days and always let him know, with a wink or a raised eyebrow, that I had my eye on him. Naturally, thoughts of him came into my head if I was working late in the office, and one night I found the temptation too much to resist.

We had recently closed our doors and the wee small hours were upon us, a time when The Paddle-Boat is all but empty, save for myself and whichever of the security hunks is on duty. The day had been one of those rare sunny ones; the sun splits the sky for far too short a lease in the west of Scotland, but when it does there is a palpable increase in the hormone levels, not least in myself. Driven by this, I left my office and made my way to my favourite window.

The lights across the street were on, but I feared I was too late to enjoy Marty's show: he was lying back on his weights bench, slowly rubbing his stiff cock and wiping his tummy, hands and cock with a tissue, clearly enjoying an orgasmic afterglow.

I waved to attract his attention and it pleased me when, standing to put on his robe, he noticed me and waved back. I suspect he always allows himself a little glance to see if I'm watching. I only regretted I had left it so late.

I found myself at a loose end and began to wander the building like a captain touring his ship. I cannot say what I was looking for; only Michael was in the building and, sexy though the young buck is, I was not really sure it was a good old-fashioned fuck I was yearning for. (Good old-fashioned fucks are Michael's stock in trade.)

I casually went by the security room anyway, just in case seeing his solid, suited body made me feel any different. The door was closed and I could hear nothing as I pressed my ear to it. As quietly as possible I eased the door open and peered around it.

The room was empty; grainy black-and-white images from around the premises flickered in the half-gloom but there was no other sign of life. I bit the corner of my sumptuous lip in anxious contemplation; was Michael investigating a problem somewhere? I opted to explore the matter and conducted a tentative search of all the public areas of the building, first the gaming floor, bar and dining rooms, then the staff areas: the common room, the Accounts department and the safe – but to no avail. Forlornly, for I scarcely expected it to bear any fruit and checked only for thoroughness, I went to The Cellar.

I received my first surprise before I had even opened the door at the top of the stairs: I heard a noise. It was muffled by the door, and I imagine distorted by the echoes of the basement walls, but it sounded to me like a thwack followed by a squeal.

I was getting quite practised at silently opening doors and I repeated the exercise once again, creeping on to the stairs and closing the door behind me with barely a shuffle or a click.

I had never before seen The Cellar so busy. Six of my staff surrounded The Wheel, in various states of undress, some standing, some supine on the basement floor, reclining on their discarded clothes. Gemma's bountiful white body shone like a beacon. She was dressed only in her lacy white bra and panties and her dark heeled shoes, which I was proud to see she had kept on. She had a deep-red stripe across one of her thighs from a single, but cruel, lashing.

Michael's granite buttocks were Gemma's main rival for attention; he was standing naked, facing her, as a smirking Maureen was tying his arms behind his back with a yellow rope and Abrille, lips pursed and obviously enjoying her task, was tying some red rope tightly around his penis and testicles. And I mean tightly: his bright-purple-red cock throbbed like a sore thumb. Jack Moyes and Peter, stripped to their boxers and T-shirts, were relaxing on the pile of clothes and enjoying the show. I too was content to watch – for the time being.

Meanwhile, Gemma had made a journey to The Dungeon and returned with one of our thick vanilla-scented candles, which she duly lit. I was very impressed with the way she used the time while she waited for the first pool of melted wax to collect around the wick, rolling the candle in her hand to play the flame over, and melt, as much tallow as possible, all the while letting Michael see his fate developing before his eyes.

Abrille and Maureen, both still in their full working uniforms, stepped back to admire their work. It wasn't exactly Black-Belt thirteenth Dan Japanese Rope Bondage but it was still a pretty good job. Michael's arms were tied behind his back at the wrists and elbows, forcing his defined back muscles and triceps into sharp relief. His cock was splendidly presented and looked fit to burst from the pressure of the restraints. As far as I could make out from my distance, Abrille had encircled the balls and cock with the rope, tying a simple knot at the top of the penis where it joins the body, and then passed the loose ends under the penis, applying a second knot and possibly a bow there to hold it all in place. The usual effect of such a restraint is to cause, and maintain, a strong erection, but it will also make the member more sensitive, something Gemma now seemed ready to exploit.

Michael's buttocks braced in a reflex clench as the tilted candle approached him. It was a sight I daresay I could watch again and again.

'The Wheel said pain,' said Gemma as she allowed the hot wax to dribble on to the head of his penis. He gasped sharply and doubled over. Gemma let him recover – the first sear of wax is always the worst, causing shock as well as pain. Michael growled, arched his back, shook his buttocks and threw his head back in reaction to the intense sensations as Gemma cruelly coated his penis, balls and nipples with the viscous liquid and everyone watched the hot oil turn to a soft carapace, encasing his most intimate areas in a new skin. There was a light ripple of applause.

Peter stood up. The tops of his thighs just under his boxers were striped with the 'lipstick' marks left by the kiss of a cane. I wondered if his was the girly 'Eeek' I had heard from outside a few moments before.

'Who's next?' he asked.

'I think that's me,' said Maureen, stepping forwards.

'Yes, it's just the two girls left,' offered Gemma as she began to untie a recovering Michael.

Peter prepared The Wheel for a spin, flicked the black ball around the rim and set The Wheel in the opposite direction. All watched intently except for Jack, who seemed strangely satisfied lying on the floor. Perhaps he had recently spent and, like the cat who got the cream, was figuratively lazing in front of the fire and purring contently.

The ball came to a stop and soon afterwards the whirr of The Wheel faded away.

'Pleasure!' cried a number of voices at once. The gang had obviously devised a system for using The Wheel to choose between Pleasure and Pain in what appeared to be the next evolutionary stage of the dice game. I felt a pang of worry in my gut, similar to the one I had felt earlier that week; I feared that the sexual freedom I was trying to instil in the folks at The Paddle-Boat might get out of hand and result in some kind of debauched anarchy. Was this a legitimate fear, or was I allowing the natural jealousy, caused by younger folk having fun, to get the better of me? Was I afraid they might have so much pleasure that they would discard me?

There was some whispering between Gemma, Peter and Abrille, and I think imaginations were at work, and decisions being made on how best to deliver Maureen her consignment of pleasure. Eventually, agreement was reached and Gemma directed the troops into action.

Maureen was roughly stripped of her clothes by a myriad of eager hands. The pleasure on her face was unmistakable and she remained as still as she could to allow the gang to do their work. Soon she was naked; it was as if a shoal of piranha had stripped her of her vestments, exposing her opal skin to ten hungry eyes. Her dark auburn hair and milky skin went together like caramelised demerara and crème brulée, and looked just as sweet.

Dusky Abrille and Gemma put their arms around her, and she wrapped an arm around each of them. With their free arms and some giggling, the two girls then took a leg each and parted them to an obtuse angle, exposing a hint of Maureen's pussy-lips amidst her bush.

The lads had formed a queue, Peter at the front and Michael at the back, still picking wax from his penis and wrestling with the rope around his cock, which was obviously rather tight.

Peter's curly head was lowered to Maureen's exposed delights and, on his knees, he began nibbling on her strawberry pearl. Maureen's gasp was loud and full of passion. I found myself tingling in empathy.

Peter readjusted himself, parting Maureen's cunt-lips with tender thumbs and applying his tongue to her love-button, licking back and forth between her swollen petals. Maureen's gasps were now punctuated by throaty growls that spoke to me and made me tingle even more. Peter continued his excellent work until he felt the hand of Jack Moyes on his shoulder. It was like a 'Gentlemen's Excuse Me' from an old period drama, as Peter stood aside and allowed Jack to lap at Maureen's glistening sex.

Even where I was, way up on the stairs, I could hear the tacky moistness of Maureen's pussy as the cute barman pressed his electric eel of a tongue against her and flicked it over her clitoris. The pleasure must have been intense: held in a position where she was unable to move her crotch, she had no choice but to endure the riot of nerve signals emanating from her sex. Her gasps and growls gave way to ambiguous cries of ecstasy and torment.

There was a tap on Jack's shoulder. Michael had freed himself from the genital bond and cleaned most of the wax from his tender areas, and clearly felt he had recovered enough to join the throng. Still naked, he took to his knees and buried his head between Maureen's milky thighs. I knew from experience that Michael was a clitoris man, which must make him a very popular lover. I imagined how the tip of his warm, wet tongue must now be caressing, then pressing, then flicking, then massaging Maureen's love-bud. She freed one arm and clutched his head with clawed fingers, before Abrille grabbed it and returned it to its place around her neck. Peter and Jack then stepped up alongside Maureen, taking a leg each and relieving Abrille and Gemma of their burden, allowing them to join the line behind Michael. My eyes widened at this development; Maureen was barely able to take what she was receiving from the boys, and I feared she might expire from the treatment of two female tongues.

She was breathing short, shallow breaths through her gritted teeth and her face looked more stressed.

'Oh, God, yes, yes!' she cried, her words echoing around the walls of The Cellar like raucous laughter in a banquet hall.

Gemma kissed Michael on the neck and whispered something to him that I could not catch from my distance, but he got the message that his job was done. He stood up and stepped away, greedily licking his fingers as he wiped the pussy juice from his chin.

Gemma crouched down, causing her thighs and buttocks to bulge beautifully. She looked up at

Maureen with a naughty smile and I saw the thinner lass steel herself as voluptuous Gemma burrowed into her pussy. Maureen was completely pinned now by the stronger lads and all she could do to express her nervous energy was throw her head around and cry out. Her noises were verging on the orgasmic and I tingled to hear them, instinctively rubbing myself as I watched and listened.

Gemma's tongue teased and prodded her to her first plateau of pleasure and she squealed like some high-pitched jet engine as she came, squirting droplets of her juice on to Gemma's face as she spasmed inside. Gemma laughed gleefully as she was spattered and softly spanked Maureen's dripping sex a couple of times. I could hear the moist sound of each playful slap.

I would surely have been jealous of Maureen's position had it not now been for the presence of Abrille, who seemed most eager of all to get between her legs, and dived into her quim with no regard for Maureen's need to recover from her orgasm. I do not think I could have taken another oral lover had I been in Mo's position, although I would not have had any choice, held from escape and apparently bound by the rules of this strange game.

Abrille slurped and lapped at Maureen, whose now hypersensitive genitals must have burnt with pleasure from each touch of her lips and tongue. Abrille was thirsty for honey and suckled on Maureen's pussy for every drop she could get. When Abrille had finished feasting, Maureen was carried, breathing heavily, to the clothes pile, where she was left to recover.

Peter was now readying The Wheel again. 'Abrille's turn,' he announced to some interest.

My vantage point was too far away for me to be

able to see the action, and I had to wait for the onlookers' responses to glean what was going on.

'Pleasure!' they chorused again as the black ball came to rest.

Abrille was sent away to a corner while the five other revellers met in committee for a few moments. Soon, after some nodding and assenting noises, Abrille was called back and directed to strip completely; she was the only one still wearing her work clothes. I presumed that the rules of this game precluded good old vanilla shagging and that the delivery of pleasure in each case had to involve something a little more imaginative. I waited to see what they had come up with.

As Abrille knelt, Maureen and Gemma had skipped off to The Boudoir and were now returning, to my great amusement, with 'Daisy' and 'Doris'. These are the two strap-ons that I like to use on my Cissy Sluts. 'Daisy' is thin, six inches long and bright pink – useful for anal virgins; 'Doris' is thicker, eight inches long and a deep-purple colour. Gemma had had the presence of mind to pick up a tube of lubricant, too.

With the help of Michael's strong hands, Maureen donned 'Daisy' as Jack helped Gemma to strap herself into 'Doris'. Both dildos have a tail: a shorter, curved stump that can be inserted into the vagina of the wearer so that it plays on the g-spot with each thrust. So I little doubted that Abrille would be the only girl receiving 'Pleasure' during this forfeit.

Meantime, Peter had instructed the now naked Abrille (how gorgeous she looked!) to get on all fours and was applying glistening gel on and into her rear and front entrances. Abrille was already moaning with pleasure.

It was like watching one of those porn movies where the shameless little tart gets fucked by two well-hung studs in the pussy and arse – only, as a delicious twist, the parts of the two studs were being played by two sexy young ladies armed with rubber weapons that never go soft or come too soon. I frigged myself again in anticipation, my sex now wet indeed. There was a passionless, vacant stare on Abrille's face as she compliantly waited for her fate.

Gemma lay down on her back, on top of the pile of discarded clothing, allowing 'Doris' to jut upwards into the air. Abrille was pulled to her feet and led to stand astride the Head Croupier, before being lowered, gently but firmly, on to the big rubber cock. Abrille had been lubed so well that it only took three or four thrusts for her cunt to devour the purple rod completely.

She rocked enthusiastically back on to 'Doris' and Gemma assisted, gyrating her pelvis to make the most of each thrust. Abrille's vacant stare was replaced by the curled lips of gratification and the half-closed eyelids of bliss.

They allowed Gemma to warm her up a bit more with some of the wildest dildo fucking I've ever seen. Meanwhile, the boys took turns to twiddle her nipples between stroking their own cocks. When Abrille's moans became animalistic growls, they judged that the time had come and Maureen stepped up to the plate.

How had my liberated staff turned into libertines? How had this happened, under my nose, with me almost unaware of the change? I thought about this while my breasts and clitoris buzzed with excitement from what I was seeing, and in a vulnerable part of me, I feared that I might become unneeded and unwanted.

Maureen knelt behind Abrille, who peered over her shoulder in anticipation of her double penetration, watching Mo as she eased 'Daisy' between her gorgeously brown arse-globes into her tight coffee-coloured rose. The thrusts were slow and short at first but, as Abrille became acclimatised to her invasion, Gemma recommenced her gyrations, pushing the purple monster in and out of her seeping crack. Abrille's face was now a picture of ambiguity as she endured and enjoyed the sensations stretching and stimulating her. Her hand clutched and squeezed at the pile of garments underneath her, scrunching a skirt in one hand and a discarded stocking in the other.

'Look at me,' Maureen said as she shafted Abrille's arse. 'Come on, look at me.'

Abrille turned to look over her shoulder and their eyes met in a lusty gaze that remained unbroken as slim and sexy Maureen pushed the bright-pink phallus in and out of that tight French ring.

I caught a glimpse of Abrille's stretched holes as the girls pounded away at her, both moaning themselves, clearly enjoying the motions of 'Daisy' and 'Doris' within their own succulent walls. The boys wanked their cocks, trancelike, as they watched.

'You like that, do you, little French girl?' panted Maureen, fixing her helpless, horny victim with a haughty stare.

'Yes, she does,' said Gemma.

Abrille was unable to answer, but her jaw dropped in a silent scream of rapture. Maureen sensed that the bawdy talk was paying dividends

'You like some Scots cock? You like a Scottish cock in your pussy and arse, aye? You want these three boys in you, you French slut?'

I nearly came myself, hearing all of that, so heaven knows what ripples of electricity went through Abrille's well-worked holes. She cried out again, lost in pleasure – I think she was trying to reply to Maureen but was unable to, so deeply were Maureen's questions turning her on.

Eventually, Abrille found the strength to form a coherent word, although who knows if she was answering Maureen or expressing the thought we all express during a five-alarm orgasm.

'Yeess!' she squealed. The girls, sensing her climax, quickened their strokes, increasing the pleasure, until the storm had fully passed and Abrille's squeals turned to satisfied whimpers. Both Gemma and Maureen laughed and clapped gleefully at their handiwork. They had every right to feel proud: it was indeed some seeing-to they had given her.

I chose this as my moment to descend from the top of the stairs.

'Very nice. Very nice indeed. And may I ask how long this has been going on down here without my permission?'

The six of them looked up at me, stunned and speechless, glancing to each other for support. Gemma it was who eventually rose to her feet and spoke first.

'Sorry, Ms McKnight, we didn't think you'd mind. This is only our second time at this, I promise.'

'I only mind that I was not invited, especially after our recent conversation on the subject. Michael, are you not on security detail tonight?'

Michael was hurriedly trying to retrieve his clothes from the pile and, I presume, get dressed and return to his post.

'Wait a minute, Michael, don't get dressed yet,' said Gemma. 'We have to spin The Wheel one more time.'

'What are you talking about?' I demanded, but I did not get a straight reply to my question.

'Grab her, boys,' I heard Maureen say as two hands closed around my arms and I was frogmarched by Jack and Peter to the centre of the room.

'You said you wanted to play, Ms McKnight, so here is your chance. Spin it,' said Gemma.

Naked save for her strap-on erection, Maureen spun The Wheel and the sound of the running ball and the clicking of the axle filled the room.

I narrowed my eyes at the impish Gemma but, to be honest, I was too horny to protest; the thought of a licking, in any sense of the word, was thrilling me greatly at this point. My heart thumped and my cunt trickled in anticipation of the outcome.

'Pain!' came the cry.

The ball had landed in a red segment of the modified roulette wheel. I guessed therefore that the black segments had been designated as 'Pleasure', although I had no guarantee that I was not being hoodwinked. Whatever the truth, 'Pain' was certainly a popular outcome.

Another huddle of naked flesh and skimpy underwear was convened and I waited to learn my fate. My stomach fluttered in fearful excitement as, amidst the trepidation, part of me longed for the hot kiss of a lash on my naked flesh. I wanted them to strip me, strap me and stripe me.

Finally Gemma stepped forwards, flicking her flame of red hair, and with mischief in her eye. She must have known that her next beating at my hands would be a spicy one after all this, but did not seem to care.

'We've decided that your torment shall be linked in some way to the wonderful playroom you have built here, Ms McKnight. First, you will be stripped, then tied with an item from each of The Cellar's rooms, and then laced once across the backside, again with an item from each room. Strip her, folks.'

It was my turn to experience the piranha-like flurry of hands removing my clothing from me.

'You must tell me the name of the lingerie shop where you buy your invisible knickers,' remarked Gemma drily, referring to my tendency to go panty-less.

'It's called "Tarts R Us",' quipped Abrille.

Red-faced but unbowed, I ignored their sarcasm.

'Leave her in her stockings and suspenders and her heels,' called Gemma.

Again I rouged as the twelve eyes drank in the sight of my dark bush, framed by a garter belt and silks, and of my full breasts heaving with each excited breath. My curvaceous buttocks clenched in expectancy.

Gemma's five helpers scuttled off in all directions and returned, proudly carrying artefacts pilfered from the eight realms within The Cellar, leaving them in two piles at Gemma's feet. I caught glimpses of leather and metal, rope and even plastic, and my imagination ran wild, pushing my exposed nipples to the hardness of bullets. I felt as though everyone must have seen how they throbbed.

My wrists were tied together first, in front of my body, by two pink ribbons from The Nursery. Clients in The Nursery are sometimes transformed into little girls and such pretty ribbons have been known to bunch the ringlets of their golden wigs to give them that sweet little princess look.

Gemma took up a yellow rope from The Dungeon and looped it cruelly and tightly around each of my breasts, making them throb and sit up like puppy-dogs. A knot was tied behind my back. I was self-conscious about my sweet red cherries already and now I felt as though the whole world must be staring at them and knowing how aroused I was.

Next, one of the chains from the Throne, which had been detached from its usual collar, was attached

153

to a leather strap from The White Room's treatment table; Michael was drafted in to squeeze the leather strap through one of the links. The strap itself was then buckled around my neck. It was a tight fit and the pressure on my breathing and circulation flushed my face and made my clitty swell. A school tie from The School Room was then passed through the link at the other end of the chain. They left it to dangle for the time being.

Maureen took up a pair of red seamed stockings from The Boudoir and rolled one into a ball, forcing it into my mouth with her thumbs. She then used the other stocking as a gag, knotting it behind my neck. I was beginning to feel helpless and I could not stop my sex from gushing its sugary syrup.

Abrille had detached a length of flex from the telephone prop that we use in The Office. I was relieved to see that I was to be tied with it rather than whipped. It was wound around the ribbons on my wrists at one end and, like the school tie, left to dangle for the time being.

A set of reins from The Stable were then wrapped tightly around my knees, the leather creaking as Jack tied the knot. I had to concentrate on keeping my balance in my heels with my knees so tightly pressed together.

The school tie was then used to tie my ankles together, forcing me to bend over, because the chain between the tie and the neck-collar would not stretch all the way from foot to throat. My buttocks were now wonderfully exposed.

Finally, my arms were restricted by tying the telephone flex, which was attached to my pretty wrist-bond, to the school tie between my ankles. Now trussed and able to make only the smallest of movements, I truly realised my helplessness and my body coursed with the electricity of pleasure. I wobbled on my heels.

'If you lose your balance during any of the strokes, that stroke will be repeated,' decreed Gemma. 'What's first?'

'The shoe,' said Michael, taking up a large size-eight shoe from The Boudoir. (The feminisation of men requires a collection of footwear in the upper size range.)

Michael slapped me on the left buttock with the flat of the sole, and did not spare the leather. It scuffed and stung me, giving me cause to gasp. Jack made a similar mark across my right buttock using a fluffy pink slipper from The Nursery. I felt the sear of its signature, followed by a pleasing hot glow.

Peter had picked up a long ruler from The Office and slapped me across both buttocks with it, bringing it down from shoulder height. I swear I felt the graduations on it imprinted on my tender, quivering flesh. Gemma blew on the sore as she leant in to examine the mark.

'How lovely, well done,' she said to him.

This was the first stroke to create real discomfort in the luscious skin on my bottom and I began to fear the forthcoming strokes, a fear that caused a fresh wave of juice to gush from my pussy.

Abrille picked up the next instrument of punishment and began to unwrap it from its packaging. My eyes widened with disbelief and I think I made a grunt of urgency from behind my gag. It was a catheter tube from The White Room: a thin, bendy plastic tube no more than a few millimetres in width. I knew such an item would cut like a whip and braced myself as it sang like a swanee-whistle on its journey through the air and sliced at my buttocks. I let out a sob through the mass of red nylon in my mouth, teetering on my heels.

On its own, the riding crop that followed, fittingly applied by Maureen after our recent session in The Stable, would have been mild by comparison, but after the previous blow it stung doubly.

Gemma approached with an eyebrow arched, slapping The School Room belt in her hand. In Scotland such belts are made from a harder leather than the sort of belt used to hold trousers up, as anyone who has compared the sting left by the two will tell you. Gemma gave the stroke everything she had and my buttocks smarted like magma.

I tried to regulate my breathing, knowing that the end was in sight. Maureen had taken up a flogger from The Dungeon and she swung it cruelly in circles behind me before allowing it to bite me. Again my body shook as the strands cascaded on to my bare arse.

'One to go,' said Abrille as she uncoiled the golden whip from The Throne Room. It is largely decorative and softer than the whips you might find in The Dungeon – it spends most of its time hanging on a hook behind the Throne – but I still feared it and took a fearful breath through flaring nostrils to brace myself.

The whip scored my sensitive flesh like a hot blade, and my knees buckled from the shock. With my mind swirling from the sweet, glorious agony I toppled sideways at last and would surely have struck the hard floor like a felled redwood had Michael and Peter not stepped forwards to catch me in their arms and stand me up again.

Gemma took the whip from Abrille.

'The stroke is to be repeated,' she said, and I breathed hard once more at the news, adjusting my position as best I could to take the lash. I glanced at my bush, which was now glistening.

Thank heavens, I was able to retain my balance as the whip branded me again. At last it was over and I savoured the feelings in my nipples, on my buttocks, in my loins – indeed I could barely feel any other part of my body. It was as though I was nothing but glowing arse-cheeks, engorged breasts and throbbing crotch.

Delicately, lovingly, I was untied and allowed to rise to my full height again. In turn, each of my croupiers hugged and kissed me.

'You are truly the best boss anyone could have, Ms McKnight,' said Gemma, and for the moment my fears and insecurity were banished.

Eleven

For once the west of Scotland kept its midsummer contract with us and gave us a run of sun-filled days. Clothing became more and more optional out on the streets and at lunchtimes in the squares, and the banks of grass along the Clyde hosted a strip show. I loved every voyeuristic minute of it.

My experiences in The Cellar had calmed my mind about the loyalty of the staff. They still considered me, quite rightly of course, the doyenne of matters sexual but, like a mother learning to let go of her child as she grows up, I now accepted their need to experiment and learn for themselves, away from the sometimes intimidating maternal eye. In the end, I knew, they would always come back to me. The eagerness with which they had involved me in their game convinced me of that.

Outside influences were still a worry. I was less than content with Marty, flaunting his fine frame and playing the cute fake-nervousness card. I still felt he was only out to work his way through my croupiers before moving on to further conquests, and as I thought about him the dominatrix within me took over, elevating my musings to outlandish heights. At first I thought about teasing and seducing him, denying him orgasm until he begged for a spanking or to lick my feet, but more and more I wanted to bring him down, for many reasons: protecting my girls, feeding my ego, extending my power, turning myself on . . . until I was imagining the day when his tongue was flicking between my toes, his neck on a leash and his signature wet on the contract that signed his precious gymnasium over to me. It may have seemed like wild fancy, but Mistress Valerie adored the idea and, whether the rest of me believed it or not, it became a resolution.

It was approximately four o'clock, the hottest part of a summer's day. I leant on the balcony above the gaming floor and, like a foreign tourist watching the changing of the guard through the railings of Buckingham Palace, surveyed the shift change. Gemma, Kirsty, Abrille and Chloe came off their tables and Nhyla, Maureen, Amber and Lily relieved them – a procession of beautiful nymphs, with jiggling breasts, swinging arses and flashing stocking tops. I wondered if any of the gamblers turned up just to watch the changeover.

As the girls who had been relieved made their way to the staff areas to gather their things, I noticed something rather more interesting: Marty arriving in the foyer, accompanied by a tall, slim, older man whom I did not recognise. They were both dressed for summer, in oh-so-pretentious deck shoes, short trousers and loose, pale V-neck T-shirts. Marty had his hair held back by a pair of sunglasses, while his companion hung his tinted spectacles on the neck of his top. Despite his age, he skilfully made himself look younger by sporting a golden tan and a coral neck-chain.

Three of the girls, Kirsty, Gemma and Chloe, now off-duty, appeared again, chatting and laughing and making their way together across the floor towards the exit. I was most gratified to note that my shy English rose, Kirsty, was still in her croupier's uniform, something she had previously thought too tarty to wear in public – she had apparently grown to accept her beauty and was now willing to go outside The Paddle-Boat in an ensemble that displayed it brazenly. I was proud indeed.

My swelling bosom was soon deflated, however, when, to my astonishment, the three girls greeted Marty and his companion with kisses and hugs and no little familiarity. After some conversation, all five left by the front entrance. I urgently made for the stairs.

Needing to move fast, I could not maintain my usual alluring gait, and I was forced to take off my heels and go silk-footed. I ran like a tomboy down the stairwell. Thank goodness there was no one on the stairs – none should ever see me in such unlady-like circumstances. I was about to breathe a sigh of relief, having reached ground level, where I could put my shoes back on and regain my poise, when I ran nose first into a solid, fridge-freezer-like chest in a shirt and tie. It was Michael.

'Oh! Michael? Did you see where the girls went?' I asked breathlessly.

'They're still out there, squeezing into some convertible across the street. Peter has taken them some food out in a hamper,' he told me. 'May I help you back on with those, Ms McKnight?' He was pointing at the high heels I held in my hand.

'Hmmm? Oh, yes, yes, you may,' I said, letting them fall to the floor before me and pointing my right foot to allow him to replace the shoe.

Michael went down on one knee and bowed his head slightly as he cradled my shoe on to my foot.

'Are you on duty tonight?' I asked him.

'No, Ms McKnight, it's Gordon's shift.'

'Have you your car?' I asked as his strong hands eased my left shoe on.

'Yes, Ms McKnight.'

'Fetch it and bring it around the front. We have some work to do this afternoon.'

I lingered in the foyer unseen until Peter returned from the car and Marty's red convertible pulled away, heading west. As soon as it was out of sight I stepped out into the street looking for Michael. After about twenty anxious seconds his car appeared and drew up at the kerb, and he opened the passenger door for me from the inside. I would ordinarily have had him get out, walk around the car and let me in like a gentleman, but speed was of the essence.

'I think you know what to do,' I said as I buckled up, 'and before you ask: yes, this is a spying mission.'

Michael nodded and engaged the engine. 'Yes, Ms McKnight.'

We were lucky. We caught sight of them at the Exhibition Centre junction and were able to follow them on to the motorway.

'Where do you think they will be heading, Ms McKnight?' asked Michael over the hum of the engine.

'Some secluded spot in Ayrshire for a picnic and a frolic, I imagine, or maybe north for a skinny-dip in a loch – who knows what wild ideas Marty and his friend have put into their heads?'

Michael expertly maintained a few cars' distance between us and I began to wonder where he had picked up such a skill; they do say many in the security business are ex-SAS or former spies, and I imagined a spy-thriller fantasy with Michael in the lead role and me as the irresistible *femme fatale*. My nipples were quite hard by the time we left the motorway.

Gradually the roads became narrower and more winding, and traffic scarcer. Soon we were the only two cars in sight. Eventually our quarry swung left into a country lane that meandered through dense woodland. Slowly, so as not to be seen at all, we followed the road. A sign – 'Aucheninnan Priory' – told us where we were and, sensing the red sports car ahead would have done the same thing, we parked in a lay-by. Michael argued that the rest of the journey should be on foot, to maintain a level of stealth.

'That's easy for you to say, Michael, dear – you're not in heels.'

I tried my best nonetheless, only removing my shoes where the dirt road became particularly treacherous. My silk stockings were taking a battering and becoming very dusty indeed, but I could always get Michael to lick them clean later.

Through the trees we heard laughter and voices and the lapping of water. I caught glimpses of a grand Edwardian building through the branches and leaves.

'Ms McKnight, if you would allow me to carry you, I think we should continue under the cover of woods,' Michael suggested.

'That would be agreeable, Michael, provided you do not expect me to go piggy-back,' I told him.

Michael picked his way through the woodland, bearing my sculpted form in his privileged arms like a loving husband carrying his new bride over the threshold of their love nest.

We took cover behind a fallen tree, over which we could see the three girls and two men sitting on a grassy bank preparing to enjoy a picnic. The girls had altered their garb in the car; Gemma and Kirsty were both in bikini tops and sarongs, and Chloe McIntyre had slipped into a tankini and cut-off denims. Near by was a loch with a fine shingled shore and a wooden jetty. It was getting close to five o'clock now, and Michael and I were quite jealous as they snacked on sandwiches, wraps, salad and dips and sipped beer or wine in the sun.

Marty was the first to announce that he was going for a swim, and ripped off his T-shirt displaying his gorgeous pectoral muscles. After kicking his shoes to one side, and stepping out of his shorts, he trotted up on to the jetty naked. There was laughter and applause as Marty, the exhibitionist, posed long enough for us all to get a nice view of his cock. Then he leapt in with a splash.

Not be outdone, and I daresay governed by a testosterone-driven need for one-upmanship, Marty's friend, who (for anyone without the revealing insight into the male psyche that a life in fetish brings) might seem too old for such behaviour, responded to the challenge, throwing off his own clothes and steaming down the shore into the water with a series of foamy splashes. His tanned arse was indeed pert for its age, and indicated that he might have some link to Marty's gymnasium. It was an arse that would certainly have looked good in The School Room or The Nursery, bent over my knee and reddening under a spanking. I watched it disappear into the cool blue sheen of the loch.

The girls laughed and clapped, applauding the display. I wondered if any of them would be brazen enough to join them in the pure highland water. Marty and his friend were certainly keen on the idea, beckoning the girls with hoots and waves. I wondered who would be first to relent. Gemma was a game lass, but unless something was her own idea she preferred to remain reserved, in keeping with her supervisory position. Kirsty, we knew, was coming out of her shell, but I doubted she was feeling loose enough to plunge naked into the water with two irresponsible chaps. No, my chips were on Chloe. Blondes, after all, know how to have more fun.

Sure enough she was first to stand up. She implored the other two to join her in the water – perhaps she was a bit wary of going in on her own with two childish and excitable men – but I knew she would not be able to resist the fun, even if Gemma and Kirsty kept their bums on the blanket. They shook their heads and made it clear they were quite comfortable where they were, nibbling and sipping wine. Chloe eventually gave up, giving a dismissive gesture and promptly released her sweet little breasts from her tankini as she pulled it over her head.

Michael shifted in the brush for a better look, and together we watched and lusted from behind the moss-covered trunk. Chloe unbuttoned her shorts and curved her back as she reached under the waistband with her thumb to wiggle out of them. She knows how to strip, that lassie – even a simple task like removing two skimpy vestments becomes a performance. The boys in the water howled like wolves.

Chloe has those dimples in the small of her back that so many men find irresistible, and they certainly mesmerised me as her feet crunched the quartz pebbles on the shore. The awesome backdrop of Ben Lomond looming behind her was the perfect context for the natural beauty of her succulent white globes.

When the water had reached her waist, she dived gracefully, demurely, into the loch and swam past the two lads who watched, captivated. Out beyond the jetty she stopped and, treading water expertly, dared them to chase her. Marty and his friend did just that as Chloe swam away, parallel to the shore.

Michael nudged me to draw my attention back to Gemma and Kirsty, who had suddenly realised what they might be missing and after a single, almost telepathic, glance between them had begun undressing each other, embracing and kissing as they released the strings of bikini tops and unknotted their sarongs. They stepped out of their bikini bottoms and ran to the lapping water, their beautiful white bodies shining in the summer sun. We watched them swim out.

Chloe had swum round in a big horseshoe and found her way back to the little wooden pier, where she began treading water once again, goading her pursuers as they trailed behind. I only wished I could see her body through the lens of Scotland's clear waters; how her fresh breasts must have been swaying with the currents.

As the boys swam nearer she came ashore, emerging from the water like a newborn Venus, her blond pubic brush soaked into invisibility. Marty and his friend watched from the water, captivated.

Gemma and Kirsty had now caught up and swam behind the broad shoulders of Marty and the stranger, playfully grabbing them around the neck and drawing them under. There was much coughing and spluttering, many splashed reprisals and duckings. Marty noticed Chloe retreating and called out for her to return to the water. She was keen to get back to the blanket. Judging from the hardness of her nipples, she may have found the water colder than she had expected.

Marty tapped his friend on the arm and, wading as fast as they could, they gave chase again, intent, I assumed, on dragging her back to the loch – but I reconsidered that theory when I saw their fully erect cocks emerging from the water like a pair of Nessies. Even Chloe froze as she saw them, so raw and rustic did those timber-hard rods look.

No words were spoken as they approached. Chloe looked at their twitching cocks and then at their lustful eyes. Automatically she dropped to her knees upon the blanket and reached up to place a graceful hand under Marty's testicles, guiding him towards her so that she could suck on his tasty penis. She bobbed her head upon it, sucking her cheeks in as she drew her head back. Marty made encouraging noises and Chloe looked up at him, moaning her own approval. Her other hand found its way to the stranger's scrotum and, after a few farewell sucks on Marty, she switched to the other cock, barely missing a beat. There were groans of approval from all corners and my own petals became moist.

In spite of my natural arousal, I was racked with ambivalence. My moistening sex, upon which I can usually rely for most of my decision-making, wanted me to watch and enjoy the show. What is there not to like about a beautiful girl giving mouth-watering oral pleasure to two horny males? What's more, two, perhaps even hornier, nymphs were emerging from the water not fifteen metres away, and were sure to add to the entertainment.

Something, however, did not sit right with me. The feelings of intense doubt, which I thought my recent experiences in The Cellar had banished, returned. Oh, would that one of my well-heeled clients had been a psychiatrist; I could have swapped him a session under my heel for a session on his leather couch, to help me get to the deliciously plump bottom of my uncertainty.

It was Marty's next act that gave me my first inkling of what the problem might be. He pulled Chloe's hips towards him as she continued to hum contentedly and suck the stranger's cock. She stuck her rump out for Marty as best she could, but was as surprised as any of us when, rather than mount and invade her now sopping wet slit, he gave her a resounding slap on her buttock with the flat of his hand. The crack was so loud that a pheasant in the woods behind me noisily took to the air.

Chloe loved it, wriggling and squirming delightfully under it – and the salvo that followed it. Her cock-sucking took on a new charged intensity.

So this was it, I realised: my problem, my discomfort. I had decided, after much inward debate, that I was content for Paddle-Boat staff to submit to and dominate each other to their hearts' content but, when outsiders waltzed into my coven and thought they could take the whip hand with my croupiers, I had a problem. As far as I was concerned, the role of any male, once within the walls of The Paddle-Boat Casino, was to serve and be dominated. All men have a desire for this deep within them and the *raison d'être* of my establishment was to find it and exploit it in every way: emotionally, erotically and financially. I chastised myself for allowing my baser urges to blur that focus. Peter and Marty both should have been broken first, then, if judged to be fine enough specimens, ridden later.

If I could have, I would have stopped these proceedings then and there, but I was afraid to blow my cover. Splendid as it would have been to have Marty and his equally cocky chum crawling in the sand and pebbles at my feet, their balls as blue as plums, I did not want my girls to know the regrettable truth that I had felt the need to follow them outside their working hours. I resolved to allow Marty and the stranger their day in the sun, then make them pay for it dearly.

Chloe was now playing the party-girl role to perfection, the wee slut. She hopped from cock to cock as a bee flits from flower to flower. Gemma and Kirsty, who had emerged from the water, their skin shiny and wet, took turns to spank her and tickle her anus with their tongues. All four were punishing her for her impudence and showing-off in the water.

Michael shifted uncomfortably behind the tree, the bulge in his black trousers giving a clue as to why he was finding it so difficult to get in a position of comfort. I tutted.

'Michael, if this is too much for you, you may wank yourself,' I told him with a haughty air.

He nodded. 'Thank you, Ms McKnight.'

I decided to let him debase himself like a mindless monkey, while I, aloof and exuding feminine superiority, ignored him, turning my attention back to the action on the blanket.

Gemma was now lying underneath Chloe, her face reaching up to Chloe's fuzzy clam. Although it could not be seen, I am sure her tongue was working feverishly. Meanwhile, she pawed her own sex.

Marty was enjoying the privilege of exploring Chloe's mouth. He could no longer spank her from there, but he kept Chloe mindful of her status in the sexual hierarchy by holding her blond hair scrunched behind her head in his closed fist. At times she submissively allowed him to fuck her mouth with short jabbing thrusts, at others she bobbed up and down sucking his penis like a lollipop and humming rhythmically with each movement.

Marty's friend was now behind Chloe, with Kirsty's pumping hand preparing him for his second plunge of the day. Even from a distance I could hear Gemma slurping and lapping at Chloe's pussy, which must have resembled the taste and consistency of a ripe melon, so juicy and sweet had it become. The older man's penis entered her with the soft, yielding squelch of a spoon going into a whipped dessert, and I was not surprised to hear him express the glorious sensations in a flood of random words and grunts of affirmation. I noted that he had a local accent.

His thrusts were long, slow and deliberate, like the drawing and plunging of the pole on a leisurely river punt. Chloe's eyes widened as she was rogered from both ends and received a tongue lashing on her 'wee-man' (a Scots lass's nickname for her clitoris: 'the wee-man-in-the-boat'). I thought it a most excit-ing show, even if I had misgivings about my girls submitting to outsiders. My own 'wee-man' was calling out for attention, and the walls of my sex were not exactly silent on the matter either, dripping freely with my sweet love-potion. I could not respond to their demand for a frigging, though; I had just made Michael feel inferior for having a wank like some horny chimpanzee, and it would hardly maintain the tone if I started shoving a finger or two into my own pie.

Kirsty though, was not so impressed with the show and, to my great surprise, delight and arousal, began to spank the stranger's sunbed-tinted backside with her hand, goading him to put some effort into it and up the tempo. He liked it – I made a mental note of that – and did as he was bade, ramping up the speed until he slapped against Chloe's buttocks and they rippled with each thrust.

Cock-muffled whimpers of ecstasy began to ema-nate from Chloe's mouth as the action became more frenzied. Marty and his friend were on a race to the finish-line, and who would bet on the winner? Marty had the head-start but Chloe's cock-sucking was being distracted by the bucking bronco at her rear.

Soon it became clear that the momentum was with the stranger and he would surely take Marty on the rails, which he did, spending loudly, howling with joy and pushing right up inside her, bathing her deeply. Marty was not to be outdone, though, and now that Chloe was no longer rocked by her vigorous seeing-to, he was able to get some real face-fucking done, finally decorating Chloe's chin with opals of semen.

I had seen enough, and did not want to hang around so long that we ended up being seen. We needed to be away well before our friends had started to pack up.

'Finish that,' I said to Michael, clicking my fingers and pointing to Michael's penis.

Michael gritted his teeth to quieten his orgasm and quickly pumped himself on to the rich woodland soil.

'Carry me back to the car,' I said as he zipped himself up.

'Yes, Ms McKnight,' he answered.

Twelve

I paced up and down in my office waiting for the appointed hour. I had changed my normal attire to something more striking: a tight black bodice that pushed up my tremendous breasts into a merciless cleavage, a black leather skirt to contrast with my bare legs and give me a sleek line about the hips and thighs, and my cruellest set of high heels. My make-up was bold: a deep burnt red on my lips, thick eyeliner and electric-blue eye-shadow.

I had picked the belt and the cane as my instruments of discipline. They may not be in use any more in schools north or south of the border, but they still had symbolism, an iconic influence on the psyche.

I paced a bit more, strutting back and forth; perhaps I was rehearsing the performance to come. The girls would be here in a few minutes. Gemma and Chloe had been in the building since late morning, but I wanted to see all three girls together and Kirsty was not due to appear until nearer lunchtime.

I wondered if Gemma and Chloe had surmised what their summons was about. I know that Michael would not have betrayed me, but perhaps one of the other girls had mentioned that the two of us had disappeared shortly after their departure. They might well have deduced that I saw them leave and was looking for an explanation.

Like naughty schoolgirls, their minds must have raced with all the things they knew they had done and hurried evaluations of whether I could have found out about it. No doubt their behaviour in the sun the afternoon before entered into their minds, but there was no way I could have known about that, was there? Perhaps Gemma and Chloe were discussing it even now as they waited for Kirsty to arrive.

I checked my timepiece. Kirsty would indeed be here any moment and, as I had told them to come up as soon as she arrived, I began selecting my pose. The legs, as ever, were the most important element of the image; their splendour must intimidate and inspire awe. I decided therefore to sit in the armchair, rather than on the desk or in the chair behind it. I pointed the armchair so that it was almost side-on to the door, just slightly oblique. Those entering would first see my heels and ankles, then the long straight avenues of smooth silk that are my legs, crossed at the knee, then the belt and cane across my lap, then finally my eyes, glowering at them from behind my colourful mask of make-up. To my right was the sofa, where I would have the three sit.

The time was near and I listened for their approach. They were not talking as they came down the hallway; only the sound of their feet on the carpet reached my ears. There was a soft, nervous knock on my door.

'Come in.'

The door opened and Gemma entered.

'You wanted to see us, Ms McKnight?'

'Yes, Gemma. Please all sit down.' I pointed to the sofa. My armchair was not facing the sofa directly, but I liked that: it created a detached atmosphere, ideal for a dressing-down.

None of them met my gaze as they filed to the sofa and sat down. I was pleased to see that their training had become habit: each one exposed the inside of her thigh as she sat, but my stern face betrayed neither pleasure nor pride.

'I know I have spoken to at least one of you before now about a certain looseness of behaviour that seems to be pervading The Paddle-Boat. Since that discussion I have come to the difficult decision not to stand in the way of sexual fraternisation within the building – it is, after all, no more than harmless enjoyment, and harmless enjoyment is what The Paddle-Boat is all about, don't you think?'

'Yes, Ms McKnight,' they returned in a ragged chorus.

'Having said that, croupiers at this establishment have a role to play in relation to the population beyond these walls: the role of Mistress and sexual superior.'

The girls glanced at each other.

'Yes, Ms McKnight.'

'In short, if you are to be a Paddle-Boat croupier, I do not want you to be giving it up to the males of this town – dominate them by all means, as much as they want or need, for money preferably; tease them with the prospect of sex if it helps you to entrap them; but, unless they are on my payroll, intercourse in any context is not an option.'

This statement was given some consideration and, soon enough, unanimous assent.

'Now I know what occurred yesterday afternoon with two outsiders, and I do not intend to let it pass without some form of correctional stimulus. There will be no option of a wage-fine.' I glanced at Kirsty, furthest away from me, reminding her of the option she had been given for punishment a short while ago.

A look of worry and surprise came across all three faces, as they tried to agree an alibi or excuse through facial expressions and eye contact. Of course it was impossible. Gemma looked at me with a most quizzical expression.

'Never mind how I know, Miss Jarvie. I simply do,' I returned, guessing the question on her mind.

'We weren't doing anything wrong, Ms McKnight,' protested Chloe.

'I do hope you're not about to launch into mentally rehearsed arguments about being responsible, independent adults – I would accept that readily, Chloe, but I have already given reasons why these arguments do not stand up on their own.'

'Ms McKnight, may I speak candidly before we receive our discipline?' asked Gemma. There was such an earnest look on her face that I had to agree.

She spoke nervously but with conviction.

'Ms McKnight, we, that is, the girls, the croupiers, all adore you, and we are so, so grateful for everything you have taught us, so we are, but some of us are beginning to wonder if being our teacher, our instructor, in these matters really gives you the authority to, to, well, dictate our sex lives. I mean, now we've all learnt what we have, can we not choose our own sexual destinies?'

I wondered if she had finished, or there was more to come. I let the silence linger to draw any further thoughts out of her.

'I mean to say, Ms McKnight, are you really so much more knowledgeable than us that we should follow your every decree and not choose for ourselves how to use, enjoy or dominate men? Should we really be punished just for exploring these things ourselves?'

I was mortified; I could have slapped her across the face with my open hand, or brought the belt down across her bare knees as my mother used to do to me if I put my elbows on the table or committed some other crime against decency. I kept myself composed, however, answering her comment with a fixed gaze before I began my speech.

'I am laying down these rules to you, and all of the girls, not to control you, but to educate you. You have all of you come very far since I took you on, but you all still have very far to go. My rules are simply part of your training and, once you have learnt all you need to know, you will realise the power that you possess and come to know I am not laying down arbitrary rules, but showing you the path to truth, a path I am confident you will ultimately all follow by choice. Until then, you must trust my judgement. I blame myself for this; it is good for any Mistress to give in to her desires now and then and receive the pleasure she richly deserves – provided it is from one of her select slaves, an Alpha male – but I have done this far too freely and often of late. I fear my example has been misinterpreted as licence to allow male acquaintances to take liberties with you. It must stop.'

My oratory seemed to have found a receptive and comprehending audience, but Gemma, flame-haired and feisty, was unconvinced.

'Ms McKnight, is there really all that much to learn? I mean, surely we are almost as skilled as you.'

I laughed out loud at the suggestion, and at the idea that the poor little angel could even think such a thing. My words had evidently not yet reached their mark, and I dreamt up a little exercise to illustrate my point.

'Gemma, would you agree to a wee contest to determine which of the two of us is right?'

'What like, Ms McKnight?'

'A contest of sexual prowess, of course.'

Gemma did not take long to decide.

'I accept.'

'There will need to be more at stake than simply the arguments in hand. If I win, you will have to accept my restrictions on your behaviour, of course, but also accept further discipline.'

Gemma nodded.

'And if I win, Ms McKnight, you will allow me more licence sexually, and there will be no punishment?'

'There is no possibility of you winning, Gemma, so I can readily accept your terms without trepidation.'

Gemma smiled and arched an eyebrow at my bravado.

'What is the challenge, Ms McKnight?'

'Kirsty, will you fetch Michael and Gordon please? I will explain when they arrive.'

Kirsty skipped away and returned a short while later, with Gordon and Michael looking very serious, following behind. They had not been told why they were summoned and probably assumed that a security issue needed their attention.

'Thanks for coming, boys, I need your help to settle an argument that has grown into something of a wager: Gemma and I will be having a contest to see who can make you come the quickest. Gemma will go first, and I second. We are each free to use whatever method or body part we see fit to bring you off. I trust you boys are happy to give it your all and to put in an earnest effort to spend as soon as possible?'

'Yes, Ms McKnight,' they answered as one, bowing their heads slightly.

'Gemma, as you're to go first, you may have the choice of partner.'

'Michael,' Gemma answered, after a moment's consideration. It was a good tactical choice; she knew

Michael and I had dallied together before and wanted to cheat me of any advantage familiarity might give me.

'Gordon, would you wait outside for us? Oh, and leave your watch,' I said.

Gordon unclipped his watch from his thick wrist and handed it to me. The door clicked behind him.

'Ready?' I said to Michael and Gemma.

They nodded.

'Begin,' I called, starting the stopwatch.

Kirsty and Chloe watched eagerly.

Gemma began by getting Michael in the mood, breathing heavily in his ear and talking huskily, so that we could all hear.

'You want me to get your cock out, Michael, in front of these girls and suck it? Aye? You do? Suck it nice and hard? Lick it like a lollipop? Suck it like a straw? That be good, aye?' she said, rubbing against him with her breasts and running spidery fingers over his crotch, tickling his cock through his trousers.

The overwhelming rush that unsurprisingly came over Michael on hearing all this was a pleasing sight, and suddenly my private place was longing to see his hard rod, its skin tight and smooth around the engorged flesh. Fortunately, Gemma did not keep my eyes and privates waiting long; she slid down Michael's body to her knees, unzipped his fly and pulled his lovely penis out into the open. It pulsated with every one of Michael's excited heartbeats, expanding a little with each throb, as a balloon inflates with each breath.

Gemma pressed her tongue to it, licking its length from base to tip. She held Michael's gaze all the way up, turning him on even more. I glanced at the watch: we were just approaching the first minute.

Gemma blew his now hard cock, spitting on it to make it slide pleasurably over her eager lips. She

177

hummed with enthusiasm as Michael's knees buckled slightly, causing him to place his hands on her head for some stability. Gemma was putting on quite a show and seemed very likely to make Michael reach orgasm in good time. Indeed, if she continued in the same vein she had an outside chance of making me come too; I was getting very damp watching her go like this. I am sure Kirsty and Chloe felt the same way as they watched intently.

The clock had reached four minutes when Gemma sensed the time had come to up the ante. She stood, Michael's cock in her hand, and led him to my desk. She pumped him with long, slow movements of her slender, feminine hand, squeezing the head of his penis at the peak of each stroke. Michael howled with pleasure each time those wet fingers gripped his glans. Gemma pulled him closer and spoke once again in his ear.

'You want to fuck my tight ginger pussy? Fuck it deep and hard? Aye, you do. Fuck my ginger pussy from behind and watch my arsehole at the same time, come on!'

She bent over the desk (with no regard for the paperwork I had neatly piled there), pulled up her skirt and wiggled her hips to slide her knickers down to her thighs, revealing her ample white arse and the furry, peach-coloured vulva beneath. Michael did not wait around but grabbed a shoulder in each hand and manoeuvred his cock to push against the opening of her sex. Rocking back and forth, Michael eased inside her, fucking her as hard as he could – perhaps remembering my instruction to give it his all, or perhaps just caught up in the moment.

Michael did as Gemma had told him, opening her buttocks with his thumbs and watching her anus dance with each thrust of his cock up her pussy. He called out with joy as the sight electrified him.

We were hypnotised by the sight of his muscular arse pumping harder and harder, propelling that excited penis into her warm and welcoming haven. Gemma had turned her head to face Michael and was doing a nice line in bawdy talk as Michael powered into her. She certainly knew how to turn a man on, but I would have questioned her methods; and I looked forward to showing her how it really should have been done.

Eventually, as the watch in my hand swept past seven minutes, Gemma played what she obviously considered her trump card.

'Come on, fuck my arse. Take it out of there and come in my arsehole – I know you've been thinking about it, so do it!'

Michael was on it like a pouncing cat, easing the head of his penis in first and using the same rocking motion as before to push all the way in. Once inside, he was not for holding back and reamed her arse.

'Ohhhhh, God, yeah!' screamed Gemma, clearly intoxicated by this cocktail of pain and pleasure.

Michael was getting close now, growling like a bear and making tighter, choppier strokes. The moment arrived and Michael, always the gentleman, withdrew his cock in time to spray Gemma's buttocks with milky white rain. I stopped the watch.

'Nine minutes and fifty-three seconds,' I said. 'Very good indeed, Gemma. You certainly know how to please a man.'

'Indeed, Ms McKnight,' she replied, wiping the spunk from her buttocks and licking her fingers clean.

I was not too impressed with her manners: the ignorant girl did not offer a single drop to myself, Chloe or Kirsty!

Gemma reinstalled her knickers and made other adjustments for comfort before returning to her seat on the couch. Michael was dressed and looking his smart self again in seconds.

'Thank you, Michael. You can return to work. Please send Gordon in on your way out.'

'Yes, Ms McKnight.'

Gordon entered and I guided him with a pointed finger to the centre of the room. I handed Gemma the watch.

'I'm ready when you are, Gemma dear,' I said.

Gemma nodded.

'Go!' she said, starting the watch.

I stood, slowly rising to my full height, and approached Gordon, who looked at me lustily; he would have heard the sounds of dirty, hot sex through the door and might well have anticipated he would get something similar.

I did so hate to disappoint him, but such is life.

'Do not look your superior Goddess in the eye. Look straight ahead,' I snapped, slapping him across the back of the thigh with the belt I was holding.

'Remove all of your clothes and kneel with your head bowed. You have thirty seconds.'

Young Gordon began to undress. I whacked him again across the thigh.

'Say, "Yes, Mistress," whenever I give you a command,' I hissed.

'Yes, Mistress.'

In no time Gordon's young body was naked, his slim legs, supple as the branches of a sapling, curled underneath him. I would normally have admonished a slave for not folding his clothes, but on this occasion there was scarcely the time.

'On all fours,' I commanded.

Gordon adopted the prescribed position.

I raised the belt to my shoulder and struck him across his pert buttocks with a stinging swipe. He shuddered and his buttocks clenched beautifully.

'Thank you, Mistress.'

'You may now masturbate, like the snivelling little dog you are, in front of these three beautiful females. I know you have lusted for them for a long time, so don't bother to deny it! We also know you masturbate while thinking about at least one of them every day. You have five minutes: begin!'

'Yes, Mistress,' said Gordon, his face reddening.

He grasped his penis and began stimulating it, coaxing it to hardness. It was quite a pathetic sight.

'Is that it?' I said, taking it in my hand and caressing it delicately. 'It's not very responsive, is it?' How did you ever think that you could get this near one of these girls? Not a chance.' I cupped his balls. 'These balls are rather tight: usually a sign of excessive masturbation, ladies.'

'Yes, Mistress,' he said, not realising that it was tantamount to a confession. His cock was now rock-hard.

'Continue,' I said without emotion.

Gordon, now humiliated in front of girls he knew and worked with, wanked furiously, while Kirsty and Chloe teased him from the couch by dangling their shoes, crossing and uncrossing their legs and, bless them, giggling and whispering to each other.

Gemma, on the other hand, feared defeat, the poor lamb, and was not so enthusiastic about titillating him. Underneath the façade, though part of her appreciated the lesson she was receiving, while outwardly her face burnt that she had prostituted her body for the wager unnecessarily.

I let the belt softly run up Gordon's back as a reminder to him to keep his elbow in fifth gear or face the consequences.

'Come on, Gordon, show Chloe how hard you wank for her when you go home at night. That's it, show Kirsty how you spurt for her in the toilets during your break. They know, we all know,' I taunted.

Of course, I had no idea how much truth there was in what I was saying, although, if I had to bet on it, I would guess that at least some of it was true. I was playing on Gordon's fundamental male need to worship the female form and to trade in his dignity for the privilege.

Soon enough, my tactics had paid dividends and Gordon cried out as his body electrified in orgasm. I wondered if his own fetish chakra was radiating as his penis spewed forth three thick strings of his essence. From the way an abdominal spasm hunched him over involuntarily, I concluded that it probably was.

Gemma stopped the watch and without even looking at it handed it over to me. I took it gratefully and, keen to see how I had performed, read the time: an even six minutes.

I was so pleased with myself and felt so triumphant that I could have grabbed the back of her head and pressed my moist fanny to her sweet mouth, ordering her to lick for her life or never breathe again. I had to restrain myself, though; that would have been too enjoyable for her, and the whole purpose of this meeting was to punish her. To her credit, she was magnanimous in defeat.

'I am sorry, Ms McKnight. You were right,' she conceded.

'Indeed I was, and the time has come for discipline. There'll be six strokes for each of you followed by an extra six for Gemma.'

I had a deliciously wicked idea as I dismissed the crimson-faced Gordon from the room: to make them lash each other. Yes! The cruel ambiguity of being forced to apply punishment to their colleagues on my

182

behalf would increase the effect. I, of course, would apply Gemma's extra six strokes. I must save some of the fun for myself.

'Gemma, please kneel on the floor in front of the couch.'

Without hesitation, Gemma knelt on the floor and leant forward so that her stomach and chest rested on the couch. I handed the cane I had brought to Kirsty. Since Kirsty is English, I felt it more fitting to have her apply the cane to Gemma's butt; I wondered if she knew how to wield it. I would soon know.

'Kirsty, please apply six of your best to Gemma's backside. Be warned – they must be your best. If I suspect you have pulled any of your strokes, I shall add it to your own quota.'

Quite embarrassed about the task I had given her, a deferential Kirsty lifted Gemma's skirt, revealing again the contrast of her opal flesh against her lacy black knickers and stockings. With her eyes on the floor, betraying guilty pleasure, Kirsty pulled the knickers down to Gemma's thighs, where they seemed to be spending a lot of time that afternoon. Kirsty readied herself, glancing at me for confirmation of her orders. I nodded firmly, urging her to take the plunge.

The cane swept through the air with a swoosh and cracked on to Gemma's behind, which quivered and squirmed. Perhaps Kirsty was no longer as innocent as she seemed – she wielded the cane competently and knew to apply only the centre of the stalk to the target area.

Chloe and I watched with moistening crotches as the punishment was applied with vigour, though I knew Kirsty would be very uncomfortable about being asked to betray her colleague in this way.

The sound of Gemma's sluttish panting and the sight of her reddening flesh drew the juice from my pussy. After the sixth swipe, I ran my fingertips over the tender, pinking flesh on Gemma's backside.

I handed Gemma the belt, and pointed silently for Chloe to take her place on the carpet, leaning on the couch. Gemma, her mind and heart probably still racing from her beating, did not hang about but lifted Chloe's skirt to expose her plain black g-string and the sun-kissed skin on her slimmer, oval behind. It was covered in tiny, fine golden hairs, giving it a beguiling sheen. Gemma chose to leave Chloe's g-string where it was, rightly judging that it would not lessen the impact of the blows. The recipe of witnessing a beating and anticipating one's own is a potent one and sparkles of sugary solution had begun to seep from Chloe on to the thin gusset. I suspected my own pussy would have looked much the same.

Gemma held nothing back, and Chloe's bottom danced under the sting of each backhanded swipe of the belt. It did not wobble quite so much as Gemma's, being of firmer constitution, but it was no less entertaining for all that. Chloe was still panting when I ran my fingers over the bands left by the leather. Gently, I lifted her to her feet. Gemma handed her the belt.

Now Kirsty was placed in position. I watched with pursed lips and aching pussy as her globes were exposed. The gusset of her panty was clearly damp and I could not resist sampling her flavour with the tip of my finger.

Chloe performed her beating, displaying her growing expertise at the discipline of discipline; it was so pleasing to see all three girls applying each and every stroke so earnestly. I nearly died from the enjoyment of watching Kirsty's pure white flesh ripple and redden and her cries of lusty anguish were the perfect musical accompaniment.

As the last lash was laid, I applauded the girls for taking and giving their punishments so well – although we all knew that there was more to be done.

'Assume the position again, Gemma,' I said. 'I trust, after this lacing, I can rely on you to follow the directions I give you about your sexual activity?'

'Yes, Ms McKnight,' Gemma assented, most solemnly I thought.

Her pink and tender rear was exposed and ready but, as I raised the belt, I had a change of heart: her attitude had persuaded me that she had been convinced and was ready for change.

I let the belt fall on to the sofa cushion with a loud slap. Surprised, Gemma gasped and turned to face me, a questioning look on her face.

'Let us call it a suspended sentence. I expect to see changes around here, or the remaining six strokes will find their mark.'

Thirteen

The past day or two had witnessed a sea change in my outlook on things. Boundaries had been defined, thoughts and feelings crystallised, ambiguities banished. I had every confidence that Marty's next visit to the casino would not bear the sweet fruit he was used to plucking, and that went for his friend too.

His friend? Spank me sideways! I had completely forgotten about him, and in the mêlée of the meeting with the girls yesterday I had neglected to ask them who he was. To think, I had been fantasising recently about being a secret agent's assistant: I would have been next to useless, distracted from my mission by the sight of freshly flogged flesh. I picked up the phone.

'Hello?'

'Hello, Gemma, angel. It is I.'

'Ms McKnight. How can I help?'

'I meant to ask you something yesterday but forgot.'

'I am sure you didn't forget, Ms McKnight. Perhaps you judged that yesterday was not the right time.' After her day of rebellion, Miss Jarvie seemed to have returned to a submissive mode, and I liked it.

'Yes, yes, perhaps I did,' I agreed, accepting her complimentary version of events. 'I was wondering who was the second fellow who left with you in the car, the afternoon before last?'

'Oh, him. That's Alex Dougall – he works at the gym with Marty.'

I had surmised that he had some connection with the establishment as he had an exceptionally lithe and athletic body for someone past forty.

'What does he do there?' I asked. 'Did he mention at all?'

'Yes, Ms McKnight. He owns the other half of it.'

'The other half?'

'The half that Marty does not own.'

I raised my eyebrows.

'Thank you, Gemma.'

So, Marty and Alex were partners in business as well as crime: running their fitness concern by day and no doubt hunting as a pair for fresh, fit, nubile pussy to sink their teeth into by night. Their laddish behaviour filled the Mistress in me with spite, even though, or perhaps because, I myself had been complicit in Marty's pursuit of carnal conquest. My focus was clear: I would find Marty's fetish, his weakness, and exploit it fully. His next hunting trip to the casino would not be successful – yesterday's meeting had seen to that. I would be keeping my eye out for him, and be ready to pounce on his poor rejected soul when it happened. I picked up the phone again, but as I dialled there was a knock on the door.

'Who is it?'

'It is Gordon, Ms McKnight.'

'Come in.'

Gordon entered tentatively. I put the phone back down.

'Are you on the door today?' I asked him.

'Yes, Ms McKnight.'

'Good, I was just about to phone you. I need you

187

to watch for someone at the door for me today. You know Marty from the gymnasium across the street?'

Gordon nodded.

'Please alert me if he attends the casino today, and, if he does, make sure he is held up for a few minutes.'

'Yes, Ms McKnight.' He nodded again.

'Now what can I do for you?'

'It's about yesterday afternoon, Ms McKnight.'

'Yes. I hope you are not too embarrassed about what I made you do in front of the girls?'

'That's the exact thing. I am. I am, and I like it, Ms McKnight. I came to ask if it could be done again.'

I leapt with joy inside; my actions appeared to have had the happy side-effect of freeing another mind – and enslaving a soul.

'You have never been dominated and humiliated in that way before?'

'No, Ms McKnight.'

'Gordon, if we are not in company, you must now call me Mistress.'

'Yes, Mistress,' he said, his eyes falling automatically to the floor.

'Report to me after work every night before you go home. If I am not busy, then I may take you down to The Cellar to explore this part of you. For now, you are dismissed.'

'Thank you, Mistress.'

I smiled a smug, self-satisfied smile; if it was as easy as this to fish a man or boy in to domination and humiliation, then ensnaring Marty, and even his friend, should not be difficult.

No sooner had Gordon left than Chloe entered, very excited indeed and holding Gemma's key to The Cellar. I knew it must be important as she had risked a spanking by not knocking.

'Ms McKnight! You'll never guess,' she blurted. Mr and Mrs Finlay have come in – both – and are asking for a session with me, you know, joint!'

'A joint session? Surely not?' I had, of course, hoped for such a result from this couple, but never really believed that it would happen. Could my machinations truly bear such fruit?

'It's true, Ms McKnight.'

'What did they ask for?'

'They asked for me, I presume because I saw Mr Finlay before. When I arrived, Mrs Finlay did all the talking. They asked that I show her a session and teach her how to join in or do this for herself.'

'This is tremendous! Are you confident enough to run this by yourself?'

'Och, aye, no problem!' she answered positively.

'Then I look forward to reading your report,' I said. I shared her confidence in her ability to make this one of the most remarkable sessions The Cellar has ever witnessed, and I had no qualms about letting her run it.

Alone with my thoughts again, I gave a satisfied sigh.

It was into the afternoon, around three o'clock, before Gordon relayed the message to me that Marty was at the door. I guessed that Marty had calculated this to be the best time to talk to a girl at her table – it gave him an hour to get her interested and propositioned before whisking her away at the shift-change.

I appeared in the foyer and found Gordon scrutinising the items in Marty's wallet, taking at least thirty seconds on each card before carefully inserting it back into the small leather case. When he had finished, he led Marty to the side for a search.

189

'You've not needed to search me before,' commented Marty.

'I'm sorry, sir, it's new anti-money-laundering regulations,' lied Gordon.

I approached to interrupt. 'Thank you, Gordon, I'll conduct the search of this guest.

'Of course, Ms McKnight,' said Gordon, withdrawing to deal with the next, rather impatient-looking, customer.

A look of relief came over Marty's face; he was glad to see me, and obviously assumed that the search was over.

'Hold your arms out,' I said to him. I did not say 'please', which marked my first dominant act over him. He did not respond well.

'What? You're actually going to search me?' He was incredulous, but not angry.

It can take a little time for a gentleman to catch on that something said to them is a command, especially when he has not yet been told that he is a slave.

'Hold your arms out,' I repeated.

He released a quiet and very nasal sigh and complied. He looked at me ruefully.

'Look straight ahead,' I told him.

His face showed me that he was puzzled indeed by the command but I knew I had made the first breakthrough, forged the first link in his chain of bondage, when he did as I ordered.

I felt along his muscular arms and around his broad torso, my hands stroking him seductively; the more I aroused and titillated him, the more his burgeoning loins would short-circuit his common sense, causing him to make decisions that a cold observer might find questionable, even unbelievable.

'Turn around and lean against the wall,' I said.

Marty's eyes flicked at the other customers who were signing in to the casino and glancing at him as they filed by. The second link in the chain of his bondage was forged as he tasted his first small dose of humiliation. His eyes flicked once more to mine, as he tried to see in me the sex-crazed nymph who masturbated so flagrantly for him in the window and took his penis so eagerly in the gymnasium. But she was no longer here. He saw only blue ice in my brown eyes.

'Look straight ahead, not at me,' I told him

There was another look of puzzlement, but he obeyed, averting his eyes from mine and turning to lean against the wall.

'Bend over more. Legs apart.'

He shuffled away from the wall a little and inched his feet a little further apart. I strode over and kicked them apart with my heeled shoes, striking him firmly but not violently on the side of the calf. He took the hint, opening his legs wide, now at the limit of his comfort.

I ran my hands up each calf, looking for the concealed weapon that I knew full well was neither there nor anywhere on his person. Then my hands administered the same cruel, sweet touch to his thighs, inside and out, running over his crotch for a fleeting moment. He looked over his shoulder.

'Look straight ahead,' I told him again.

This time he turned back to face the wall without pause or question. As a reward, or perhaps as further torture, I repeated the frisking of his legs and crotch. His cock would be tingling now, I was sure.

'Stand.' I said.

He did so, but paused for more than a moment before turning away from the wall, as he considered if he should wait for my order to turn. A very good sign.

'Thank you. You may proceed,' I said.

191

He entered the gaming floor without a word or gesture, and a warmth grew inside my torso, causing my nipples to tighten.

'That,' I said under my breath, 'went extremely well.'

I returned to the balcony overlooking the gambling area and watched Marty as Hera watched her husband's little clay pawns from atop Olympus. Apparently unfazed by my treatment of him at the entrance, he continued where he felt he had left off before, choosing a girl at one of the tables and flirting with her in his pseudo-shy way. It was Nhyla he had chosen today. Although Nhyla was not present at the dressing-down of the three girls from the picnic, I prayed that word had reached her about its outcome.

She was receptive at first, smiling and simpering a little in his direction and causing me flutters of dread that this swaggering beefcake would notch another conquest within my walls, but she was unresponsive to any further suggestion and the smiling and the simpering were all Marty got. After a dozen or so hands, he appeared to lose heart and, after picking up his chips, moved to another table.

Kirsty was running the roulette wheel that Marty homed in on next. He was no doubt hoping to cash in on the familiarity between them, and perhaps looking for the comfort of some safe ground after his rejection by Nhyla, but my dread grew to smugness when he met the same reception at Kirsty's table.

Marty had now spent the best part of an hour in the casino (losing a fair proportion of his chips, I am pleased to say) with no joy, and now the girls were preparing for a shift-change; he had missed his chance of a four o'clock rendezvous. I saw him rub his chin and look around, as though searching for inspiration. His eyes lit on mine, up above him. I folded my arms and looked down on him as a genie looks down on a mere mortal. His discomfort increased, causing him to turn away and wander to another table. I made my way down.

'Come with me, Marty. I think I can help you with what you are looking for,' I said, leaning in behind him, breathing softly in his ear. No sooner said, I turned away and walked towards the staff-area door. I did not look back, since it would have appeared weak to check that my instruction had been obeyed; I simply walked, confident that my tone was authoritative enough and that the beacon of my swaying arse would draw him like a moth to a campfire.

I opened the door, turning for the first time since I had spoken. He was following – behind me by some ten yards, but following. Unsurprisingly the turmoil within him had taken some seconds to resolve, and he had not immediately acted upon my instructions. Ultimately, however, he had chosen obedience. He stepped through the door as I waited for him, but this time he did not meet my gaze.

'You will no longer find what you have been looking for at The Paddle-Boat,' I said to him sternly as I closed the door behind me. 'This is a place where male sexuality is not self-serving, and if you wish to continue fraternising with my croupiers it must be on my terms. The girls have been told, and know what is expected. That is the reason for your fruitless hour.'

His eyes met mine again as he replied. 'Terms? What do you mean, terms?'

The back of my hand swept through the air and smacked his face, following through in a full arc.

'Do not look me in the eye,' I snapped.

It was the moment of truth. If my curt superiority during the door-search had not awoken Marty's natural need for domination, then he would not yet have come to terms with the true meaning of my behaviour. To him my blow would be an assault, and he would protest robustly, perhaps even laying his strong hands upon me to prevent another blow before pushing me aside and leaving in a rage. I felt like the lion-tamer who enters the cage unprotected for the first time, knowing that the beast he faces is physically stronger and placing all his faith in his power to control it.

On the other hand, if my manner had awoken stirrings in him, feelings and excitement such as simple sexual conquest had never given him, his need for more would overpower his pride, and he would submit.

He hung his head. 'What are your terms, Madam?' he asked.

'Mistress,' I corrected.

'Mistress.'

'Obedience, submission and monetary tribute for all forms of private contact with myself or any of the croupiers. If the superficial male needs to be in the presence of beauty, he must pay for the privilege, do you not agree?'

'I do, Mistress.'

'One hundred and fifty pounds,' I said.

Marty looked up at me in surprise and then remembered himself and quickly returned his gaze to the floor.

'Mistress?' he said.

'Pay me one hundred and fifty pounds now.'

Marty had no idea, of course, what he was paying for. Was I going to offer some service to him for this money? Was he indeed paying this extortionate price just for our conversation? He would not know until after he had paid – that was all part of the thrill of his submission. He handed me ten casino chips and one hundred pounds in notes. The gesture rubber-stamped his acceptance of his inferiority and I felt that some action was needed to mark the moment. Calmly and coldly I spat in his face.

'Loser,' I said. 'Follow me.'

'Yes, Mistress.'

I paused for a moment's thought. The Cellar was still occupied by Mistress Chloe and Mr and Mrs Finlay, and our presence might ruin their fantasy. We had never had the place double-booked like this before. I concluded that it was more than big enough to accommodate two sessions, provided they were not in the same room.

As we made our way down the stairs, the echoes of distant stern female voices rattled on the walls, which must have added curiosity to Marty's feelings of trepidation as he followed me to The Wheel. I saw the two Mistresses and the (un)fortunate Mr Finlay playing in The Nursery. Marty would have heard them, but he had his head bowed – proving what a fast-learning slave he was – and would not have seen the activity in the chamber.

'Kneel,' I said.

He knelt.

'In The Cellar of The Paddle-Boat, we ask our slaves to submit to the whims of chance – how else would a casino operate? Do you submit your fate to The Wheel?' There really was not much of a choice for him, but ceremony was an important part of this experience.

'I do, Mistress.'

I spun The Wheel and flicked the black ball around in the opposite direction. It rested in the section marked 'The Office'.

'Come, we will go to The Office area. I walk, you crawl.'

What would I have done if The Wheel, in its wisdom, had chosen The Nursery, which was already occupied? Why, I would have chosen one myself and pretended that The Wheel had decided. I am, after all, The Mistress.

Our Office is furnished with office cast-offs like an old computer, two old desks and some chairs, but we keep them in good condition and it certainly has the right feel for the fantasies that tend to be requested in there: humiliation, cruel lady boss, blackmail, financial domination, tease and denial. I had had a partition put into this room, inside which is the Top's office; the Bottom sits out at the older desk, on the older chair, with the old computer, but he can see the Top's legs through a window in the partition door.

One advantage of an Office fantasy is that I am already dressed for it: I *am* an Office tease, I dress and act like one outside this room, so no change is required.

'Normally I would play an elaborate fantasy in this room, one of exploitation and harassment,' I said as I swung my arse over to the desk and perched it on the corner, extending my legs towards him. He stopped crawling, kneeling only a few inches away from the tip of my stiletto, my legs stretching upwards like a mountain path as he looked upon me. He was nervous now and his mouth was dry; he licked his lips. I laughed.

'I think you would be the office geek, the pervert who stares at the legs of his female colleagues all morning then wanks in the gents' at lunchtime,' I told him.

He enjoyed the fantasy; his eyes closed as he took an excited breath at the thought.

'Gradually, though, your cruel colleagues catch on to your little habit and taunt you deliberately, dangling their shoes absent-mindedly and smoothing their nylons when they know you are watching out of the corner of your eye. Would that send you wild? Would that make your cock tingle all day?'

I dangled my own shoe on the tip of my left foot as I spoke.

'Yes, Mistress,' he answered, breathing deeply through flared nostrils as he imagined the scenario and watched my stockinged foot.

'And would you wank in the toilets after lunch, even though you knew it was common knowledge what you were up to?'

'Yes, Mistress.' He swallowed, and once more licked his lips.

'Or would that make it better for you I wonder? Knowing that every girl you were thinking about was outside at her desk smirking to herself at what a loser you were? Yes, it would, I know it would. And they would all start to compete to be the one, the one who sends you over the edge, the one whose cute backside or shapely calf sends you bent double into the cubicle.'

He groaned. 'Yes, Mistress.'

His trousers now contained an uncomfortable bulge, I noticed. I stood up and stretched out my foot, pressing the sole of my shoe to the prominence and rubbing it slightly.

'Then you would start a ritual of coming out holding the tissue containing your slime and placing it in the wastepaper basket of the girl you were thinking about. It would be just for your own thrill at first, to give you one last frisson of shame as you passed her desk and dropped off your tribute, but eventually the girls would begin to catch on, and watch eagerly to see if they were the one that you'd been jerking yourself to today. Oh! How they would compete, counting up their tissues at the end of the day and acting so jealously when the winner was announced. You know how girls are.'

He was fidgeting with frustration as the story turned him on. I upped the ante.

'Then one day your uncompromising boss, Ms McKnight, can be seen through the door in her office, dangling her shiny black shoe, flexing the sexiest silk-covered ankle you have ever leered at. She uncrosses and crosses her legs and, as you see the sheen on her stockings disappear into the shadows between her legs, your little cocky springs to attention. You rush to the toilets and let your silly-looking appendage spring forth, pumping it as if you were shaking a champagne bottle and soon the foam sprays over your hands and trousers as you savour the vision of Ms McKnight's form, so fresh in your mind.'

I reached down to unzip Marty's trousers and popped the button to open them. His stiff erection, that I had known so intimately before, leapt for freedom and he leant back in his kneeling position, displaying it to me as a totem of his devotion. I wanked it softly and delicately with spidery fingers.

'You wipe yourself with another tissue,' I whispered, 'and you do your trousers back up. Your cheeks are burning with the combination of the orgasmic glow and the shame of your action. Clutching the tissue, you shuffle to her office and, slipping through the half-open door, you complete your duty by dropping the tissue into her wastepaper basket. She looks up and scowls at you. Can you guess why?' I asked, my hands still feathering over his cock.

'No, Mistress.'

'Because she does not know about the competition, Marty. She bellows at you: "What the hell are you doing in here? Can you not use your own bin?" and you stutter a reply: "I thought . . . thought you knew . . . The oth . . . other girls, Ms McKnight . . ."

'She picks up the bin. "What about the other girls?" she demands and steps out into the main office, holding up the bin for all to see. "Can anyone explain why this loser just came into my office to put a used tissue in my bin?" she says. There is silence for a moment, and Kirsty, the nearest girl, the girl you wanked your dirty little penis to yesterday . . .'

I gave his cock a hard squeeze here, before continuing again with the light wanking.

'. . . explains *everything* to Ms McKnight. She glares at you with her obsidian eyes. "Get in my office," she commands.'

I stopped playing with his cock and stood up. He was gasping now, his eyes half-closed like a customer in an opium den, almost in a trance. I waited until he was looking up at me once again, and when he did his eyes widened and begged for more of this fantasy.

'Get in my office,' I commanded.

Fourteen

Marty crawled through the partition door into the office, his erect member rocking from side to side. I followed, closing the door, and sat on the desk in front of him.

'This sort of behaviour is not acceptable in a respectable office, Marty. I am going to have to think seriously about disciplinary procedures. Is there anything you can say in your defence?'

'No, Mistress.'

'Look, your cock is erect even now – have you no control, you loser?'

'No, Mistress.'

'I am sorry but I cannot tolerate regular masturbation on these premises like this, I am going to have to impose a fine of fifty pounds, payable now,' I pronounced, folding my arms.

It took a few seconds before Marty realised I meant him to pay me fifty pounds from his own pocket.

'You may wank yourself while you pay me, if it thrills you.'

Marty's look of disbelief was a picture, but the logic subroutines in the male psyche are bypassed when an erection is present and, to my huge excitement, he wanked his cock vigorously as he reached into his pocket with his left hand and handed me three notes, totalling fifty pounds. The act excited him. Indeed, the whole session had excited him. I could tell just by looking he had never before experienced sexual pleasure this intensely.

I would have let any ordinary client come at this point, but I wanted to exploit Marty further while his mind raced with lust and the addictive rush of sexual humiliation.

'Do not come just yet,' I said coldly. 'Have you enjoyed your session with me, Loser?'

'Yes, Mistress,' he replied, still making monkey-like 'ook' sounds as he jerked himelf.

'You would like to come to The Cellar with me again?'

'Ohhh, yes, Mistress.'

'How does the idea of unlimited sessions for a month sound?' I was tantalising him with something I knew he wanted with every fibre of his soul. I hoped he would not come too soon and break the spell.

'Oh, God, yes, Mistress, please!'

'One thousand pounds?'

His wanking quickened slightly at the mention of the amount.

'Yes, Mistress.'

'And what about after that, a year's supply of sessions? Would that interest a loser like you?'

'Ohhhhhhh, yes.'

'That represents a lot of my time. Shall we agree a more substantial investment? How about five per cent of the health club?'

His eyes widened as he contemplated the proposal. A crisis was boiling away inside him as the nervous excitement sent pleasure coursing through his whole body. I watched his dribbling cock and his quickening hand, hoping that he would not find release before he could agree.

The words 'Yes, Mistress' finally crawled out of his throat followed by a huge groan of pleasure.

'Of course, I could be very generous indeed, Marty. After that year was up, I could offer you a lifetime of sessions with me – how does that grab you? We could play in each of the rooms here: The White Room, The School Room, The Dungeon, three, four, five times a week, fulfilling whatever fantasy comes into your head, Marty dear. I would only ask a further twenty-one per cent share in your gymnasium. Think about the value of that, though, against the value of maybe two hundred sessions a year for the next twenty, thirty, forty years.'

I chuckled inside. I am a woman of my word and would make good on any arrangement we agreed, but I knew very well how unlikely it was that Marty would still know me in even a decade, let alone the scores of years I was promising him. I was relying on his heightened state to cloud his vision.

The decision raged like a tornado inside him; if the previous one had been a struggle this was causing an internal tumult of no small proportion. But the thought of agreeing, and thereby submitting to me in such a real and affirming way, turned him on, accelerating his wrist and causing him to growl like an excited dog. Only the thoughts of the consequences held him back, as the last sensible part of him fought the yearning. But it was a losing battle.

'Yes, Mistress, I agree!' The words strained out of him through clenched teeth as the thrill of giving in pounded through his loins and sent a fountain of semen flying into the air. Literally spent, he flopped back from his kneeling position on to his bared arse and then toppled on to the floor, still slowly pumping his cock, desperate to coax every ampere of pleasure through it.

I went to the desk drawer, where a supply of tissues is kept, and threw the packet down to him.

'Clean yourself,' I told him. I wondered if any pangs of regret had yet begun to form inside him. It did not matter, for I knew they would soon disappear when his testicles had once again recharged themselves.

'Bring the paperwork in tomorrow,' I said, 'and perhaps we'll have time for another session.'

The following morning I arrived at my usual time to find young Gordon waiting outside my office with his finest puppy-dog face on.

'Good morning, Gordon,' I said.

'Good morning, Ms McKnight,' he replied. 'I came by last night like you said, but I am afraid you weren't here,' he added deferentially.

'Yes, Gordon, I was otherwise disposed with an important client.' I made no apology for my lack of availability. 'Do come back tonight and see if I am available.'

Gordon nodded and withdrew. I am sure he had duties at the door or bar that he was neglecting. It does well for one learning humiliation to be shunned by a woman at first: it makes them more hungry.

Flushed with my incredible success with Marty, I had clean forgotten about Chloe's simultaneous session in The Nursery, so it was a pleasant surprise to be reminded by the presence of a report lying on my desk as I walked in. I would read that later, but for now I had work to do: all evening, in between trying on new lingerie with my curtains open or sitting in my armchair and rubbing my clit as I listened to music, I devoted a lot of thought to Marty, his partner Alex and the grand plan, and concluded that the time was right to move on to this Alex character.

I knew little about him, and had never seen him in the casino as a customer, so the problem facing me was how to lure him in. I say problem, but in truth, with so many alluring sirens at my disposal, it was hardly that. My course was clear: send one of the girls he already knew, Kirsty, Gemma or Chloe, over to the gymnasium to entice him into a session. Once he was in my domain, I could work my charms on him. I picked up the phone and gave Gemma another summons.

'Morning, Ms McKnight,' she said breezily as she stepped in.

'Gemma, I have an extraordinary task for you.'

Gemma immediately knew the significance of the word 'extraordinary', which I used before with her to mean that the request is not related to the running of the casino but rather a direct service for me, as her Mistress. She knelt before my desk, her head bowed.

'What is your bidding, my Mistress?'

'I need you to spend some time in the gym across the street, Gemma, with the aim of luring Alex Dougall to The Cellar. You know him better than I, and I want you to find some way of dominating and titillating him that will bring him crawling back for more. Can you complete the task?'

'Yes, Mistress.'

'This is a very important task, Gemma. Failure will mean suspension from the rack and six strokes of the cat.'

'Yes, Mistress.'

'I appreciate that I have made recent comments on the matter of giving your body to outsiders, but where this is done under my orders, and to ensnare a slave, it is acceptable. There are no boundaries – even if bringing him here means letting six of his friends squirt their gloop into your puckered little anus, you are to comply, do you understand?'

'Yes, Mistress.'

'Good. You have four days. You may work half-hours at the casino until your task is completed. Go.'

Gemma rose to her feet, bowed her head and skipped prettily out of the room. I shut the door behind her and went to my desk, picking up Chloe's report:

Croupier: Chloe McIntyre
Date: Friday 25th June
Client: Mr and Mrs Finlay

My previous report for a session was written in some nervousness, Ms McKnight, but this occasion filled me with such enthusiasm that I felt only excitement. I fully appreciate the unusual nature of the session; it is not often we are asked to perform such a sacred task – that is to say, bringing two loving people closer together.

There was only the very minimum of conversation on our way down to The Cellar. I think Mr and Mrs Finlay were a wee bit fearful of what was to come – Mrs Finlay especially, since she would have had no idea what to expect. Mr Finlay, we suspect, has acted his natural part in many a session, although even he had never done one with his wife present!

We stopped at The Wheel, and I turned to ask: 'Have you a particular session in mind?' On his first visit, if you remember, Mr Finlay had a very definite idea of the session he was looking for and chose not to use The Wheel on that occasion. This time was not much different.

'Jeffrey and I are looking to play in The School Room or The Nursery,' replied Mrs Finlay.

'Shall we let The Wheel decide between the two?' I suggested, and reached over to spin it. 'Black for The School Room and red for The Nursery.'

The black ball danced around the slowing wheel and came to rest in a red segment.

'The Nursery.' I smiled. 'Have you anything in mind for The Nursery, Mr Finlay,' I asked, 'or would you like me to dream something up for you?'

'Please run the session as you see fit, knowing what you do of me already,' he answered.

We made our way to the 'Pink Room'. I showed them around pointing out the oversize cot, the toys and teddies, the baby and toddler clothing available and the nappy-changing facilities.

'Where did you get all this?' Mrs Finlay asked incredulously. She was particularly aghast at the idea of the outsize nappies and the babygros in adult sizes.

'Oh, you can usually find a specialist for anything if you know where to look, Mrs Finlay, and, if I can tell you one thing about Ms McKnight, it's that she knows where to look.'

She shook her head, I seem to recall.

'May I suggest that we play the parts of two nannies, Mrs Finlay, and we give your husband some tough but motherly love.'

They nodded bashfully, the pair of them still unsure of themselves in this new environment. I could see I was going to have to take the lead with them both, even though Mrs Finlay was officially one of the 'Tops' in this scene, she was perhaps going to need as much instruction as the little baby girl we would be dominating.

'From now, Mr Finlay, you are Wendy. I expect you to look and sound like a wee lassie. And you are to address us both as Matron. Now remove your clothes and kneel.'

'Yes, Matron,' Mr Finlay said in a pathetic attempt at a girl's voice.

'Useless,' I said. 'I expect it to be more girly by the end of the session. Don't you agree, Matron?'

Mrs Finlay looked a little unsure at the way I had suddenly, and subtly, brought her into the conversation, and hesitated before she answered, but I am glad to report that she did respond, and in character, and the ice was broken.

'Yes, I certainly do, Matron. Perhaps once we have her dressed she will feel more girly.' She glanced at me quizzically while her husband undressed in front of us, looking for some indication as to how she was doing. I put a discreet thumb up to show that she had done well.

I went over to the pink and blue wardrobe, where the makeover things are kept, and fetched a curly brown wig, a brown eyebrow pencil, rouge, some subtle lipstick and two pink ribbons. I did not think Mr Finlay's Wendy would want to be a baby; my previous session with him suggested a definite penchant for girly-ness rather than the more neutral adult-baby option.

Wendy had now stripped and was kneeling on the floor waiting for 'her' humiliation. I handed the things to Mrs Finlay.

'Matron, would you get Wendy looking nice and pretty today? Start with her hair – put it in ribbons while I do her face.'

We set to work on Wendy, with Mrs Finlay affixing the wig and tying it into pigtails, using the pink ribbons I had found. She knew what she was doing, tying off two perfect loops on the bows. I gave Wendy some freckles using the brown pencil, and applied the pale-red lipstick to Wendy's lips.

'She will look a very pretty little girl today,' I cooed. 'Tell me, Matron, has Wendy been a good little girl recently?'

I winked at Mrs Finlay, hoping she would understand.

'No, she hasn't,' she replied, getting the right idea.

'Oh dear, I hope that doesn't mean we're going to have to punish her.'

Mrs Finlay thought for just a second before replying.

'Oh, I'm afraid I think it does.'

'Do you think a spanking over the knee will suffice?'

Mrs Finlay seemed surprised that such an activity was a possibility; perhaps it had not dawned on her that the activities we would take part in would be appropriate to the costume and surroundings, or perhaps she was still getting used to the whole idea.

'I think so, Matron,' she answered.

'Would you like to finish Wendy's face, Matron?' I asked.

'Yes, of course,' she replied, picking up the rouge from me.

Soon Wendy's face and hair were finished and we made her look at herself in a handheld mirror. The sight of the girly hair and freckles certainly made that cock twitch.

'Time for some knickers, Matron,' I said, pointing to the pink and sky-blue chest of drawers in the corner, next to the cot. I was not going to take any further part if I could help it; I hoped that Mrs Finlay would be able to continue on her own, with my occasional guidance.

Mrs Finlay opened the top drawer and selected a very frilly pair of adult-sized white knickers for her Wendy to don. She held them up to me for approval.

'I think Wendy needs some help with putting them on, Matron,' I said helpfully.

Mrs Finlay stepped over to her husband.

'Stand up, Wendy,' she said.

Wendy stood and Mrs Finlay placed the knickers on the floor in front of her.

'Step into the knickers.'

Wendy put her feet through the holes and Mrs Finlay pulled the frilly underwear right up to Wendy's his crotch, almost lifting her off the floor, so tightly did she pull them into place.

'There.'

'Don't forget to tell her how girly and pretty she looks, Matron,' I prompted.

Mrs Finlay looked unsure what to say, and so I chipped in with a suggestion.

'Wendy, you do look awfully dainty in those knickers,' I said. 'Let's see how you look with a pretty dress over them.'

I pointed to the wardrobe for Mrs Finlay, who went over to pick out a dress. Unsurprisingly she picked out the pink dress with the puffy sleeves and frilly hem – it's easily the best dress in that wardrobe, Ms McKnight.

I did not need to instruct her what to do next – she was clearly getting the idea. Indeed, she was getting the idea very well and I could not hide my surprise when, without prompting from me, she said, 'Yes, let's get this nice pretty dress on you and see what a sweet little girl you make, Wendy.'

I clapped twice. 'Well done, Matron.'

Wendy was soon in her dress and I helped out again by pointing to the next drawer down and then to the bottom of the wardrobe.

'Socks, and shoes,' I said.

Mrs Finlay picked out a pair of humiliating knee-length virgin socks from the drawer and a pair of black Oxford pumps from the wardrobe, after deciding that the alternative (a pair of pink sandals) did not have enough of a heel.

The effect was finished and I pointed to the full-length mirror inside the wardrobe door.

'This way, Wendy, so you can see what a pretty little girly you are,' Mrs Finlay said to her feminised husband as she positioned him in front of the glass.

'Do a curtsy for us, Wendy,' I requested.

'Yes, Matron,' said Wendy in a voice perhaps a little bit more girly than before, but not much. She did the best curtsy that I would have expected any person to manage at their first attempt in unfamiliar heels, but I was not in the mood to give her any credit for his efforts – she was here for humiliation, after all.

'Oh, dear, that's not very good. I think Matron Elizabeth will have to get you working on that at home before you come back to The Nursery again,' I said, referring of course to Mrs Finlay. 'Shall we see if you're any better at skipping like a girly?'

Mrs Finlay closed the wardrobe door and gestured across the room. 'Yes, Wendy, show us how you skip across the room like a wee sissy.' Again I gave Mrs Finlay a discreet gesture to show that I approved.

Wendy took a quick gasp to steel herself against the humiliation she was feeling and then did her best to skip across the room and back. It was garbage.

'Oh, dear me, no,' I said. 'Do it again properly.'

Wendy tried again. This time things were much improved – I think maybe he was getting used to the pumps.

'What did you think of that, Matron?' I asked.

'Better, but I still think she needs to be more fairy-like,' Mrs Finlay replied.

So we made Wendy go again. By the time he returned this time, I could definitely make out a bulge in her frilly knickers.

'Better again, Matron Elizabeth, but I still think you're going to have to work on it at home. Be strict:

if she shows no improvement, then make sure she is spanked until she does.'

'Yes, Matron Chloe. Should we administer a spanking today?'

'Yes, I think we should – right now, in fact.'

I took a seat in the pink and yellow chair and smoothed down my black uniform skirt. I did my best to look prim and proper, just as a nanny would, with my shoes flat on the floor. I straightened my back and held my head high and aloof.

'Over my knee, Wendy, you pathetic little girl,' I snapped.

Wendy came over shyly and bent over my lap with her knees and hands on the floor either side of me. It was obviously Wendy's first taste of over the knee punishment, as she seemed unaware of the very important aspect that you taught me, Ms McKnight: the full weight of the naughty girl or boy should be on the Mistress's knee.

'Hands and knees off the floor, you silly little girl,' I said with disdain.

Wendy complied.

'Matron Elizabeth, would you pull down the wee lassie's knickers for me?' I said, knowing it would be especially humiliating for Wendy to have her wife bare that arse for me.

Mrs Finlay lifted the ruffled hem of the dress up and pulled the white, flouncy knickers down, exposing two ripe and ready cheeks. I felt Wendy's erect cock tickle me under my right leg as it stood to attention. I rubbed the bared buttocks with my open hand and felt the penis twitch again under my leg; it was quite exciting.

I made the first slap, short and sharp, and resumed my circular caressing.

'Naughty girl,' I whispered and slapped her again, harder and louder. I noticed the wig-covered head bob and felt that cock twitch in response. Again I softly rubbed the reddening area with my hand to sensitise it.

It was time for a more stringent spanking now and I made three hard smacks across that cleavage causing Wendy to give a girly gasp and her white globes to glow bright pink in the shape of my hand.

I caressed the area again, and then, judging when the time was right, I delivered a volley of five or six loud smacks one after the other. Under my leg, I felt the cock tickle my nylon-covered thigh at least three times as it twitched in response.

I do not know if either of us can imagine the humiliation of being dressed as a wee girly and spanked over an attractive woman's knee in front of one's wife, but whatever Wendy was feeling it was certainly doing the trick for that excited cock.

It was time for Mrs Finlay to have a go. I gave Wendy a light tap on the buttock.

'Stand up,' I said.

Wendy stood up, allowing the dress to fall down and cover her modesty. The knickers remained around her legs, so that the elevated cock lifted the dress up at the front. She did look a silly little horny girl.

I stood up.

'Matron Elizabeth, would you like to sit down and continue the spanking?'

'Why, yes, I would,' she answered enthusiastically, sitting on the chair and adjusting the creases in her skirt ready for Wendy to drape herself over it. When she was ready, she peered over her glasses (which I was rather jealous about, because they really lend an authentic nanny-like look to a woman) at Wendy and patted her lap to signify she was to mount.

Wendy complied, taking position in the right manner and without need for correction this time.

Mrs Finlay lifted the dress to expose once more those pink buttocks. The rawness was fading, which was a shame, but I was sure Mrs Finlay would soon bring it back. She caressed the buttocks in the same way I had shown her, teasing and sensitising the area before delivering the slap. I was amazed at how Mrs Finlay savoured the spanking, caressing the buttocks between each blow, which was delivered suddenly and without warning. It was a joy to watch and I felt my pussy moisten quite markedly. If Gemma were watching, she would have been wanking herself by now, I think!

Mrs Finlay was intense, putting all her attention into delivering discipline to her sissy husband. After about a dozen smacks the buttocks were almost red, but I wanted them redder.

'Deliver another twelve, Matron – it's always best to finish with a flurry, I think.'

Mrs Finlay was most pleased to hear my suggestion and really went to town on Wendy's bottom, with twelve fast, hard and loud smacks that really brought out a lovely magenta shade on the skin. You may have heard them being applied, Ms McKnight, as I noticed you and, to my surprise, Marty coming into The Cellar at this time.

Remembering the way I had milked Wendy's cock in our previous session, I reached between her legs and did the same again to her as she bent over her wife's knee. Wendy's moans gave away her enjoyment and soon Mrs Finlay was spanking her arse in response to every whimper. There are few men who can resist that sort of arousing treatment and I'm surprised that Wendy lasted as long as she did before squirting a dribbly but substantial load on to The Nursery's floor.

Wendy stood up, red-faced and red-arsed.

'Good girl. Now clean yourself up, get dressed, tidy the playroom and come upstairs. Mrs Finlay and I will be in the bar enjoying a coffee, waiting for you,' I said.

We left Mr Finlay to transform herself from Wendy back to Mr Finlay unsupervised. I hope she was a good little girl in our absence. Mrs Finlay was delighted with how it went, confessing to me over coffee that, although she was terrified on arrival, we had opened her eyes and quite possibly changed the lives of them both for ever. I told her you would be pleased to hear this!

Indeed I was. I was over the moon, and filled with a most satisfying joy. To think that The Paddle-Boat had achieved such a wondrous thing for two loving people was beyond my wildest dreams for the establishment and I hope that I would one day be given the opportunity to repeat the feat for another of Scotland's repressed population. I left my office with the sole intent of finding Chloe and giving her the wettest, slurpiest, horniest kiss of congratulations.

Fifteen

'Where's Gemma?' I asked. It was the following afternoon and I stepped into the staff common room wearing my red skirt suit and matching heels. Slim, chestnut-haired Maureen and platinum blonde Amber were there, relaxing on their break. Amber shrugged.

'Search me!' she answered in her loud, strident manner.

I would have liked to take her up on that offer, but doubted that I would find Gemma upon Amber's saucy little person, and strongly feared that I might be sidetracked from my goal of finding Gemma if I did conduct such a search.

Maureen, delicate Maureen, gave a more considered response.

'She said she had half-days until Wednesday,' she ventured.

'Oh, yes. Right you are.' I smiled, suddenly realising that the very reason I wanted to see her was the very reason why it was proving difficult to find her.

I reasoned that, as Gemma had had two afternoons and one evening to track her prey, she would at least be stalking him by now. It was therefore perfectly reasonable for me to go looking for her to see how she was getting on.

I crossed the street in the broken afternoon sun that you have to get used to in this part of the world and entered the health club. I was stopped at the gymnasium reception by a lean blond youth with athletic shoulders.

'Could I see your membership, please, Miss?'

I felt a bit ambivalent about this: whilst it was pleasing to be called 'Miss' by a man some ten years my junior, I was rather cross that an employee of this establishment, which I now part-owned, would have the effrontery to ask me for identification. Still, he was not to know, I suppose, and he did have a pair of sexy, rounded shoulders and cobalt-blue eyes.

'I regret I do not yet have my full membership through. Would you call Marty to reception for me, please? I'm sure he'll let me in.'

The shiny young specimen nodded and picked up the cheap plastic reception phone, an accessory strangely at odds with the modern feel of the establishment, and buzzed Marty for me. Soon enough, my latest conquest appeared. He looked a little embarrassed, perhaps even worried at the sight of me. Maybe he feared I was going to tell his employee, ahem, *our* employee, exactly what a jerk-off loser slave-pig he was, but he need not have feared: discretion is my middle name.

'Marty, I wonder if I might gain entry,' I asked.

'Yes, of course,' he replied a little vacantly, perhaps thinking of what to say to cover up any embarrassment should I spill any beans. 'Ricky, in future Ms McKnight is to be let straight in,' he told the man at reception, who nodded and smiled at me.

Marty ushered me into the ground-floor gymnasium, which consisted of a small area set aside for rowing machines and a refectory that smelt of coffee and oatmeal flapjacks.

I placed my right hand on my hip and put my left foot forwards, the toe of my scarlet shoe pointing towards him. A very teasing, very dominant pose.

'I'm looking for my croupier Gemma. Have you seen her?' I asked with cold eyes. His face flickered as, I presume, his heart skipped a beat; nothing turns a submissive on like bringing him a touch of arrogance into his real life.

'Yes, she is in the coffee-shop, talking to Alex.'

'Thank you, Marty, that's all.'

As I turned away, Marty's eyes said 'Yes, Mistress,' but he was not yet brave enough to hear himself say the words out here in the real world.

I found Alex and Gemma chatting at a table over some ridiculously expensive and outlandishly foamy coffee. She saw me approach and managed to smuggle an undetected smile out to me, over the borders of her conversation.

'Hello, Gemma.'

'Hello, Ms McKnight.'

'I don't believe I've been introduced to your friend, Gemma,' I said.

Alex Dougall turned to take his first real look at me. I loved to see the features of lust being painted on a man's face when first we meet: the eyes dilate, the mouth eases open and lips purse.

'Ms McKnight, this is Alex Dougall. He owns part of this health club.'

I presented my hand for him to kiss; would that it could have been my sweet foot. He kissed it, looking up to me with hungry eyes, betraying an appetite that he longed to feed but I alone knew would never be sated.

'Your loyal employee was just telling me about you.'

'I have invited Alex to come and play poker with me tomorrow, and enjoy a tour of The Paddle-Boat,' explained Gemma. 'Would you like to come along?'

'I'd be most interested in coming along, thank you,' I said. 'But I'm afraid for now I must call you back to your duties. Something has come up,' I lied. I could see that Gemma had already completed her mission in two days and I felt there was little mileage to be gained from leaving her in temptation's way. She looked somewhat disappointed.

'Yes, Ms McKnight, of course.'

'Nice to meet you, Alex,' I said as we took our leave.

Alex watched us longingly as we both left. Yes, it was certainly the right decision to pull Gemma away – always leave them wanting more, they say, don't they?

Alex turned up right on time, his greying hair coiffed and his gym clothes replaced by a charcoal suit and white shirt. I patrolled my gaming floor, smiling at my girls reassuringly as they looked up from their games. I stopped at an unoccupied poker table and ran my hand across Gordon's back to tease him. He was preparing the table for a private game.

'Everything ready? Fetch some drinks, please – something fruity and refreshing for summer,' I asked.

Gordon nodded and I patted his bum to send him on his way.

Michael arrived, perching his wide frame on one of the players' stools.

'Who is the croupier today?' he asked as he shuffled his behind on the cushion, looking for a comfortable position.

'I am,' I said, arching an eyebrow.

I had asked Michael to join in the game with us, with strict instructions for him to drop out after a few hands. I had told Gemma to do the same a few hands later. Her brief for play was to flirt and tease our mark as much as she could and, once he was nice and hard under his trousers, and the blood had drained from his brain to his cock, follow Michael away from the table, leaving Alex alone with me to work my magic.

Gemma led Alex by the arm from reception, down to the gaming floor. She was in her croupier's uniform, so very flattering to her voluptuous figure. She smiled up at her escort, batting her eyelashes and swaying her hips so that they brushed against Alex's legs as the couple promenaded to our table. I effected an introduction between Michael and Alex as our two new players took their seats.

Gordon arrived with orange juice and ice in a jug, serving us each a glassful. It was rare to see such silver-service from an untrained bouncer, and I was a little disappointed that I had not had the foresight to set up the table in a more private area and make Gordon dress up as a maid to serve us; he certainly showed a talent for it.

'Have you played before, Alex?' I asked as I prepared the deck and chips.

'Funnily enough, I've never been to a casino here at home, but I do go regularly if I'm in the East or the South of France,' he answered.

'It's often the way, we find licence to do things while we're on holiday that we feel too inhibited to do at home,' I observed.

'I agree.' Alex smiled wistfully.

'Indeed, sometimes even a short trip to the country can get some of us as horny as a nymph, don't you think?' I directed the comment ostensibly to Michael, but it was meant, of course, to resonate with Alex.

Michael agreed guardedly, his noncommittal reply allowing the comment to retain its ambiguity and subtlety.

I clicked my fingers and Kirsty, her alabaster skin blushing profusely, I believe from horniness for Alex

219

rather than embarrassment or discomfort, skipped over with a supply of chips for play. Alex bought a generous sum and Michael and Gemma did the same, using the cash I had loaded them with from The Paddle-Boat's coffers.

'Shall we begin with a five-pound ante and increment?' I suggested to no dissent.

We began. Gemma did her best to play one-handed as she softly ran one finger of her right hand along the inside of Alex's knee. I hoped that this continual low-level stimulus would build up and and distract him from his game. I remember many years ago, on my first date with a young female, she did this to me as we sat over drinks in a public house; at first it had only a pleasant tickling effect, but after half an hour it was making my clitty glow like a beacon. I hoped the same effect would soon be in evidence in Alex's penis.

We played a few harmless hands. Alex lost all of his first few but more than recovered his antes with a Three-of-a-Kind: as dealer I had to pay him odds on the win. This pleased me; I needed Alex to be abuzz with hormones and endorphins if I was to reach beyond his guard and ensnare him.

Michael politely made his excuses and left with his chips; I winked at him as he went, to let him know he had played his part well and, in choosing the right time to withdraw, had also shown a talent that can be so important in a male stud. He really was a devoted wee servant and I resolved to reward him soon for unquestioning co-operation in helping me with my many and varied whimsies.

Gemma's hand was moving surreptitiously up Alex's leg and his play began to be distracted. As I dealt, I spoke to him with my eyes, flashing them here, winking there, perhaps widening them, flicking an eyebrow or glancing down towards his crotch suggestively. With myself acting like a hussy and Gemma feeling him up, it must have been overload for him.

Gemma sensed her moment – she really was becoming adept at male manipulation, both in-session and out in the real world – and stood to take her leave. Alex looked disappointed, and his yearning puppy-dog glance at her spoke volumes. She kissed him on the cheek as her right hand squeezed his thigh.

'Don't worry, Alex, Valerie will look after you. I'll be back to give you your tour,' she cooed, running her hand lightly over his shoulders and back as she departed. We both watched her arse cheeks oscillate and her calf muscles tightening and flexing as she walked away.

'Alex, playing just for money is so boring at times. What do you say to me changing my betting currency to something a little more exciting?'

Alex shrugged his shoulders in an easy-going manner. 'What do you have in mind?' he asked.

'You continue to wager your cash chips, but how about if my chips began to represent certain forfeits on my part?'

'You mean like strip poker?' he said with a smirk.

'A little like that, only better.'

I took out some training chips from the drawer of the poker table. They are much the same as our real chips, except that they have a black band around the circumference and so cannot be exchanged for cash.

'Let us say that a ten-pound chip forfeits me to give you a kiss,' I said, holding up the relevant disk.

Alex exhaled deeply at the idea.

'And a twenty-five-pound chip makes it a topless kiss,' I added, raising my eyebrows cockily.

He did the same, but out of surprise rather than cockiness.

I held up a fifty-pound chip.

'Let's call this a topless lap dance, shall we?'

Alex bit his lip. He was already hornier than an alley-cat and the sight of a woman as striking and attractive as I offering herself so playfully was not reducing his lust.

'This one we can call a topless lap dance followed by delicately applied and highly pleasurable hand relief,' I said, holding up the hundred-pound chip. Alex's hands went to his crotch in a vain attempt to cover his increasing manhood.

'And finally this can only be all of the above followed by the silkiest and slickest fellatio you ever experienced,' I said, referring to the five-hundred-pound chip, 'There, that sounds much more interesting, doesn't it?'

'Yes, ahem, yes, it does,' agreed Alex.

'All you have to do, Alex, is put up a real chip of equal face value. Simple. How high the stakes go is up to you and what you desire. Shall we play four hands and see how lucky we get?'

Alex nodded and threw in a ten-pound chip: we were playing for a kiss at first then. I covered it and dealt the first hand: five cards face down for my opponent and five for me, the last one face up for him to see – the six of clubs. Alex examined his hand, frowned slightly and raised for another two chips, which he placed neatly on the green baize. We had started modestly then, playing only for three kisses.

I revealed my hand, a rag-tag collection of misfits that failed to reach the dealer's minimum requirement of an ace or a king: a loser's hand if ever there was one.

'I look forward to my kisses,' he said with a grin, collecting my three chips from me.

'If you don't get a bit more daring, that's all you'll be getting,' I told him.

Alex was goaded into showing some balls and placed a £25 chip on the table. I covered it with a training chip of equal face value and dealt the hands. My showing card was a pathetic three of diamonds. Alex viewed his hand and placed two more £25 chips down.

'That's more like it,' I said. We were playing now for three topless kisses and I rather looked forward to revealing my succulent breasts to him, seeing the look in his eyes and then drawing closer to kiss him.

I turned over my hand, which looked far more promising than the first, containing a pair of twos alongside the aforesaid three of diamonds and two other inconsequential cards. I gave a sulky pout: this gave me a good chance of winning the hand and I would not get to give Alex those unfettered kisses I had been looking forward to.

But Alex's smug grin changed my mood. He turned over his hand to reveal three unmatched red court cards and two black eights. He had beaten me and as dealer I had to pay odds of two to one on a pair. Blushing, and with my heart thumping, I handed over four more £25 chips.

You may ask why, having resolved to take a harsher line with the males of the city, I was allowing myself to be won like some cheap slapper in a pool hall. Please rest assured, it was all part of the ruse: the bait in the trap, if you will.

Alex was cocky as hell now, and flipped a £50 chip on to the table as ante. I covered it and dealt. We looked each other in the eye across the table and the air between us ionised with sexual tension. If I lost this hand I really would be flaunting myself for him – we were playing for a lap dance now. I dealt.

My showing card was the eight of diamonds, again not a promising sight as I had no guarantee of a playable hand. Alex did not seem too much more pleased with his own cards either but, after a moment's indecision, opted to raise with a £100 chip. Now one of my locally renowned hand-jobs was at stake. I turned the rest of my cards.

The ace of spades proudly shone forth, but no other card of consequence joined it. Alex revealed his hand too, which contained only the ace of clubs. He screwed up his lips in disappointment. Ordinarily, two equal hands would mean a stand-off and the return of bets, but the exception was the highest card in the deck – the ace of spades, which acts as a tie-breaker whenever it appears. I scooped the chips towards me. I wonder if in his lust and excitement Alex had even noticed that he had just lost one hundred and fifty pounds.

'Last hand,' I said.

Alex threw in another £100 chip, this time as his ante. I covered it with a 'hand-job and lap-dance token' and dealt the final hand.

My showing card was the king of spades. At last, I had a decent card showing and I was guaranteed a playable hand. Alex gave himself pause as he examined his own hand, smiled and threw two more chips as his raise. There was now three hundred at stake from him, and if I lost I would be finding myself dancing for him, wanking him and sucking him in my office for the rest of the week.

I turned over my cards. The three of spades and the seven and ace of hearts all showed themselves, but most importantly so did the rather handsome king of hearts, giving me a pair of kings. Alex clicked his fingers at his poor luck. He had been given a reasonably good hand containing the two black sevens, but it was not enough. I smiled at my lucky escape and scooped up the chips.

'Now that was exciting,' I said, 'and you appear to have won eight kisses from me, five of them topless.'

I wondered if the grinning Mr Dougall had even noticed that the entire experience had cost him four hundred and fifty pounds. I hoped not, because, like the vampire bat, my plans rather depended on being able to bleed him painlessly.

I came out from behind the table and approached my prey, slinking between his legs as he sat. I cared not for who else in the hall might see and, placing a fingertip along his jaw, I kissed him three times, each one wetter and more passionate than the first. I felt his cock tense inside his trousers.

'Shall we do your tour and I can pay you the rest I owe you,' I said.

Alex nodded wordlessly.

We fetched Gemma from her table, where a number of oriental gentleman had been drooling over their blackjack hands as they watched her running the table. She took her leave of them and came to join us.

'Gemma, would you mind taking Alex on his tour of the facilities? I'll meet you both downstairs in twenty minutes,' I said. 'If you like what you see, I hope we'll see you as a regular customer, Alex.' I smiled and winked as I left them to each other.

I used the spare time to find some privacy upstairs. In my office I retouched my make-up for a more striking, vampish look, reapplied my perfume and gave my breasts a light brushing with baby oil, so that my nipples glistened like rubies. I put my clothes back on and made my way to the door of The Cellar where I waited for Alex and Gemma.

'Thank you, Gemma, you can return to your table,' I said as they appeared.

Gemma kissed Alex on the cheek and took her leave of us. Alex looked very frustrated that Gemma had made an escape again; the poor chap thought he was on a 'promise', not realising that Gemma had only gone across the street to flirt with him on my orders to lure him into my lair.

'Come on, Alex, I'll give you a glimpse of our most important facility.'

I ushered him down the stairs into our chamber of delights and turned on the atmospheric main lighting. Alex strained to survey the shapes and sights in the half-light. From his vantage, though, he would have clearly seen the outlines of whips and restraints, cages and leatherwear, buckles and chains, dildos and masks.

'Our Cellar contains a cornucopia of delights for the daring and deviant. Perhaps for our next game of poker, if you are willing to up the stakes, we can play for something a little more exciting.'

Alex was lost for words; disbelief came over his distinguished good looks. But I could tell he was interested.

'I've always been curious to try . . .' he stuttered.

'I'm sure you have.' But, for now, I think I owe you five more kisses. Wait here.'

I led Alex to the spot where I wanted him to tarry and strode off to The School Room – I needed a chair.

'Sit,' I said, bringing it to him.

Alex, with his eyes locked on me and my splendid body, relaxed into the chair like a man hypnotised, his arms loose and lifeless at his sides. I inched closer to him, gyrating my torso as I approached. I let the jacket of my suit slip from my back and fall to the floor. He could now see the shape of my breasts under my top. He stared intently as I put one stockinged leg over his knee and began to unbutton my top. Slowly I disrobed as I inched my pelvis towards him, pushing the now exposed cleavage towards his face; it gleamed from its shimmer of oil.

I grabbed the back of his head and lifted my other leg over his; I was now sitting astride him, my skirt stretched tightly between my parted legs, pulling the fabric close to the contours of my hips like a second skin. My stocking tops could be seen in the shadows. I began to grind my crotch into his and pulled his nose into my cleavage, eliciting a moan of pleasure as he smelt my scent and felt my flesh brush his face.

With his pole now tenting his trousers, I reached behind me and unclasped my bra, brought my arms together and allowed the bra to fall on to his lap. I squeezed my breasts together with my upper arms and then let them bounce freely as I continued to dry hump him. My pussy leaked with joy.

My nipples were lip-red and they tightened like bullets under his breath. He gasped hungrily, staring at them and then looking up towards me.

I smiled down at him and drew closer for his first kiss, encasing his mouth in my open lips and drawing them in together before pulling back. Again I let my nipples brush his lips, before kissing him again, this time slipping my tongue into his mouth and flicking the tip of it against his. I pulled back, smiled an evil smile – for I knew this was turning him on immensely and that he was about to be left high and dry – and kissed him again, now lapping hungrily with my tongue.

Again I kissed him and the writhing of his body under me told me how horny he was getting. He desperately pushed his crotch upwards as I kissed him, hoping that his rampant member would brush some part of me. I cut short the kiss and gave him an admonishing look that only seemed to turn him on even more. Cruelly, I gave him his final kiss, as teasing as the first, and little more than a sensual peck.

'There, I believe we are now quits – until we play again, that is.' I grinned and stood up to put my bra and top back on. Alex watched me. I deliberately ignored him, as if I were a queen and he a peasant on the roadside, catching a glimpse of me through the curtain on the carriage door. I decided, on reflection, not to give him time for his erection to subside before escorting him up the stairs and across the gaming floor and out of the building. Many of the women in the casino flicked their eyes down at his bulge as we passed, causing him to blush. I kissed him goodbye on the cheek and saw him out of the door with a wave.

'Bye for now, Alex,' I said. I knew he would be back.

Sixteen

The evening was wearing on and I was thinking about heading home when Gordon entered, cap in hand, so to speak.

'How can I help you, Gordon?' I asked, as though I had no idea.

'Em, Mistress McKnight, you said I was to come see you every night and if you weren't busy we could, erm, play?' he stuttered.

'It's Ms McKnight or Mistress Valerie,' I said icily.

'Yes, Mistress Valerie,' he said. His voice was much quieter than normal; it seemed that the idea of humiliation at my hand had a real and tangible effect on Gordon's personality. I liked that.

'You are lucky this evening: I am not busy, so I can play with you a little, but not for long – I was thinking of knocking off soon.'

'Thank you, Mistress Valerie.'

'You know, when you were serving the drinks today I had the most fabulous vision of you in a maid's uniform. I think I shall try you in one just now.'

Gordon experienced a rush of adrenalin at the thought of being dressed up by me and I pressed the idea to really get the kinky juices flowing in his brain.

'I've got lots of underwear in my cupboard here that would suit you – how do you think your wee bobby will look in a pair of lacy knickers? – and I have a nice blond wig. I'll put you in them first, then fetch the uniform from downstairs,' I said.

Gordon closed his eyes and gasped again as my words seemed to pass through him like a wave of excitement.

'Strip while I root about, fold your clothes and kneel naked in front of my desk,' I said.

I left Gordon to complete his task as I selected a bra (rolled-up tissues would have to do as breasts today, since I do not keep falsies in my office) and a pair of black lacy knickers.

I sucked a thoughtful tooth for a moment while considering whether Gordon's maid would have her cock tightly encased in my flesh-coloured tights, or if she would be saucy enough to go with suspenders and stockings. I decided on black stockings. I gathered everything together, picked up some shiny black heels and turned to Gordon, who was now obediently kneeling at the desk, his head bowed.

I began by wrapping the bra around him and tightening it at the back. Next I rolled up some soft tissues and stuffed them in the cups.

'Show off your boobs, you silly tart,' I told him.

He swung his chest from side to side in a very stilted fashion.

'More feminine,' I insisted.

He tried again, this time with a hand on his hip, swinging more gracefully.

'Better. Stand on the coffee table,' I said.

'Yes, Mistress.' He stood on the table.

Now his twitching cock was at my eye-level. I wanted him raised; I felt this would make him feel more self-conscious.

I made him step into the knickers and pulled them up to his waist, grabbed his cock and pulled it a couple of times, just to get the blood running, and stuffed it inside the thin gusset. Next, I fastened the suspender belt around his waist, set the clasps and gave his thin, fleet legs a stroke with my fingers and nails.

'These slender, almost feminine, pins will look fine in nylon or silk,' I commented. 'Put your toe forward.'

'Yes, Mistress.'

I rolled up the stocking and Gordon wobbled slightly on the table as he lifted his foot.

'Point your toe, be more dainty,' I said.

'Yes, Mistress.'

I rolled the stocking sensuously up his leg. I remember the first time I wore a stocking: it was such a new and rich experience that I could have rubbed my thighs and clit all day. If this was Gordon's first time he would now be feeling the same way too and indeed his 'clit' bulged against the lace pattern of the panties. I placed the second stocking on him and fastened them both to their clasps. Next the shoes were slipped on to his feet, tightening his calves and buttocks.

'Very nice. Do you feel pretty?' I asked.

'Yes, Mistress.'

'Good, you look pretty. Step down.'

'Yes, Mistress.'

Lastly, I placed the blond bobbed wig on his head, fluffing it out as best I could to give it a bouncy feel.

'Lovely. Now I want you to practise walking gracefully and sexily in those heels while I fetch the maid's uniform,' I said, leaving the room and locking the door behind me as Gordon did his best to strut up and down the length of the office.

I had no intention of getting the maid's uniform for him. Instead I ran around the building looking for someone with no current duties at any of the tables; I needed a croupier to help me humiliate Gordon fully. I finally found Abrille at a loose end in the staff room.

'Abrille, do you fancy some fun?'

'Yes, of course,' she replied. 'Have you a client in The Cellar?'

'No, Gordon is in my office dressed in lingerie. He expects me to come back with a maid's uniform for him. Here's the key: bust in on him and give him a telling off for me,' I said, giggling.

'With pleasure,' said Abrille, joining in my laughter.

I followed her up the stairs and waited, listening, at the door as she unlocked it and flew in.

'What is this!?' she snapped. 'Does Ms McKnight know what you are doing in here, Gordon, you little pervert?'

Gordon, unsure whether to be exhilarated by the intrusion or mortified, answered weakly in the affirmative.

'I think that is highly unlikely,' Abrille retorted. 'I think it is more likely that you sneaked in here to sniff her underthings and got carried away, putting them on yourself and prancing around like a Jessie-girl.'

I heard some moving around and the sound of my couch taking someone's weight.

'Are you a Jessie-girl, Gordon? Do you like to be a dotty tart? Shall I call you Gabrielle from now on?'

There was a long pause as Gordon tried to deal with his emotions.

'Yes, Mistress,' he confessed.

'Over my knee, Gabrielle, or I shall tell Mistress Valerie what a juicy slut you are.'

I heard more movement.

'Pull down your knickers,' said Abrille.

There was a pause followed by a barrage of slaps and spanks. The sound was most exciting and amusing to hear and my hand went to my mouth to cover the huge smile I had, and also to stop any audible laugh escaping. The spanking continued, culminating in a huge slap that fair rattled my ear-drum and made 'Gabrielle' gasp. I entered the room.

Gordon was over Abrille's knee on the couch. His bottom, framed by the black lace of my knickers, suspender belt and the two straps, was bright red.

'Dirty little girl! Stand up!' I shouted. 'Take your shoes off and put your clothes back on over your lingerie.'

'Yes, Mistress.'

Gordon stood up, his cock standing proudly at 45 degrees to the ground.

'Leave your underpants in the wastepaper basket,' I added.

Abrille and I watched as Gordon stuffed his aching cock inside his knickers and pulled his clothes back on over my lingerie. He threw his Y-fronts in the bin.

I picked up the shoes and handed them to him.

'Good. Now go straight home, take off your clothes, put on the shoes, dance in front of the mirror and wank yourself for all you're worth. You can bring back my things tomorrow.'

'Yes, Mistress,' said Gordon, shaping to leave.

'Leave the wig here, Gordon, you idiot,' I chided.

Gordon returned the garments to me late the following afternoon. I made him bow down with his nose in the carpet in front of my desk as he confessed to his overnight activities. He had apparently carried out my wanking assignment as soon as he got home in the evening, then again first thing in the morning and again after breakfast. He had then spent the rest of

233

the morning and early afternoon washing them and drying them so as to have them ready to return to me by the start of his evening shift.

'My, you are a keen and ever-so horny little sissy, aren't you?' I chided.

'Yes, Mistress,' he said.

I had no further use for him at that time and I dismissed him.

That was only the first of three interesting visits to my office that afternoon. The next was in the pussy-watering form of Maureen Stewart, who crept in the half-open door and evaded my field of vision until she was standing directly in front of my desk. I looked up from my accounts.

'Maureen, you ignorant wee besom, do you ever knock?' I joked.

'Sorry, Ms McKnight, but Gemma said that I had a better chance of catching you with a dildo up your fanny if I just walked in.'

'Did she,' I said dryly. 'Are you trying to catch me with a dildo up my fanny?'

She tactfully ignored the question.

'Ms McKnight, a number of us are planning another session of our little game Pleasure or Pain, and wondered if you would give permission for us to use The Cellar.'

'Is it just Paddle-Boat staff?' I asked.

'Yes, Ms.'

I was bound by my recent resolutions to allow the game.

'Then of course, but on two conditions.'

Maureen did not speak but waited expectantly to hear my caveats.

'First, that, if a client arrives in the evening, you all clear out in ten minutes flat and, secondly, that I can play too.'

Maureen beamed at the idea of my participation.

'Of course, Ms McKnight. We're starting at the back of six thirty,' she said, breezing out of the room.

No sooner had she exited than there was a knuckle rap on the door, and I looked up again from my accounts. This time I stood up, so eagerly had I been anticipating this visit.

'May I speak with you, Ms McKnight?' said a voice.

'Come in, Marty,' I said.

Marty entered. He was in a brown leather jacket and dark-blue jeans, a departure from his usual sporty ensemble, and carried a small black zippable portfolio.

I knew already what this visit was about and growled within like a well-fed tigress. Marty was about to make good on our deal for a share in California Fitness in exchange for unlimited Cellar play sessions.

'What have you there?' I said, feigning innocence.

'Ms McKnight, I've been thinking about the deal we made in our session, and I think that your offer is just far too special for me to decline. I have had my solicitor draw up the paperwork to transfer twenty-six per cent of the gym to your name.'

Of course he had been thinking about the deal, I guarantee that nothing else had entered his thoughts since I last saw him. Let me expand on exactly what had been going through poor helpless Marty's mind since I left him. Firstly, after the initial sated glow of satisfaction had died away, Marty had become racked with guilt and regret about the unrealistic stupidity of trading part of his future for something as frankly luxurious and unnecessary as my attention. He had resolved never to come back, simply not to speak to me again, and silently back out of the deal.

Then the following morning, he would have caught a glimpse of some female, either an office-tease on her way to work or perhaps one of his customers working out on a legs machine, and his guilty cock had sprung to life. The first thoughts of revisiting me for another session came into his head. Then, that afternoon, I had turned up at the gym, stirring in him undeniable urges that now stayed with him the whole of the evening and night – every time he thought of another session with me, his fetish chakra sang in his gut and once again the thought of paying me his part of the bargain started to turn him on: regret dissipated.

Now, with his testicles fully recharged from the draining I had supervised two days before, he was once again under my spell.

'Let me see the paperwork,' I said.

'It requires a witness,' he told me as he unzipped his folio.

I picked up the phone to accounts and asked Gemma to send Maureen back up to me. As I set the phone down again, I asked, 'Is Alex aware of your intention to make this deal?'

'No, Ms McKnight.'

Good, I thought.

'Then I have one more condition to this agreement: that you do not tell him until one week has passed.'

Marty paused at this, but with his loins tingling with excitement was not able to get his brain around why I might make such a request.

'Yes, if you wish, Ms McKnight,' he agreed solemnly.

Maureen arrived, a little less surreptitiously this time.

'Maureen, I need you to witness two signatures,' I informed her as I handed my gold-plated fountain pen to Marty. Seeing it again reminded me of the gentleman who had given it to me, a lovely man who was, when I met him at least, the owner of a casino on the banks of the Clyde river. He had kindly given me the beautiful pen after signing the ownership over to me. I wondered what he was doing these days.

Marty scratched his name on to the legal paper, shakily passed me back the pen and I did the same. I applied my signature with a flourish before passing the pen to Maureen, who completed her own details and added her mark. Marty, his hands trembling now, handed me my copy and forced his own back into his portfolio, as though he were hiding a shameful magazine in his briefcase.

'Thank you, Ms McKnight,' he said, bowing his head slightly.

'Ms McKnight, we're about ready to play in the basement, if you're still coming?' Maureen interjected, perhaps sensing that the arrival of a visitor might put a crimp in my plans.

'Yes, I'm ready. Who is playing?'

'Myself, Amber and Abrille,' she answered.

I looked at her quizzically. 'No fellers?' I asked.

'The girls and I thought we would try it without them, just for once. It might be more sensuous.' She giggled.

'There's no need to giggle, I think you might be right,' I answered.

Marty had been listening as we spoke and, braving my wrath, he swallowed hard before interrupting. 'Ms McKnight, may I be permitted to attend?' His voice was tremulous.

I glanced at Maureen before replying. 'Well, I would not want your presence to spoil Maureen's plans. Perhaps if you begged her,' I suggested.

'Miss Maureen, I wonder if you might allow me the privilege of attending your play session,' he pleaded.

'Silly arse! Lick her shoes!' I scolded.

Marty obeyed immediately, falling to his knees and applying his tongue to her shiny black heels. He repeated his request.

'Well, OK, but only as a spectator.'

'Red,' I announced. 'Pain!'

The girls all clapped with excitement, save Maureen, who breathed deeply in anticipation of her fate.

'What shall we do with her?' asked Amber, gleefully.

'I have an idea I'd like to try on her. Get her stripped and bring her over,' said Abrille, strutting her lovely stuff over to The Dungeon Room.

Maureen stared innocently and compliantly at us, like a deer in the headlights, as Amber and I removed her clothes from her. Stripped, she did look sweet, standing there naked – but not quite right. I stepped forwards to slip her black heels back on her feet, improving the look of her nakedness tenfold, before leading her by the hand towards the dungeon. I noticed Marty's eyes helplessly following the sight of her as he knelt in his restrained position, his hands tied to his ankles. He wore a black leather hood with opened eyeholes and I had fed his cock and balls through his fly and pulled the zip tightly up under his scrotum, probably pinching some skin with the metal teeth – I did not bother to check. Now his only exposed parts were his eyes and genitals, which I generally consider the only things you need to read a man.

In The Dungeon Abrille had lit all of the many candles that were there and was preparing a couple of wall-mounted cuffs for Maureen's wrists. We bound Maureen into them, with her back to the wall. Her wrists were fixed quite high and she had to stretch to keep her heels on the Dungeon floor.

'I want to see her slim little body writhing under hot wax,' said Abrille.

We nodded our approval.

'Grab a candle each,' she said.

Eagerly, dancing away into the yellow light, the three of us selected a candle each, removing it from its sconce and cupping a hand behind the flame, nursing it with kisses of air. I swirled mine around gently, building up the pool of melted wax around the wick.

Abrille went first, brashly splashing all of the wax from her white candle over Maureen's right breast with one flick. The droplets gleamed like fresh spunk as they solidified on her exposed skin. Maureen jerked and squirmed beautifully from the sudden searing jolt. Abrille closed in and took relish in allowing the still burning candle to dribble wax directly on to her nipple.

Amber took the same tack, splashing the wax from her darkblue candle over the other breast. The three of us watched her lithe wee form writhe from the sting, and then tremble from the intensity of the dribbles on to her nipple. Maureen's tense moans brought forth a dewy sap from my petals and I stepped up eagerly to apply the wax from my candle. I put my arm around her, twisting her round so that her forearms crossed over each other and her slim buttocks faced me. I dribbled my wax rather than splash like the other two, letting it trail over her buttocks and into her arse crack. She shook again and we watched her jerk and clench her buttocks as the hot gloop fused on her skin.

Amber and Abrille clapped behind me in appreciation of the show. Indeed, when I turned I saw that Amber was playing with her clit under her skirt.

Our arousal was interrupted, however, by the sound of someone entering The Cellar, and we turned to see Gemma making her way across the central area, past the kneeling and trussed Marty, at whom she glanced as if he was a whimpering dog, to where we stood. She looked at Maureen chained to the wall, naked but for her heels and a second skin of coloured wax. She found the image pleasing and even rubbed her crotch with her hand as she looked.

'Can I help you, Gemma dearest?' I asked.

Gemma answered vacantly, her mind, and eye, still on the gorgeous sight of the suffering Maureen. 'Alex is back to see you, Ms McKnight. He wants another private game.'

I was surprised but pleased to hear that Alex had returned so eagerly and so soon, although his timing could have certainly been better; I was anxious for Marty and Alex not to see each other, lest they become suspicious and awake from their stupor.

'Thank you, Gemma, I will go and meet him. Girls, after your play is over, please see to it that Marty is released from his bonds and led discreetly back to the gym, preferably by the back way.'

I kissed them all, except Maureen, who received a slap on the thigh, and skipped up the stairs.

'You've certainly caught me unawares, Alex, I did not expect you back for at least a day or two.'

Alex unbuttoned his suit jacket and slid a hand coolly into his pocket, but I was not convinced by the show of nonchalance. I knew he was like a sack of monkeys inside, whatever his outward appearance.

'Well, I find myself at a loose end this evening and I must admit to rather enjoying the game last night, and I'll be honest: I want more.'

'You could do worse with your evening than playing me again, but I must warn you that, for me to retain an interest, the stakes will have to be higher, and a lot more attractive.'

'You mean, I'm playing for time in The Cellar?'

I admired his insight.

'Yes, you are and I'll need you to put up more than mere petty cash against it.'

He ruminated on the proposal, but did not answer.

'Alex, let me get you a drink on the house, while I arrange for us to have a room set up.'

I led him to the bar and instructed Jack to furnish him with a malt whisky, while I skipped again up the stairs to the mezzanine and set up a poker table in one of the private diners. I opened a case of larger-denomination rectangular chips, both real and training varieties, and unwrapped a pack of cards. I set out a bottle of wine for us to enjoy as we played, and ran around to my office.

I wanted to change my attire to something more dominant, more mercilessly provocative. A pair of simple black heels were ideal for what I had in mind and I rummaged in my cupboard for a matching skirt and top I knew I had somewhere: the black skirt reached mid-thigh and was cut away at the side, only five thin straps obscuring the sides of my thighs and buttocks. It had a matching top, cut away in a similar fashion at the cleavage and back. Eventually, no thanks to my organisational skills and my habit of changing my clothes halfway through the day and not putting things away properly, I found the two garments and threw them on. I decided I would go bare-legged as well as bare-pussied and peeled off my stockings before slipping my feet into the shoes. It was time to slide back down the stairs to fetch my quarry.

I stepped into the bar, causing Jack to drop a glass and stand frozen like a statue staring at me. I was indeed quite a sight – I only wished I could shag myself sometimes. There were two customers relaxing in the bar at the time, whose reaction was much the same as Jack's, becoming mesmerised as I walked in. I did my best to ignore them.

Alex turned to face me from his seat at the bar and again I saw his lips part softly and his eyes dilate: two of the involuntary responses I live to induce and thrive to exploit.

'You are in luck. There is a free private table on the mezzanine. Would you care to join me?' I said to him, running a finger softly across his shoulders.

'You look – you are – amazing,' he said, trying his best to remain cool as he fumbled out the compliment.

'Yes,' I said, leading the way.

In the private room we sat at the table, not, as before, on opposite sides but next to each other at the corner, my legs crossed out to the side where he could see them. I planned to swing my leg and dangle my shoe throughout to distract and dazzle him.

'As the stakes are going to be so much higher, Alex, it is only fair that we play on equal terms, instead of the casino tradition of dealer versus player,' I said as I shuffled the deck. 'Also, we will be playing Draw instead of Stud – it makes the hands more interesting.'

'Suits me,' he said, glancing helplessly at my cleavage and down to my shining legs. 'What are the stakes?'

I placed fifty £1,000 chips in front of him.

'It's very simple: you bet on your first hand, and again on your second hand. Each one of the dummy chips I put up represents a session in The Cellar.'

'And what am I betting?'

'Like I say, I am not willing to play for boring old cash any more. I need something with more collateral.'

'Such as?'

'Each chip will represent a one per cent share in California Fitness,' I declared.

Seventeen

Alex laughed quietly at my suggestion.

'What makes you think I will agree to that?' he asked guardedly.

I stood up and paced slowly around behind him, extending my legs demurely with each step. His eyes followed me.

'Because I know what you have been through this past day. I know how much you enjoyed being teased and denied yesterday. I know how much extra you felt it because you knew I had taken money, part of your power, away from you. I know that the idea of submission to me and my girls excites and intrigues you. And –' I put my leg over his and clasped the back of his head to punctuate my point '– know how you need it, need it all.'

I threw my head back disdainfully and returned to my seat.

His face was shrouded in turmoil as his pulsating loins fought with his mind for control. It was a losing battle, as ever.

'I will accept on the condition that you put up part of the casino against me.'

Oh, how he wanted this! Despite knowing that no sane man would ever agree to such idiocy, he was actually considering my proposal! Desperately, he had tried to rationalise the proposal by bringing in a business element to the wager. I decided to throw him a bone, to match the one pushing against his trouser fabric, but still drove a hard bargain.

'Seems agreeable, Alex, but the sessions on offer, and the greater value of my Paddle-Boat, must be taken into consideration. I shall offer you a half per cent share and a session, against one per cent of the gym.'

This was the true meaning of 'edge-play', the art of bringing real risk into sexual fantasy. Again Alex was in crisis, but the need in him to feel that frisson of excitement won out.

'Agreed.'

'Four hands, as before?' I asked.

Alex nodded for me to proceed and I poured us both a glass of wine to drink to the agreement before we threw in a chip each. I dealt the cards, swinging my leg all the while with a hypnotic rhythm, and picked up my hand with an arrogant smile in Alex's direction. He was trying to concentrate on his cards.

'Are you going to play on?' I asked.

'Yes. I'll raise you just the one chip, and change two cards,' he said, sliding his rejected cards in my direction.

I changed them.

My hand was a mish-mash, the only possibility being that I held three disparately numbered cards of the same suit, which, with a bit of luck, might become a flush. I decided to stay in, though, and met his bet. I exuded as much confidence as I could to unnerve Alex, but inside I was very nervous: after all, one per cent of my casino was on the line.

I too rejected two cards, and received the queen of hearts and king of clubs in return – not much use to me, as my attempted flush needed spades. Fortunately, though, I held the queen of spades already and so finished with a pair.

'I raise another chip,' announced Alex, clearly confident of his hand.

I felt my own hand was worth a tipple and met his bet, laying my two queens down on the table. Alex clicked his tongue and threw down his hand – he too had two queens but his next highest card was a ten. I held the king of clubs as my spare, and therefore won the hand. I scooped up the chips and I could not help my eyes taking on a predatory glare as I contemplated the three per cent share in the gym I had just won.

'Unlucky in cards, unlucky in lust,' I gloated.

I crossed my legs over the other way, displaying a flash of my pussy as I did, and adjusted my position so I sat more side-on to Alex, exposing my thigh and buttock to dazzle him through the cut-away skirt. I put in my ante and I dealt another hand. Alex threw in his ante.

I was in clover when I picked up my hand to see two jacks and two fours looking up at me. I had been blessed with a good hand and resolved then and there to get the most I could from it. It was my turn to play first and I raised the pot with two chips.

Alex paused to consider my brave bet and I leant forward to distract him with my cleavage; flustered, he reluctantly met my bet with two chips. I changed my one card with a confident smirk, and could barely suppress my joy at the sight of another handsome jack. I now had a practically unassailable full house.

Alex changed two cards, but I was unable to tell for certain whether he felt they improved his position or not. I hoped he had a hand that he felt he could win with as I planned to throw down the gauntlet with my final raise. Dangling my shoe and pushing my breasts forwards, I raised the pot with three more chips and looked at Alex smugly. But my heart skipped a beat as Alex's demeanour changed to one of confidence.

He eagerly met my raise without a second's pause and laid his cards on the table: the jack, ace, eight, four and ten of hearts revealed themselves – a flush.

'Oh, very good,' I said to him. 'Very well played.'

'Thank you.' He grinned suavely and reached for the pot.

'Ah, ah, ah,' I said, placing the warm palm of my hand on the back of his and laying my full house down on the table. 'But not well played enough,' I added, taking the chips.

Alex bit his lip.

'I am determined to get something out of this game,' he told me as I pinned him to the table, like a lioness with her paw on a mouse's tail.

'Then you are going to have to up the ante to make it worth your while,' I goaded.

I lifted my hand to let him go and sat back, crossing my legs again, just to remind him what a pussy looks like in the shadows of a short skirt. Alex blew his cheeks out slightly and flared his nostrils as he again wrestled with his thoughts and urges.

'Shall we double the minimum bet, then?' he finally said, giving in.

I put in my two chips and dealt.

My hand consisted of the two, three and five of spades and the six and seven of clubs – the makings of a straight at first sight, but I knew that three of the fours had just been played in the previous hand, so the chances of a straight were greatly reduced, and going for it was not recommended. I should be careful.

It was Alex's turn to bet and he raised for another two chips, responding to my taunting as his heart and loins pounded. I had got to him, and the sexual pressure on him was starting to tell. He felt good, the kind of good we all feel when we think we might be 'in' with some super-sexy girl or boy: the nervous

247

taste in the mouth, the tingling fingers and tongue, vertigo in the stomach – I was turning him on and offering him the very real chance of fulfilling fantasies he had not dared to contemplate before. The result was that he started to give himself away – what poker players call a 'tell': he tried to hand in his three rejected cards before I had met his bet. This faux pas told me that he was very likely indeed to have a pair already. I needed an eight and a nine or the lonely remaining four to make a good hand. The odds were too long and I decided to cut my losses and threw in my hand. Alex seemed pleased and collected the pot, which contained dummy chips worth two sessions in The Cellar and one per cent of The Paddle-Boat to him. I cared not, it was a small price to pay for the ultimate end.

I took some wine and casually crossed my arms, placing the cold of the wineglass against my nipple, where I kept it, leaning back on my chair.

'You deal,' I said as I felt my nipple tighten and protrude through the material of my top. As Alex dealt, I moved the glass to my other hand, applying it to the other nipple, which I felt harden. I uncrossed my legs, leaving them wide open this time and reached forwards to place the ante of four chips into the pot. I put the wineglass down, revealing my unmissable nipples to him.

'Four chips is OK for you, isn't it?' I asked.

'Yes, no problem,' he answered absently, trying to divide his attention between the cards in his hand and the two red studs straining against my tight top. Alex had reached the point I had been aiming for and was now totally oblivious to the cost of his lust, concerned only with satisfying it.

I was as nervous as a white-socked virgin schoolgirl behind the bike-sheds: the continuation of my plan now depended on being dealt a decent hand and on distracting Alex from playing his properly. I picked up my cards with trepidation. At first glance, they seemed to present no hope: the six of diamonds, the nine of spades, the five of diamonds, the eight of spades, the seven of diamonds. But as my mind came into focus I leapt inside and turned cartwheels; I had been dealt a straight right out of the deck!

I needed to keep the betting high, but without scaring my prey away. 'As it's the last hand I think I'll raise the same amount both times. Here's another four sessions and two per cent of the casino,' I said chirpily, hoping Alex would buy the justification for my bold raised bet, and concentrate on the possibilities rather than the realities. Whatever his reasoning, he made the bet.

He handed in three cards and I smiled inside: again this meant he was probably holding a pair. Unless the next three cards he took as replacement were three of a kind – very unlikely – I had him beat.

Now I had to keep him in the hand; I was about to keep my five cards, a sure-fire 'tell' to him that my hand was a dancer. I either had to convince him I was bluffing, or distract him. I decided, given that Alex was the owner of one of these penises that seem to put such a crimp in the thought processes of their owners, that it would be easier to do the latter.

I brought my right foot up on to my chair and laid my right arm on my knee, locking his eyes. My skirt was now riding up into my crotch, fully revealing my bushy cunt to him. I let my left hand slide along my left thigh to my crotch and started to burrow into the pink opening inside my labia..

'Aren't you going to raise your bet?' I said, knowing that with the sight of me masturbating myself he would overlook the fact that I had not taken any cards, or even that it was my turn to raise, not his.

'Hmm? Oh, sure,' he said, placing his four chips down in the pot.

I made sure four of mine were there to meet them before he had a chance to realise what had happened.

'I call your hand,' I told him, deceitfully.

I held my breath and my heart froze as he revealed his cards – even my finger stopped moving in my love tunnel. I breathed a soft sigh of relief as two red nines looked up at me, but naught else of consequence. I proudly turned my hand over on the table, and spread them out with my finger, deliberately dabbing a little of my nectar on each one.

'A straight,' I said.

Alex sighed, a beaten and disappointed man, as I collected my chips. I piled my winnings up on the table to count them, as I had not been able to keep track of them up to now; I had been concentrating on counting something else. There were two piles of ten and one left over. With Marty's 26 per cent, I now owned 47 per cent of the gym, just four per cent short of my goal. Alex of course, had no idea of how close I was to a controlling share of his gym, as Marty had not told him of my other little deal this week.

I needed another gambit to squeeze from him one final drop.

'I want a chance to win my one per cent of the casino back,' I said, still nonchalantly rubbing my pussy in front of him. 'How about you put up the two chips you won from me, plus four of your own and I put up ten of the chips I won from you. We can play a straight dealt hand with no draw for the winnings.'

Alex could barely resist the offer: my stake was significantly larger than his, and he agreed. I sensed that victory was close. I had deliberately placed the two queens from my first hand on top as I returned them to the bottom of the deck. Since then, 45 cards had been drawn and I knew that those queens now sat eighth and ninth in the pack. The peculiar dealing pattern of poker would work in my favour here.

I dealt Alex three cards, then myself two, then two to him, leaving me to be dealt the two queens, plus the third card in my original hand. He failed to notice the ruse. He turned his hand over to reveal only a single card hand, eight high. I did the same, revealing the two queens and the king that had helped me to win the very first hand.

My sex squirted with the delight of my victory, and I quite shamelessly wanked my clit and came defiantly in front of the deflated loser. I took back my portion of the casino and piled my gym chips into five piles of five.

'I trust I can expect you to return tomorrow with the necessary paperwork to transfer twenty-five per cent of California Fitness to me?' I asked, standing to pull my skirt down.

Alex nodded. He was honourable, I am sure, even if he was far too horny to be a good businessman. I sneered down at him.

'If it's any consolation, you are more than welcome to attend The Cellar as a paying customer,' I said comfortingly, placing my juice-soaked middle finger in his mouth for him to suck it clean.

A few days later I sat at my desk completing the paperwork required to install myself as director of California Fitness. I stroked the luscious locks of red hair between my thighs as I read through the accounts of the establishment. My clit and pussy were wet and sopping, tingling and burning with pleasure. I rubbed my breasts with my other hand and felt the feeling spread all over me. I forgot my work for the moment; I was close to coming.

'Of course, Gemma, you will have to take on many more duties in The Paddle-Boat if I am to share my time between here and the health club,' I said. 'I'm thinking of starting a massage service over there, once I've got settled in,' I added. 'Do you fancy it?'

Gemma made the most effective affirmative noise she could manage considering she had her tongue inside a hot juicy cunt. I held the back of her head under the desk and pulled her upwards a little, drawing her to my clitoris. She took the hint like a truly considerate lover and worked the tip of her tongue on to it eagerly. I forgot my work.

'Fingers! Fingers!' I gasped.

Gemma responded immediately, inserting two fingers into my velvet-lined canal to seek out my g-spot, and soon I spent hard and loud, squeezing Gemma between my nylon-covered thighs as she diligently pressed on with her duties in the face of my writhing and bucking.

I looked down at her as she lifted her head and smiled at the sight of her face, glistening with my love-honey around her lips and on her chin.

'Gordon,' I called.

Gordon stepped out of the corner where he had been patiently waiting on my next command. He was all the more resplendent in his maid's uniform for the fact that we had picked one too small for him and consequently the suspender belt, his buttocks and stocking tops were constantly on view.

'Yes, Mistress Valerie,' he answered.

'Bring a tissue for Gemma, would you, there's a wee dear.'

The leading publisher of fetish and adult fiction

TELL US WHAT YOU THINK!

Readers' ideas and opinions matter to us. Take a few minutes
to fill in the questionnaire below and you'll be entered into a
prize draw to win a year's worth of Nexus books (36 titles)

Terms and conditions apply – see end of questionnaire.

1. Sex: Are you male ☐   female ☐   a couple ☐?

2. Age: Under 21 ☐   21–30 ☐   31–40 ☐   41–50 ☐   51–60 ☐   over 60 ☐

3. Where do you buy your Nexus books from?

☐ A chain book shop. If so, which one(s)?

_____

☐ An independent book shop. If so, which one(s)?

_____

☐ A used book shop/charity shop
☐ Online book store. If so, which one(s)?

_____

4. How did you find out about Nexus Books?

☐ Browsing in a book shop
☐ A review in a magazine
☐ Online
☐ Recommendation
☐ Other _____

5. In terms of settings which do you prefer? (Tick as many as you like)

☐ Down to earth and as realistic as possible
☐ Historical settings. If so, which period do you prefer?

_____

☐ Fantasy settings – barbarian worlds

- ☐ Completely escapist/surreal fantasy
- ☐ Institutional or secret academy
- ☐ Futuristic/sci fi
- ☐ Escapist but still believable
- ☐ Any settings you dislike?

_____

- ☐ Where would you like to see an adult novel set?

_____

6. In terms of storylines, would you prefer:

- ☐ Simple stories that concentrate on adult interests?
- ☐ More plot and character-driven stories with less explicit adult activity?
- ☐ We value your ideas, so give us your opinion of this book:

_____

_____

_____

7. In terms of your adult interests, what do you like to read about? (Tick as many as you like)

- ☐ Traditional corporal punishment (CP)
- ☐ Modern corporal punishment
- ☐ Spanking
- ☐ Restraint/bondage
- ☐ Rope bondage
- ☐ Latex/rubber
- ☐ Leather
- ☐ Female domination and male submission
- ☐ Female domination and female submission
- ☐ Male domination and female submission
- ☐ Willing captivity
- ☐ Uniforms
- ☐ Lingerie/underwear/hosiery/footwear (boots and high heels)
- ☐ Sex rituals
- ☐ Vanilla sex
- ☐ Swinging

☐ Cross-dressing/TV
☐ Enforced feminisation
☐ Others – tell us what you don't see enough of in adult fiction:

_____

_____

_____

8. **Would you prefer books with a more specialised approach to your interests, i.e. a novel specifically about uniforms? If so, which subject(s) would you like to read a Nexus novel about?**

_____

_____

_____

9. **Would you like to read true stories in Nexus books? For instance, the true story of a submissive woman, or a male slave? Tell us which true revelations you would most like to read about:**

_____

_____

_____

10. **What do you like best about Nexus books?**

_____

_____

11. **What do you like least about Nexus books?**

_____

_____

12. **Which are your favourite titles?**

_____

_____

13. **Who are your favourite authors?**

_____

_____

14. Which covers do you prefer? Those featuring:
(tick as many as you like)

☐ Fetish outfits
☐ More nudity
☐ Two models
☐ Unusual models or settings
☐ Classic erotic photography
☐ More contemporary images and poses
☐ A blank/non-erotic cover
☐ What would your ideal cover look like?

_____

15. Describe your ideal Nexus novel in the space provided:

_____
_____
_____
_____

16. Which celebrity would feature in one of your Nexus-style fantasies? We'll post the best suggestions on our website – anonymously!

_____

THANKS FOR YOUR TIME

Now simply write the title of this book in the space below and cut out the questionnaire pages. Post to: Nexus, Marketing Dept., Thames Wharf Studios, Rainville Rd, London W6 9HA

Book title: _____

NEXUS NEW BOOKS

To be published in April 2006

WHAT SUKI WANTS
Cat Scarlett

Suki is 21 years old and drifting; a waitress in a Midlands transport cafe, she lives alone in a motor-home and sleeps with women. Haunted by the memory of her dead girlfriend, a bisexual American with SM tastes, she takes to the road, heading north to where they first met. Whilst there, Suki is drawn back into the seductive decadence of her old life, to experience what she's secretly been missing for years.

£6.99   ISBN 0 352 34027 4

CAPTIVES OF CHEYNER CLOSE
Adriana Arden

The privileged girls of the exclusive Fernleigh Rise Estate, in England, look down with contempt on the residents of shabby Cheyner Close, and wage a secret war of vandalism and harassment against them. But they underestimate the ingenuity and determination of those they so despise. When the residents strike back, the girls find revenge is both sweet and very painful.

£6.99   ISBN 0 352 34028 2

THE SUBMISSION GALLERY
Lindsay Gordon

For her art, Poppy seeks out and recreates acts of submission and domination. Each sculpture she creates is taken from life – a life of total sensual freedom where she meets a strange cast of extreme lovers. From strangers in restaurants to tattoo artists, from a baroness to a uniformed society of fetishists, Poppy experiences obedience and tastes power. The result is her submission gallery.

Where Poppy's quest for inspiration will finally lead, and to whom, remains a mystery. But behind the scenes of her journey and the art it produces, the world's most bizarre collector waits to seize the greatest artefact of all – the artist herself.

£6.99   ISBN 0 352 34026 6

If you would like more information about Nexus titles, please visit our website at www.nexus-books.co.uk, or send a stamped addressed envelope to:

Nexus, Thames Wharf Studios,
Rainville Road, London W6 9HA

NEXUS BACKLIST

This information is correct at time of printing. For up-to-date information, please visit our website at www.nexus-books.co.uk

All books are priced at £6.99 unless another price is given.

- - - - - ✂ -

Please send me the books I have ticked above.

Name   ....

Address   ....

               ....

               ....

               .... Post code ....

Send to: **Virgin Books Cash Sales, Thames Wharf Studios, Rainville Road, London W6 9HA**

US customers: for prices and details of how to order books for delivery by mail, call 1-800-343-4499.

Please enclose a cheque or postal order, made payable to **Nexus Books Ltd**, to the value of the books you have ordered plus postage and packing costs as follows:

   UK and BFPO – £1.00 for the first book, 50p for each subsequent book.

   Overseas (including Republic of Ireland) – £2.00 for the first book, £1.00 for each subsequent book.

If you would prefer to pay by VISA, ACCESS/MASTERCARD, AMEX, DINERS CLUB or SWITCH, please write your card number and expiry date here:

....

Please allow up to 28 days for delivery.

Signature ....

Our privacy policy

We will not disclose information you supply us to any other parties. We will not disclose any information which identifies you personally to any person without your express consent.

From time to time we may send out information about Nexus books and special offers. Please tick here if you do *not* wish to receive Nexus information.   ☐

- - - - - ✂ -